MAGPIES & MAYHEM

ELSIE WINTERS

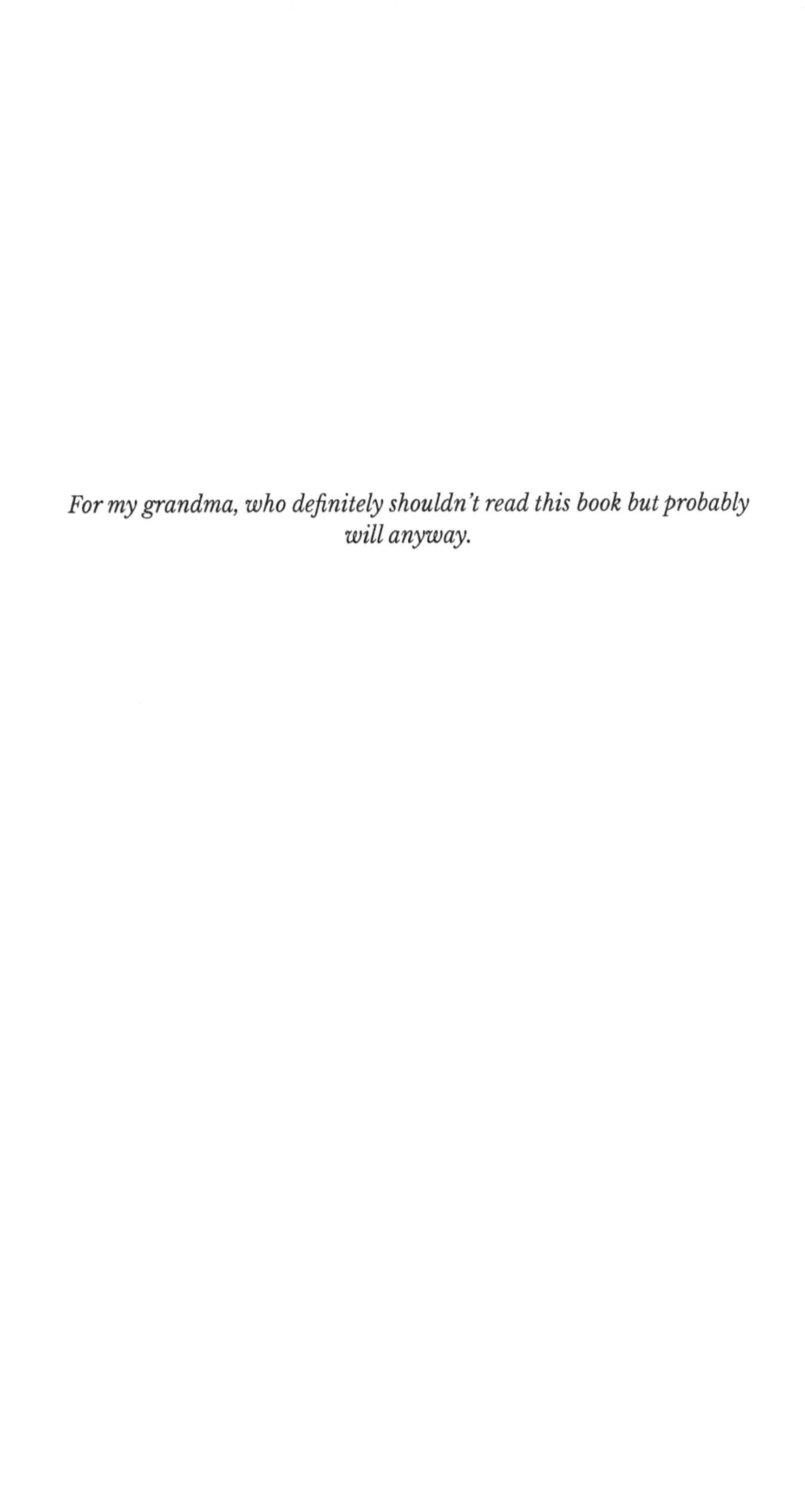

For my grandma, who definitely shouldn't read this book but probably will anyway.

Contents

Prologue

Jordan

THE MAN HANGING LIMPLY across my shoulders stank of drugs and body odor. There were many things I despised about becoming a vampire, but the heightened sense of smell was a constant annoyance. Another was my unreasonable desire to rip the throat out of the grim reaper who was currently towing me along in a loose headlock. I'd laughed a few seconds ago when he first grabbed me. I understood my roommate's roughhousing for the comfortable affection it was, but I couldn't stop the bristling defensiveness from surging through me. Thankfully, Grim was incredibly observant and released me as soon as he felt my muscles tense—before I had time to act on the violent impulses demanding I defend myself from anything that came too close.

I took a deep breath as I straightened and adjusted the body on my shoulders, using the cold, damp night air to clear his stink from my lungs. The body odor was his own fault. The drugs... hm, yes and no.

"This is far enough. I'll take it from here," Grim said, his quiet voice reaching me after we'd put a few blocks between us and the place we'd picked the men up. I looked back at Grim, watching him continue to grip the second unconscious man by the front of his collar with one hand, the man's arms swinging like a rag doll and legs dragging along the road behind him. At six feet tall, I was on the taller side—especially considering my Chinese ancestry—but Grim was easily head and shoulders taller than me, and even without vampire strength, he hefted the man's weight effortlessly.

Dark shadows swirled around Grim's body, clinging to his shoulders and spilling out around his feet like a cloak. He reached into the shadows with his free hand, pulling out a staff with a lantern hanging from a crook at the top and planting it on the wet pavement of the abandoned alleyway. To his left, a flash of light rent the air in a vertical streak, swirling purples and blues before widening into what I recognized as a Gate between worlds. I'd never seen a Gate this small before—or a portable one. In the North Seattle neighborhood where I lived with Grim and our other roommate, Levi, we had three permanent Gates into the Boundlands—a place which humans often referred to as Faery, where magic still lived. They were wide enough to fit several men abreast, and just as tall, with big stone arches around them. Very permanent.

I stiffened as this Gate, about six feet wide and tall and starting two feet off the ground, settled into focus. The view through the shimmering opening wasn't anywhere I'd ever seen before. It was a dimly lit cavern with a dirt path leading to a slow-moving river. A wooden boat floated by the near shore, a cloaked person holding another lantern-staff sitting on one end. The foreboding magic pouring out of the portal filled me with an odd kind of creeping fear, an existential dread that reminded me of the type of nightmares one wakes from where you aren't even sure what was chasing you. The person in the boat turned their head to face us, and I forced myself to ignore the dump of adrenaline and the uncomfortable feeling of my skin prickling. Nothing but shadow could be seen inside the hood.

Grim stepped toward the Gate and nonchalantly tossed the body he was carrying through it. It landed on the other side with a muffled "whump", and Grim turned to look at me expectantly, his normally human-looking blue eyes overtaken by white as his power surged in him. He stared at me for a beat before shifting his weight awkwardly—an easy tell for when he felt confused, considering he usually possessed a preternatural stillness. "You can't... follow me through here," he said.

I blinked at him. As if I would want to follow him into whatever underworld hellscape he'd just ripped a portal open into—the hair on the back of my neck was already standing on end and I still had both feet firmly planted in the land of the living.

Hard pass.

I reached up and hauled the man I was carrying off my shoulders, gripping him by his upper arm and studying his slumbering form. Wiry build, average height, clearly part human. I eyed the windrose tattooed on his hand that signified he was part of the Phantoms, a mafia group from the Boundlands. "I'm not going to get to have *any* fun tonight, am I?" I muttered.

Grim didn't respond.

"What did these Phantoms want with Levi's girl, anyway?" I finally asked, now that we were out of hearing range of our other roommate, Levi, and his girlfriend, Elara.

I'd been demolishing Levi in a late-night game of "Super Smash Bros." when he'd gotten a text from Elara that men were trying to break into her shop with her inside. Grim and I had beat him down the street to her shop, only to find the two men drugged and unconscious on the street in front of her store, with tiny little Elara standing over them, going to pieces and hyperventilating. I don't know why I'd been surprised that she'd already taken them down. The first time I'd met her, she'd nearly choked me out with her magic, and it hadn't even been on purpose. These guys clearly hadn't known who they were messing with.

Grim stared at the man in my grip for a beat, his lip pulling up in an uncharacteristic sneer. "These men accosted her at the corner of 9th and Meridian in Dry Gulch last week."

"Why?"

It didn't seem like he was going to answer at first as he studied me, until he finally said, "The fairies have requested she build them some weapons. The Phantoms want the same thing, only it seems they aren't requesting."

I eyed the small duffle bag draped over my shoulder—full of zip ties, lighters, and hunting knives—that we'd found with the men. I didn't even want to think about what they'd had in store for Elara.

I handed over the man I'd carried to Grim, and he tossed him through the Gate the way someone might toss a rolled-up rug. He turned and reached his hand out for the bag.

I was half tempted to see what would happen if I beaned the creepy guy in the boat with the bag instead. Vampire strength meant I could totally hit him from here.

I passed the bag to Grim. He took it gingerly, as if it were dirty, and held it away from his body. After stepping through the portal, he cast me a glance, gave me a nod, and bumped his staff against the ground again. The Gate immediately collapsed in on itself, flashing with a burst of blue and purple light before disappearing as if it had never been. I hadn't even known that was possible.

I stood in the empty alleyway for a long moment, until the sounds of a car turning onto a nearby street finally made me return from my thoughts. What was it Grim had said about the Phantoms accosting Elara last week in Dry Gulch? 9th and Meridian... I pushed heat into my palms and conjured a ball of flame to pass back and forth between my hands, careful to keep it away from my sleeves.

Maybe I can still have some fun tonight, after all.

Chapter 1

Sidney

HUMANS ALWAYS MAKE A big fuss about PMS, but you know what else sucks? Molting. Imagine being an angry, hormonal hot mess, losing most of your feathers, and then the prickly, itchy, bruising, painful process of growing them back. *For weeks.* Not to mention, the entire time you look like the bird equivalent of a hobo. That was me, folks.

At least I could escape some of it for a bit when I was in my "human" form. I was still an angry, hormonal hot mess, and my brain felt a little bit like it was on fire, but I could hide away the pin feathers and most of the desire to peck out the eyes of anyone who got too close. Somewhat.

Stomping up the stairwell to the nondescript third-floor apartment wasn't enough to blow off my steam—*I acknowledge that*—but even though I probably wasn't fit for company, I still wanted to be there. For one, I hadn't spent any quality time with my best friend, Elara, in over a month. She'd been busy with an important project, which could literally save lives, and was newly married to a siren with an annoyingly seductive voice.

I liked her husband, Levi, but I couldn't help begrudging him all the time and attention he'd been stealing from me. I was working on it, okay? Maturity wasn't something that came naturally to me—I had to fight for every ounce of it, tooth and claw.

Which brought me to the other reason I'd accepted Elara's invitation for a movie night at his old apartment: curiosity. Levi lived with a grim reaper, and no one could have possibly expected me to be mature enough to pass up an opportunity to see a guy like that in his natural habitat, no matter how grumpy or irritable I felt.

The problem with my impulsivity was that I'd forgotten how nervous the reaper made me. Nervous was maybe a strong word. I wasn't scared of him… much. Something about his presence made me jittery, like I should strike first and ask questions later. That was entirely inappropriate, however, because the man had never been anything but politely disinterested in me.

It didn't stop me from glaring down his front door like it had offended my mother. Who knows how long I'd been standing there like a crazy person—I hadn't even knocked—when the front door slowly creeped open. Standing on the other side was seven-foot-whatever of otherworldly maleness, holding a bowl of popcorn and staring at me like I was the weird one. *How did he even know I was here?*

"Grim," I greeted him, standing there and pretending like I wasn't nearly quivering with tension. I couldn't feel people's magic the way Elara could—that wasn't in my wheelhouse—but I think it would have been impossible for anyone to be in this guy's space and not feel something menacing emanating out of him. His aura swallowed a whole room just by him existing within it.

He simply inclined his head toward me in greeting, then gestured toward the room with his bowl, stepping back to make way for me. So nonchalant. So normal. You'd never know he could spawn all kinds of things from shadows and collect the souls of the dead. I wondered what he did with them. *Does he eat them?*

Grim's expression became more inscrutable the longer I stared at him, but I got the distinct impression he wanted to roll his eyes at me. I narrowed my own eyes at the dark-haired man and turned sideways to slide through the doorway, pretending like I wasn't trying to keep as much space between us as possible. Because I'm smooth like that.

It only took two small steps into the room to transport me back in time to twelve-year-old Sidney, because seated in front of me, glowering at me, was my childhood daydream. Jordan Houjin, my oldest brother's super-hot teammate and my pre-teen crush, was gripping the arms of his recliner like he wanted to destroy them. He still had those gorgeous cheekbones that looked like they could cut glass, those perfect, kissable-looking lips, and that glossy, raven-colored hair. Looking at him instantly took me back to days spent on the sidelines "watching my brother's matches" as a gangly, gap-toothed child.

Jordan was different too. His skin was all wrong, pallid and sickly looking, and it caught the shadows in an odd way. Elara's words came back to me, about Levi having a vampire roommate, and my heart plummeted. What had happened to him?

Worse still was how hard his eyes were as he stared at me. The playful, flirty, confident Jordan I'd watched growing up wasn't the same person I saw before me now.

But then, I guess I wasn't the same knock-kneed girl he'd known either.

"Hey! Sid's here—" Right over my shoulder, where I hadn't noticed his approach, Levi's exuberant voice sent me into a conniption fit. Between the hair-raising presence of the grim reaper on one side, and the dawning horror of discovering Jordan's fate, I had no mental space for anything else. My response to being startled was to shift—every time—and this was no exception.

Before Levi could even complete his sentence, I'd collapsed in on myself with bone-crunching speed, flaring with heat and sprouting feathers. I tucked my arms-turned-wings against my body with a snap to pump me up out of the neck hole of my shirt, flapping twice more before my clothes even hit the floor below me.

But—*CURSES!* I remembered too late. *My pin feathers!*

Outrage flooded me. I didn't consider myself terribly vain about my human form, but when it came to my feathers? Yeah, I cared what they looked like. Corvids in general are striking birds, and as a born-and-bred magpie shifter, I wore my black and white markings with pride. But right then, mid-molt, I looked like a buzzard with mange.

I had two choices here: I could remain an ugly-ass, mid-molt bird, with raging hormones and tender skin, or I could immediately shift back and be naked as the day I was born. My choice was made before my clothes had even touched the floor, but dang it, it *hurt*.

Shifting was always uncomfortable—calling magic forth and commanding a change to one's corporeal form was never a pleasant sensation. But twice? In less than a minute? The amount of magic required, and the physical exertion, caused the second shift to be downright painful. And that did terrible things to my mood.

I was poised to strike the instant my body reshaped, my leg pulling up and releasing with a snap. It was an overreaction. I knew it before the kick even connected, so I changed course just enough to strike his chest and not his face. Levi took far too much pleasure from startling me into shifting for me to let it go completely.

"Oomph!" Over the back of the couch he went as I landed on my pile of discarded clothing. "I probably deserved that," he wheezed, sucking wind for a few seconds on the floor somewhere behind the couch. "Maybe not for this time, but definitely for one of the earlier ones."

Elara stood, frozen, a few steps from where he'd landed, holding two full drinks she'd been carrying into the living area, exasperation written on every tiny elfin feature. I felt the tiniest spark of shame for punting her new husband across the room, but I ruthlessly stomped it into smithereens. I was standing here, buck naked in front of my childhood crush and a real-life-actu-al-grim-reaper, because Levi had startled me *again*. My bones still ached from the rapid double shift.

"I told you she was molting," Elara muttered.

"You did mention that." I guess Levi had decided the floor behind the sofa was a comfortable spot, because he didn't seem to be in any hurry to get up. A soft crunching sound behind me told me that Grim was eating popcorn. That was my cue to extract myself from this ridiculous situation.

I unclenched my fists and my jaw, crouching to scoop up my clothes and careful not to give Mr. Reaper more of a free show than he was already getting.

"Levi's room is the—" Elara started, but I cut her off.

"I got it." I wasn't an idiot. I headed for the closest open bedroom with my clothes and shut the door. It had a large poster of the boy who played Jacob from the movie Twilight taped to the back, and the room didn't smell like Levi at all. It smelled like vampire.

Chapter 2

One Month Later

"Sidney, if I didn't know better, I'd think you were my mother," Elara muttered distractedly.

I nudged the sandwich closer to her, half-considering what she'd do if I snatched up the project she was so intent on. Sometimes I did "mother" her a little too much, but this wasn't one of those times. "You're still recovering from knocking yourself out, and your dad said to take it easy. Also, you've missed lunch again, and—" I picked up the work log to verify that her output had indeed gone above what I'd laid out for her today, "—you're done." Elara was technically my boss, but you'd be forgiven for not realizing that at first glance.

We ran a shop together in North Seattle. She made and modified magical items, and I sourced supplies, sold the products, and ran the books. I'd also taken over planning out her daily schedule due to her inability to pace herself when she was stressed, and for the last few months, she had been intensely so.

She was still trying to catch up on the backlog of orders that had piled up due to her recent absence while working on a project for the fairies. This was against the "light duty" order by her doctors after she'd over-exerted her magic just over a week ago. She'd blacked out and ended up spending a stint in the hospital. Two days of supposed light duty, while knowing she had a pile of orders waiting for her, had been enough to make her want to tear her hair out. We'd been at odds about it ever since. She got that obstinate look on her face that meant another argument was coming, and I held up my finger for her to hold her peace. I needed a moment to *really* look at her.

Her father was old-money elvish nobility, and while it showed in her delicate, aristocratic features and darker complexion, what really stood out was the wealth of jewels she covered herself in on a daily basis. I'd known Elara for several years now, and—first meeting not-withstanding—she was always tidy and put together.

But today... the dark hair she pulled back into dainty elvish knots had tendrils creeping free of the thin chains she used to keep it contained, strands curling haphazardly about her face. Circles under her eyes had been ever-present since she'd woken up in the hospital. While she always wore her amulets—they were useful and functional, containing all kinds of magical enhancements—the last few days she'd resembled a Faberge egg. That told me she was low on energy and magic and relying too heavily on her jewels to get her through her normal tasks.

On the surface, we were very different. Our mutual friends sometimes joked that we were an "odd couple". I was taller, fair-haired, and light-skinned. Brash. Outspoken. Elara was tiny, delicate, darker, and quiet. But she was also magically powerful, and kind, and hilarious, and honestly a little too precious for this world. The first time I'd ever laid eyes on her—apart from noticing how shiny she was in all her jewelry—I'd been gleefully watching her wreak absolute mayhem at our college campus. I'd glued myself to her and had remained that way ever since.

"Hon, I know you're stressed," I started. "I get it. But I've made a plan to get all your orders finished and all of your customers have been updated with the new timelines." I settled back into my chair and pulled my hair free from my braid to redo it. "Everything is fine," I reassured her. "You don't need to work beyond what I've scheduled." I would never tell her this, but I'd been turning away new orders left and right. The last thing she needed was a larger workload.

Elara closed her eyes to rub them, and I took the opportunity to snatch the project off her desk. "Argh!" she growled. "I knew you were going to do that!"

I shrugged and batted my eyelashes at her before filing away the jewels and paperwork. "You hired me to help you and look out for the business's bottom line. That's what I'm doing." This was totally part of my job description, as far as I was concerned.

Elara let her head thump onto her workstation and hid beneath her arms. "Yeah, but you don't have to be quite so *bossy* about it," she grumped.

"Yes, I *do*," I groused back, "because *nobody* ever listens to me, and if you kill yourself by working too hard, no one else is going to pay my paycheck."

"Har, har," I thought she said. It was hard to tell with her face pressed against the wood.

"Go home. I mean it. Where is Levi?" I pulled out my fancy-shmancy Voider telephone and sent him a text, wishing for the thousandth time that spectral messengers worked here in the Void—the magicless world. It was time for me to call in the big guns and sic her new husband on her. One look at how tired she was and that over-protective siren would probably bridal-carry her out of here like the adorable sap that he was. A definite benefit to having him around was that it was nice to have another pair of eyes on Elara. I don't want to claim that she causes chaos everywhere she goes or anything, but mayhem really does seem to follow her around. It was what made me like her in the first place.

"He's spending some quality time with the guys," she mumbled as I finally finished tying off my braid and stood to head into the back room.

"Oh yeah? What are they doing?" I asked over my shoulder, careful to keep my tone mildly disinterested. "Guys," *plural*, meant Jordan was back. He'd been gone by the time I exited his room the last time I'd seen him. Elara said he'd just stood up and walked out, and according to Levi, Jordan hadn't come back for a solid week. That was weird, right? Did I offend him that badly just by using his room to put on clothes? Whatever. I hadn't asked questions, not wanting to tip my hand and show my curiosity about him. Seeing his imperious, haughty scowl had plunged me right back into my teenage fascination with him, and I'd been dodging Elara's questions about how I knew him ever since. Nobody needed to know about my childhood infatuation.

I poured some water in a mug from the electric kettle and dropped a teabag in, carrying it back to her desk as she answered.

"Levi said something about subversive cross stitch, but I don't know what that means."

I froze mid-step, trying to picture the siren and his dude-bro roommates cross-stitching dirty words onto sewing samplers. "No, he didn't." There was no way.

"He did! I swear! Why? What does it mean?"

I ignored her question. Sometimes I could swear Levi's entire goal in life was to see what kind of outlandish stuff he could tell people and get away with. "Here." I set the tea on her desk, next to the sandwich she was daintily nibbling on. "Drink this tea and I won't bring up the elephant in the room."

She squinted at me. "What elephant?" she asked after swallowing.

"The 'you need professional guards, and we need to change the nature of our business' elephant."

Elara visibly wilted. She was an extreme introvert and hated the thought of being stuck with a stranger watching her all day, and she had made her own weapons and could defend herself. She'd proven that when she'd set her wasp golems after the last guys to bother her and dropped them like rocks with the venom stored inside. But Phantoms—anarchist gangsters from the Boundlands—had sought her out three times now for her weapons-making magic, and it made me as nervous as a mama bird watching a snake climb her tree. I'd been unable to track down the group's whereabouts since their main hangout burned down, even though I'd been searching nearly every day. I just desperately wanted to protect her.

Before I had time to respond, she perked up and turned to the window expectantly. Elara was able to feel people's magic from a distance, and only one magical person would put that lovesick puppy look in her eyes. A few seconds later, Levi pushed through the door, running his hands through his blonde hair and smiling at my friend. He wore short sleeves and no coat, even though the weather was chilly, so the ocean scene tattoo snaking up his left arm was on full display.

"Oh, good, you're here. I need to go do some stuff and things. You need to take your wife home and put her in bed. She's looking pretty rough." Elara gasped and pretended to be offended, but when you'd been friends with somebody as long as we had, that was just how the cookie crumbled.

Levi cast a concerned look at Elara but held his hand out to me as I stood anyway. We had a secret handshake for the changing of the guards, which was a regular handshake, just done secretly. Elara always rolled her eyes—even though she actually loved it—but her pretty, blonde husband always cracked a grin, so I counted that as a win on both counts.

I patted him on the shoulder as I passed, making him flinch, and headed for the door. "Go make some babies or something. You two had your courthouse date two whole months ago. I expected you to make me an auntie by now. Lord knows my brothers won't."

It sounded like Levi might have choked on his tongue, but I missed it because the door swung shut. I bit back a grin as I headed down the sidewalk, cataloging every person and animal I passed.

There was something about the Seattle ambiance that had always appealed to me, although it would always pale in comparison to the grit of Dry Gulch. It didn't have the opulence of Golden Laurel, or the sleepy beach-town feel of Oars Rest, but it was so much more *interesting*. The people watching was certainly better, for one, and both cities had an industrious atmosphere that felt more honest to me than the moneyed neighborhoods of Golden Laurel.

Distress cries from a nearby robin pair caught my attention as I made my way to my Gate, and I scanned through the nearby park until I found a chestnut tree with a baby robin on the ground. It seemed late for robins to be breeding, but what did I know about Voider animals? Everyone else in the park was going about their business, never noticing the commotion. I was typically more aware of the activity of birds around me than a human, but their general lack of awareness about *everything* always managed to stun me. Even now they were walking by on the sidewalks without even glancing around, and these birds were *loud.*

I frowned down at the baby bird in the grass, all naked bumpy skin and little tufts of fluff on the head that it wasn't strong enough to hold up yet. It was clearly far too young to be out of the nest. A visual search of the lower branches didn't reveal a nest, but it had to have come from this tree. I hated this. I generally didn't interfere much with Voiders, and Voider animals by extension—circle of life and all that—but I couldn't just *leave* it there.

I bent and lifted the little nestling into my fingers, checking to make sure it was still alive. A breath and trembling movement confirmed it was, but with the chilly afternoon air, it wouldn't be for long. It already felt cool against my skin. These birds were really pushing it on the late side of mating season.

"Poor, ugly baby," I crooned, ignoring the scolding cries of its parents. I needed to find some place to shift. Not that I cared *that* much about being naked in public, but the locals tended to clutch their pearls about it. I stalked toward a nearby business with a few feet of wooden fence meant to hide some trash cans, keeping the bird curled in my fingers for warmth. The parents were already stressed, so I wanted to make this quick.

I stripped out of my torn-up jeans and the hoodie I'd stolen from my little brother, stacking them neatly on top of my shoes before setting the baby on top of the pile and quickly shifting into my bird form. One quick hop to snag the rugrat into my claws and I was airborne. It was much easier to spot the nest from above, and I circled a few times to find the best point of entry. I wanted to get this finished before the neighborhood birds started to mob me. Robins were docile, but if crows took up the alarm, I'd be annoyed.

More annoyed.

Birds could be real dicks.

There was only one other nestling in the little cup of sticks, looking plump and princely as I landed. I would have mean-mugged him if he'd been old enough to have his eyes open yet, so I told him off instead. "There are plenty of bugs around here for both of you," I groused at him as I tucked his sibling in beside him. "Fratricide isn't a good look." My magic didn't have any effect on Void creatures, unfortunately, so that was the best I could do.

Launching out of the tree and into the darkening sky to give the little family some space, I chose not to shift back just yet. There was no one nearby to disturb my clothes, and it felt good to stretch my wings for a bit. The chilled air had a bit more bite to it than I usually cared for as it sliced between my feathers, but the freedom of the updraft under my wings as I wheeled about over the streets below filled me with a giddy sort of pleasure. And if I found myself drifting toward a familiar apartment block, it was purely coincidence.

It was hard not to be curious, though, and it didn't help that I easily spotted my prey perched all alone on the empty rooftop. I didn't remember Jordan being a smoker, but he sat four stories up, arms draped over his knees and a cigarette between two fingers, gazing blankly at the horizon as the last rays of light disappeared.

An impulse grabbed me as I peered down at his rigid posture, and I didn't even attempt to fight it. I already acknowledged birds were dicks, didn't I? Pulling my wings against me for a steep dive, I swooped and snatched the cigarette from his fingers before he even knew I was coming and promptly dropped it into an open, wet dumpster below. No amount of my own cackling could drown out Jordan's swearing, but by the time I looked back, he was gone.

Chapter 3

MY ROUNDS HADN'T GONE well. I usually knew where to find the creeps hiding out here in Dry Gulch, the old Boundlands cattle town in the desert where I lived with my youngest brother. Tonight had been just as fruitless as every night since—according to rumors—a group of sparks, the little fire fairies, had rioted and burned down the main headquarters where all the local Phantoms hung out. Normally, I'd never concerned myself with Phantoms—there were all kinds of shady people who lurked around in the seedy underbelly of the city. But once they'd messed with Elara, I wanted to have my eye on them and my finger on the pulse of their group. I was frustrated that I couldn't find any. Not one. I'd been keeping an eye on all of their local haunts, leaving no stone left unturned, but... nothing.

There was also the fact that everywhere I went, I kept catching whiffs of the same brand of cigarettes Jordan smoked. But whenever I looked around, he was never there. It meant that I was constantly feeling like I was being watched, and dwelling on my one-sided and entirely misplaced infatuation with him. So, I was a little extra grumpy when I stomped into our apartment and my little brother cut off his magic to his calling stones as soon as he heard the door open. Calling stones were what we used to communicate over long distances here in the Boundlands. We fed a little magic into a special chip of stone, and spectral messengers would consume the magic and record our message to take to the person whose DNA we presented them. I guess you could use a toenail or something if you were into that, but most of us kept a lock of hair from the people we wanted or needed to talk to. It wasn't something you'd do with a casual acquaintance. For my brother to cut it off like that and act like it wasn't a big deal? Did he actually think I was that brainless?

"What are you doing?" I asked.

Josh blinked at me. "Nothing." He was sitting on our ragged couch with his ankle crossed over the knee, the blonde hair that desperately needed a cut flopping into his eyes. He grabbed a bag of jerky off the coffee table and tried to act casual.

"You think I don't know who you were talking to?" I groused.

His shoulders tensed as I walked over and took the bag of jerky from him, biting into a piece and flopping onto the seat next to him with my lower legs thrown across his lap. "You're a grown-ass man, Joshua. You don't need to hide who you're talking to. We live in a rinky-dink apartment with paper-thin walls. You think I can't hear you having flirty conversations with your boyfriend?"

His eyes went wide as he feigned shock, and he looked around as he blustered, as if there were someone else here that might hear us. "He's not my—Sidney! What are you—he's not my boyfriend." He acted like that was ridiculous. It wasn't like we hadn't ever discussed his romantic preferences, so he wasn't trying to hide *that* from me, but he hadn't ever acted on them.

I narrowed my eyes at him, not buying any of it. "Why not? Have you not asked him out yet? Ask him out."

Josh narrowed his eyes back at me and stared at me until I wasn't sure he was going to answer. He was twice my size, if not more, although he hadn't quite filled out as much as our two older brothers. I know I said he was a grown man, but that was a pretty recent change. I didn't really remember when he'd turned into this big burly guy. He'd been a lanky teenager for so long, but even then, I still saw him as the tender little boy with wispy hair who followed his big sister around and always cried when our older brothers picked on him. I'd been his champion then and I'd been his champion in everything since.

"I don't... know if he feels the same way about me," he said hesitantly.

My back was instantly up. "Are you kidding me?" I said around a bite of jerky, sitting up in my agitation. "Why wouldn't he? You're adorable and *perfect*—well, you'd be perfect if you'd stop eating my yogurt and pick up the socks you leave lying around everywhere. Everyone knows you're the best of us. That's just… this is silly, Josh. I'll ask him out for you." I reached for his calling stones—and he *squirted me in the face* with a spray bottle.

"Boundaries."

"What the hell?" I sputtered and scrubbed at my face. "Why do you even have a water bottle?"

"For my plants." He gestured at some potted shrubbery on the side table.

"What's *wrong* with you?" I asked.

"Nothing is wrong with *me*. I haven't decided how I feel about all this yet, and I don't want to be rushed. I want you to respect my boundaries and my own timeline here."

I frowned at him and finished drying my face with my sleeve. He eyed my hoodie, obviously recognizing that I'd grabbed it from his closet this morning but choosing not to mention it. This was a regular thing for us. His shirts were big on me, but I loved them. It made me feel like my family was always with me.

"What's to decide?" I asked. "Dating a dude isn't taboo in our culture like it is for some of the human cultures." Maybe he had some kind of internal hang-up with it.

He sighed. "It's not taboo in Boundlands' culture, but in shifter culture? I can't pass on my genetics with a husband. I might as well bring home a vampire for how pleased Grandma will be."

My gut clenched at his mention of a vampire and the reminder of how Jordan's life was basically ruined now. Josh was right; shifters had a different take on pairing up and producing offspring than some other groups. Our ancestors, the original shifters, could shapeshift into any animal that breathed air. All of them—any bird, mammal, reptiles, *dragons*, you name it. But as we bred with other races, our genetics got more and more diluted, and eventually family lines could only shift into certain types of animals, and now most of us could only shift into one specific animal, like my family. Some lines got so diluted that they lost the ability to shift altogether, with other magics presenting in their children instead. There was a lot of pressure and expectation around shifters pairing up with other shifters, especially ones with comparable animal forms. I'd dated a lot of different types of people, but Josh was right... I'd always kind of assumed that I'd end up with another bird shifter someday.

I leaned forward and rested my head against his shoulder. "I'll protect you from Grandma." I loved my grandma to death, but on this issue, she could kick rocks. "I just want you to be happy, Bubby," I said, using my childhood nickname for him.

He wrapped his arm around my back and gave me a squeeze with his cheek against my head. "Great. Then buy me more of that fruit-on-the-bottom yogurt."

I WAS SICK OF poking my nose into all the pubs around Dry Gulch—the drinks were terrible, and the patrons were worse—so I decided to head up to the Silver Tongue, a brewery managed by a friend of mine in the same neighborhood Elara lived in. I stepped in, half hoping to find her there, and scanned the interior. No Elara, but I did spot four familiar figures at the bar.

"Oh, drat it all! Hyrak!" A loud voice buzzing with indignation came from the big gray mothman as I threaded my way through the high-top tables. Then, barely quieter, "Can you believe it, Solandis? He's done it again." Alistair was an average-size mothman, which meant he was as tall as an orc. He picked up the drink in front of him and brought it down onto the bar top with a solid sounding *thunk*.

A tinkling laugh from the little sylvan woman next to him made my face split into an involuntary grin. Solandis was basically the plant version of a Disney princess, and she never failed to make me smile. "You should know better than to insult Hyrak's artichokes by now," she replied.

"I wasn't—uff!" Alistair squirmed away as Solandis needled him in the ribs with her boney fingers. They had been best friends since they were little kids and the two of them were like siblings when it came to bickering. "I wasn't insulting them! I only said I didn't understand why anyone would want to eat something that looks so horrifically like a thorny pinecone."

"Hyrak, baby—get him a beer!" Solandis called to her husband as he bustled around behind the bar.

"I don't want a beer; keep your *grass juice*. I wanted a smoothie." Alistair buzzed with irritation. "I'll take a cider and *stop freezing my stuff*!" The wings he kept tucked behind his back fluttered slightly before he pinned them in place again.

Hyrak was an orc I'd met in college and liked immediately because he reminded me of my oldest brother, Sam. He was an ice elementalist, and he'd married Solandis as soon as we'd graduated. They were *disgustingly* cute, and I couldn't be happier for them. I'd even helped him commission their wedding rings from Elara.

Solandis, being sylvan, was pale green with darker extremities and soft white hair that had frickin' *flowers* growing in it. Hyrak had dark green skin covered in white patches that he decorated with tattoos in some foreign script. Probably orcish. He kept his black hair shaved on the sides and back and pulled the rest into a knot at the back of his head. He always had his tusks capped with metal and wore dressy button up shirts and black-rimmed glasses like the big ol' handsome nerd that he was. They were *perfect* for each other.

There were two open seats at the bar, one next to Alistair and one next to Bane, a big panther shifter with some Latino human ancestors who graced him with golden brown skin and hair as dark as Hyrak's. On the one hand, Bane was a huge flirt and sitting next to him might give him the wrong idea. On the other, I had a hard time keeping my hands out of Alistair's fluff when

I was near him. He had a ruff of fur around his neck, like a big gray lion's mane, but it felt like rabbit fur. If I sat next to him, I'd want to pet him all night, but he also shed rainbow-colored scales from his wings constantly. The guy would be the world's worst burglar. It was like a cloud of glitter everywhere he went, and I could never get it off of me.

I decided to sit with Bane.

As I sidled up to the bar, Solandis hissed something at Alistair and he buzzed a reply, but my hearing isn't as good as my sense of smell. "Have you been listening to this all night?" I asked Bane as I slid onto the stool.

"All night," he agreed, nodding.

"Hey, Sidney!" Solandis greeted me cheerfully, and I gave her a wink and a grin as I watched her best friend pick up his frozen block of drink and use one of his four clawed hands to try to scrape some of the icy smoothie off the top. The clicking sounds coming from him sounded distinctly indignant.

Hyrak placed a dark colored cider in front of Alistair with a mischievous grin before turning to greet me. "How you doin', Sid?" The big muscles in his arm flexed as he pushed his black-rimmed glasses up his nose.

I couldn't help my chuckle. "Hy, buddy, you look like the Hulk had a baby with Clark Kent when you wear those things."

He cast a glance at his wife. "Sweetie, do you know what any of those words mean?"

"No, I do not," came her bubbly reply as she tried to steal a sip of Alistair's cider. He unfurled his long cylindrical tongue and plunged it into his drink, making her squawk.

"Never mind." I shook my head. Voider references rarely landed well here in the Boundlands. Of the five of us, only Bane and I were able to survive in the Void, or the human world. Humans couldn't pass through the Gates to the Boundlands at all, because the magic in the portals killed them instantly. Elves could survive for years in the Void before being cut off from the magic in the Boundlands started to affect their health. As a result, they'd mixed with humans and produced offspring.

Us with mixed-race ancestry could more or less pass back and forth unharmed as long as we made it back into the Boundlands to recharge occasionally, but the older races, the ones closest to the original high-fae like the orcs and fairies, they couldn't survive there for longer than a few minutes. That meant my human references and movie quotes were entirely wasted on these people.

Hyrak smiled his big, friendly smile at me as he leaned his elbows on the counter. "What can I get you, Sidney?"

I eyed the drink in front of Bane, full of leaves and limes. "Is that a mojito?"

Bane nodded and took a gulp. "Yup."

"I'll have what he's having." I turned to Bane as Hyrak left to make my drink.

"How you doing, beautiful?" Bane swayed a little on his stool.

"Ew, no. Lord, Bane, *every time*." I steadied him on his seat so he wouldn't fall on me. How strong were these mojitos? Honestly, I couldn't tell you why I wasn't attracted to Bane. Elara would tell you he checked every one of my boxes and was a dead ringer for my type. He was big and burly, which was a *must* for me. He was handsome and charismatic, which I loved. I don't know what it was, but every time he flirted with me, I couldn't help but cringe.

He smiled at me, but it looked more sleepy than flirty. I was going to have to tell Hyrak to cut him off and make sure he got home okay.

"You heard anything about the Phantoms lately?" I asked, keeping my voice low.

He shook his head. "Nothing. Maybe they're all dead."

"They're not all dead." They couldn't *all* be dead. "They're just underground."

"Maybe." He took another sip of his drink, nodding a little too much. "I got something for you."

I gave him a side-eye.

"Rowdy says his crew has some ceremonial daggers coming through the chain tomorrow. They'll be at the warehouse on

53rd in Seattle tomorrow if you wanna peep at them and see if you want dibs."

I considered this information for a moment, then placed a calling chip between him and his glass. It contained the names of some of his competitors with new shipments, and it quickly disappeared into his pocket before he nodded and took another long pull of his drink.

"Pleasure doing business with you, sir."

Chapter 4

I TOOK A BREAK from work the next day to check out the warehouse Bane had mentioned. I took a meandering flight before circling the building a couple of times, giddy with anticipation. Digging through a warehouse for supplies felt like a treasure hunt every time. I rarely found exactly what I was looking for, but I almost always found something interesting. Sparkles and baubles, and sharp, shiny tools… weapons, gemstones, and random artifacts of all kinds. Bartering, haggling, pawing through random piles of other people's treasures… this was the language of my little magpie soul.

Workers at places I didn't visit often weren't usually cool with me poking around inside, so I decided to let myself in through an open window in the loading bay.

The biggest problem with being a bird is that we don't have hands, a fact I lamented as I landed on top of a large wooden crate with no obvious openings that I could see into. If I were a box full of ceremonial daggers, where would I be? I hopped from crate to crate in the dusty, dimly lit warehouse, looking for labels and gaps large enough for me to get my head inside, growing more frustrated by the second. Stomping my foot just didn't give as much satisfaction in this form, so I let out a raucous screech instead.

Instead of the silence I expected in response—since there wasn't anyone around that I could see—I received a chirp. A really odd, pathetic, garbled-sounding chirp. Just one, and then silence. I called again and again, pausing and listening each time to the occasional response until I'd tracked the sound to the large, dilapidated wooden crate closest to the loading bay doors.

Shipping live animals wasn't illegal, but the size of this crate told me it wasn't chickens. The sound it was making wasn't exactly birdlike—it didn't sound like *any* bird I recognized. I found a gap in the shoddily built crate that was large enough to cram the top half of my body into, and once my eyes adjusted to the darkness, I saw red.

There were eggs—rough, pale yellow, and easily larger than a human soccer ball—packed in puffed stone. And these weren't Voider eggs. They were *dragon eggs*. Some greedy, half-wit *scum* were smuggling them from the Boundlands into the Void, where they should have already died. Dragons are not creatures who can survive in the Void without the magic the Boundlands provides. What's more, they need very specific conditions to incubate. Pressure and heat from the mountain fissures they're lain in, usually threaded with gold and other magical conduits by their parents.

I pushed some of my magical energy blindly toward the middle of the crate, hoping to give the little creatures a boost until I could get back. I couldn't spare much in this form, but I gave them as much as I could. Then I was out of the crate, through the hangar door, and into the sky in seconds flat, winging my way back to the shop in less than a minute. It would take longer to get back, but I repeated to myself that I could only do what I could do.

I shifted forms on the street in front of the door and wrenched it open, diving for the back room—and my clothing, phone, and weapons—talking at top speed all the while. "Elara, grab your phone. I'm going to text you an address. Call the Boundlands' Enforcement line here in the Void and tell them there are smuggled dragon eggs in a crate in the warehouse there."

I didn't hear a response, so I turned to find her still frozen in her chair, probably confused by my nude jaunt through the front of the shop, but I didn't have time for her to catch up mentally. I texted her the address and started strapping on weapons. "Can I grab your new emitters?" That snapped her into motion and she was up in a blink.

A few months ago, Elara had found a water sprite here in the Void, and like most creatures that venture into the Void and don't belong here, she died before we could get her back into the Boundlands. Neither of us had been happy about it, but Elara, being who she is, had done what she always did when presented with something that distressed her: she'd fixated on it. Fixation had led to her experimenting with magic, as it usually did, and she'd created some magical emitters. They weren't finished yet, but she had a working prototype that was created for this exact situation. If a magic-dependent creature was found in the Void and unable to get back through the Gate quickly enough, these emitters could be placed around them and, hopefully, provide enough magic to keep them alive long enough to make it safely back out of the Void.

It was genius.

It just... hadn't been tested on anything living yet.

"You won't be able to power them on or know how to set them up," she said, grabbing her coat and dashing for the make-shift case she kept them in on a back shelf.

I cursed a blue streak in my head, knowing she was right but that her coming would put her in danger. I grabbed an extra set of daggers to stuff in my boots, and my handgun went into the waistband of my pants. *Don't try this at home, kids.* "If you're coming, I'm going ahead first to make sure it's clear," I announced as I bolted for the door. My instinct to protect her warred with my acknowledgement that she had her wasp constructs full of venom with her, as well as the desire—no, the *need*—to get those eggs to safety. It felt like déjà vu from my earlier bid to rescue the water sprite, and I couldn't let the outcome be the same this time.

I made good time on the way back to the warehouse, and I knew I'd have longer than I liked to get the building secure for

Elara to arrive. Try as she might, that girl couldn't run any faster than a mountain troll taking a Sunday stroll.

I started scanning the outside grounds, but only found two workers in the main loading bay. I grimaced a bit at the force needed to overpower both of them, but there was no way these guys didn't know about the smuggling going on in there. These operations didn't hire random people they couldn't trust not to narc when they found out what was going on. Not for the first time, I wished I had the abilities that Elara possessed to control her creepy venom weapons, but then we'd probably get caught for having the venom since we were involving authorities this time. This was why I hated involving cops; they complicated everything. If Rowdy or Bane were involved in this, I was going to gut them both.

Elara arrived shortly after I'd popped the top of the crate with a pry bar. As much as I wished I could trust the Voider cops or Boundlands Enforcement to swoop in and know how to save the eggs, I absolutely, one hundred fifty percent, did not. The thought was laughable.

The eggs were nestled down neatly in the rocky medium, but there was no heat source at all. The shells were leathery and rough feeling, cold to the touch. "I don't know how to get enough heat to all of these," I grumbled. "I don't even know if they're still alive. I could hold one or maybe two against my stomach and wrap my arms around them to give them warmth, but it's not going to be enough heat and there are too many eggs for that anyway." I mimicked the chirping sound I'd heard earlier, hoping to get a response, but got none. "How do I know which ones to focus on?"

Elara glanced up to where I was perched precariously on the edge of the wooden crate. "How many eggs are there?" Her voice had an odd note as she worked carefully to set up the three small stone pillars around the crate.

I hopped down and worked to haul the wooden box away from the stack of crates it was stacked against so she could have more room to maneuver, grunting as I answered. "I'm not sure because they're all buried down in here, but there's at least three I can see from the surface."

She made a face but continued to fuss with the pillar placement as she spoke. "I can feel magic from inside there. There's something alive. I can look at them when I'm done, but I have to get these running. You should call Jordan."

That was a record scratch moment if there ever was one. I blinked at her, probably looking like a startled owl, but she wasn't looking at me. "Why on earth would I do that?"

Elara paused with her fingers on a gemstone set in the middle of the pillar she was holding and looked at me out of the corner of her eye. Her expression clearly said I was missing something. "Sidney, you said you know Jordan. What does Jordan do?" Her tone said she was trying to jog my memory.

I gently scraped some of the shipping medium away from the closest egg to examine the state of it. No mold, that was a good sign. "Uhhh, glares at me, skulks around in the shadows, smokes cheap cigarettes, and drinks blood from little plastic pouches?" I wouldn't have known about that last one if she hadn't told me, but I still had no idea what she was getting at.

"He also got hired on to some Boundlands' Enforcement task force here in the Void, and I'm pretty sure he's a fire elemental."

I blinked repeatedly, memories from my childhood flooding back. Jordan playing with a smoldering stick as he talked with another boy while they waited for a match to start. Jordan with flaming orange eyes as he fought for the ball against a boy twice his size. Jordan wearing gloves at every match, because he couldn't control his heat levels when he got amped up at a game. All of his game poles—the long sticks with curved hooks on the ends used for directing the ball in a game called hooks—were covered in scorched handprints from practices. *How could I have forgotten that?* I guess it was because those things hadn't really mattered much to a twelve-year-old with a crush. I just saw his handsome face and the way he moved with precision down the field and the confidence with which he'd held himself... I shook my head to snap out of it.

There was no way I was going to call Jordan. What good would a fire elemental do anyway? He'd be just as likely to cook the eggs as he was to warm them. I growled. "I don't even have his number; how would I call him?"

Elara just shrugged, completely ignoring my internal freak out. "Call Levi. He's already on his way, but it will save time if he calls Jordan while he's headed here."

I frowned at the top of her head and pulled out my phone to call her husband. I hated using this thing, but unfortunately, calling stones didn't work in the Void.

Jordan sat perched on the crate across from me with his hands stuffed down in the puffed stones the eggs were packed in. I could see nothing but the blank black visor of a full helmet and a head-to-toe uniform of jet-black leather. He kept a scarf made of stiff material draped over the helmet like a hood. He looked like some kind of futuristic motorcycle rider. He was just sitting there, doing what we'd asked by warming the eggs, and his uniform didn't allow me to see his reaction to anything at all. It irritated me, and I desperately wanted to *mess with him.*

"I think there's seven," Elara said beside me. I glanced over to find her staring into the crate with us. "I don't think they're all alive though." I heard the reluctance in her voice, and I hated that I'd had to drag her along to this. She had a tender heart. As for myself, I was *angry.*

"What do you feel?" I asked. Elara's magical abilities never ceased to amaze me.

"The eggs themselves have some kind of magic to them," she answered, hovering a hand over one that was exposed at the surface, and then another. "I think the shells actually emit some magic, though it's pretty weak. That's why a few are still alive.

This one has very little magic. She moved her hand to hover over another exposed egg. "While this one has much more."

"Did you guys know there's banging coming from a closet back here?" Levi's voice came from the other side of the room. The enchantment on his voice tugged at my emotions, trying to pull me into a dazed stupor, but I blinked through it.

"Yeah, that was me. Don't move that chair," I hollered back. "So, you think the ones with less magic are dead, but the shell still has some residual magic?" I asked Elara. She was frozen, clearly still stuck on the noises from the closet. "I didn't want to risk them hurting you when you arrived, so I... put them over there." I waved in their direction.

She blinked at me a few more times and answered slowly. "Yes, I think that's correct. There's only two or three with larger amounts of magic, but it's hard to tell because they're all clumped together in there and I can't see them. I could also be totally wrong about all this, but I don't think I am. When you were chirping at them earlier, I felt the magic in one of them increase more than the others. I don't know why that would be though."

Birds and reptiles both sometimes responded to their parent's sounds through their shells before they hatched. I chirped again at the eggs, cognizant of Jordan's stare through his featureless helmet and doing my best to ignore him. Elara nodded to show it was having some effect, so I focused on my animal magic and shared what I could with them. "That's helping," she said. "Whatever you're doing with your magic right now, all three of the stronger ones just increased."

"The door is rattling!" Levi's voice carried over the room, carrying a slight emotional rebuff with his enchantment. The dude's nerves must have been getting his undies in a twist. I jumped down and stalked over to the closet where I'd left the men earlier, finding Levi with his arms crossed as he stared at the door.

"One of the eggs just lost a lot of magic, Sidney," Elara called as I walked away.

This is like juggling crystal goblets.

I shoved the chair more firmly under the doorknob with my foot. "Just hit them if they get out," I told Levi, trying to hand him my gun.

"I'm not touching that," he said, eyeing it.

I mentally rolled my eyes and stuffed the gun back into my pants, jogging back over to the eggs. Elara was trying to lift one out of the crate, but she was so little she couldn't get any leverage on it from where she stood. "I've got it." I jumped back onto the ledge. The stones in the crate were nicely warmed, just above body temperature from what I could feel. I was impressed with Jordan's temperature control, though I'd never admit it. I put my hands on the egg Elara seemed most worried about and released a little more of my energy. There was a strange echo in my magic as I did, almost reverberating through me. My skin felt hot and itchy for a few seconds and my magic twinged oddly.

"Better," she commented, nodding approvingly. I shook off the odd feeling and tried not to preen.

"My team should be here any minute." Jordan's voice sounded a little muffled through the helmet. "I heard the call come through when Boundlands Enforcement's Void division redirected Elara's call." His head tipped in Levi's direction. "Should I get rid of those guys back there?"

"Nah. I didn't hurt them too much and they'll probably be too embarrassed to admit a girl did it." These types of guys never liked to admit to being strong-armed into a closet by a girl obviously smaller than them.

When his team of four others did arrive, Jordan did most of the talking and took the blame for the men I'd corralled, which was weirdly kind. None of his team seemed too worried about it. All but one were dressed in the same black leather uniforms and deep hood with a helmet underneath. They made quick work of dismantling the crate and setting all seven eggs—Elara was right—in a heated incubator the size of a table.

Elara stiffened as they wheeled it away. "No! No, that isn't going to work." She addressed the woman pushing the incubator firmly but blushed under the weight of everyone's stares as they all turned to look at her. "There's an egg, *there*,"—she pointed at a place she obviously had no clear visual of, but I knew she could feel—"that suffers somehow every time it's removed from Sidney's presence." She gestured at me.

No one spoke, but the other two wearing helmets turned to look at the lady pushing the incubator, and she raised her eyebrows.

Elara wasn't going to let it go. "I can feel its magic," she insisted, "and when Sidney walks away, or when you started to take it, the magic lessens." It was really adorable how much fight she had in her whenever anyone else's well-being was at stake. Even more adorable? The way Levi stood behind his tiny wife, towering over her by head and shoulders, his glare daring everyone in the room to question her. I could *burst* at their cuteness, but I needed to focus here.

I cleared my throat to take some of the social pressure off my friend. "I'm a shifter," I said to the group, "with some animal mage abilities. I loaned them some energy, but they still seem very weak. Maybe that one is closer to the brink than the others." The other two living ones, at least, if Elara was correct.

The group exchanged glances again, seeming unsure what to do about the situation. "Why not let her ride along to the rescue center?" Jordan asked, sounding tired.

I frowned at him. "And what, live there?" How was that supposed to work long term? "I have all the necessary brooding equipment at home. I could just bring it home with me." Assuming my incubator was large enough to hold the thing. I used it to help rehabilitate abandoned bird eggs in the Boundlands sometimes as a hobby, but it should be big enough to fit *one* dragon egg.

The lady with the incubator scoffed. "Our permits don't allow for—"

I cut her off. "I'm a *shifter*," I repeated. "We have special rights regarding protected species." Not to mention, I'd been working in animal rehabilitation since I was a pre-teen. "I can get you whatever paperwork you need."

And that's how I ended up with a dragon egg living on my kitchen counter. *I never did find those ceremonial daggers...*

Chapter 5

THE FACT WAS, WE'D all needed to ride along with the Enforcement crew. They needed to bring the magical emitters at least as far as the Gate and Elara wasn't willing to let her prototypes out of her sight yet. Both the woman who wasn't in uniform—apparently part of the Boundlands' wildlife welfare—and Jordan's team lead had peppered Elara with questions about her creation and had been disappointed to learn they were still a way off from being something rescue crews could have on hand. She'd submitted them for review but was still bogged down in the approval process.

Every government has red tape.

Elara was now at my apartment with every piece of gold she could possibly spare, helping me cram it into the incubator. I hoped the wildlife welfare office had friends with pockets as deep as Elara's for the sake of those other eggs.

"I never knew that dragons used gold as a magical conduit to brood their eggs," she said, fascination clear in her voice.

"Mm, yeah, I figure that's where the legends of them hoarding treasure comes from. How's the little guy doing?" I asked, closing the incubator and peering in through the glass.

"Much better, I think," Elara answered thoughtfully. "It didn't like it when you went into your bedroom to get your ear cuff,"—I'd finally caved and decided to grab the enchantment ward she'd created for me so that I could ignore Levi's magic more easily—"but between the heat Jordan provided and your magic, its magic level is much higher and more stable."

It felt healthier to me too, but her reassurance made me feel better. "I guess I'm going to be living in my kitchen until this thing hatches," I grumbled.

"Do they make portable incubators?" Levi asked from where he stood at the sink, looking out my kitchen window at the street below.

"Probably, but I don't have one, and something big enough for a dragon egg would be hard to come by. This thing will probably pip any day now based on the sounds it was making."

Elara wrinkled her delicate little nose. "Maybe we should have Jordan come over and carry it around for you," she said lightly.

"I'm good." I lowered myself to the kitchen floor and laid down on my back, making a show of getting comfortable. The last thing I wanted was that guy in my house making me more obsessed with his pretty brown eyes and arrogant-looking cheekbones. "I'll just hang out in here for a few days until it hatches, make sure it takes a meal or two, and then return it to the wildlife refuge so they can release it back into the wild."

She eyed me doubtfully. "You're going to live in your kitchen?"

"I might have to take a bathroom break every now and then. Josh will be home soon; we can take turns." All my brothers had some animal magic, though mine was the strongest. They'd egg-sit in shifts if I asked.

"What's the deal with you and Jordan?" she asked for the third time. I was rubbing off on her, which meant she was getting bolder with her questions. No more dancing around the edges of things like a proper elvish socialite. I'd be proud of her if it wasn't me that she was needling.

"What deal? What makes you think there's a deal?" I bit my tongue. I was as bad as Josh at deflecting attention.

The look she gave me told me she wasn't impressed. "You both act so weird around each other. You basically ignore him, and you never ignore anyone unless they're flirting with you and you don't like it. But he's not flirting with you." She thought for a moment. "And he's normally so playful and friendly, but he doesn't act like that around you."

That got my attention because that's the Jordan I remembered. So, he was still playful and friendly, but not around me? I scowled at the ceiling. *What the hell? Totally not a slap in the face or anything.*

"I dunno. I was kinda busy with the eggs," I lied. "It's not like he talked to me. He said maybe two sentences the whole time he was there. And what's the weird uniform about?"

"Sunlight," Levi said, his attention still glued to something on the street. I guess that made sense, if it were true that vampires couldn't be out in the sunlight.

"Wait, were they all vampires?" I asked.

"The ones in the leather and helmets were," he answered distractedly. "He got hired on to some special Enforcement team that's just vampires. He was probably just sleepy, Elara—it was broad daylight and he's normally dead asleep at that time."

I thought about it for a moment from my place on the kitchen tile before I decided it didn't matter. So what if the hot vampire didn't like me? *Nobody likes vampires anyway. They're as volatile as the fae, and his weird behavior proves it.* As soon as it entered my mind, I felt guilty, remembering the happy, fierce teenager I'd known, who was probably struggling with being a vampire now. I couldn't help it if he didn't like me though. I brushed the thought away as Elara gathered her things to head home.

"Levi, are you ready?" she asked.

"Hold on. There are two boys out here having a peeing contest, and a little old lady spotted them through her window. She's sneaking up on them with a broom." That would be Delores. Those boys were gonna get it; that old woman had some dryad bloodlines or something and she would *never* tolerate anyone peeing in her rose bushes.

"A peeing contest?" Elara's voice was completely baffled.

"Yeah, you know, trying to see who can pee the furthest distance away," Levi said. No, Elara would not know. Shouts erupted from outside and Levi burst out laughing. Even with my ward against enchantments, it was hard to ignore the strength of his magic as his throaty laughter echoed. "Oh man, I've never seen an old lady swing a broom so fast." He was still chuckling as I bade them farewell from my spot on the kitchen floor.

I was still laying there pondering my lot in life when my brother came home. He approached the kitchen to peer at me with raised eyebrows after noticing my legs sticking out from behind the cabinets.

"Hey, you're home," I said without moving. "I'm going to need a favor."

THIS WASN'T GOING TO work.

I'd been so excited when, after two days of camping out next to the incubator, the biggest egg I'd ever known had finally pipped. After slicing open a flap in its shell with its little egg tooth, the baby hadn't been in a hurry to come out, content to sit and soak up what was left of its yolk and peek out through the slit in its shell. Eventually, after some coaxing from me in the form of calling to it with the little squeaky chirp it used, it tried to force its way out of the hole. There hadn't been enough room for it to hatch in the incubator, so I'd hauled the egg out, and watched in awe as a baby *dragon* had hatched on my kitchen table. My magic had echoed oddly again as he climbed out of his shell, and my skin prickled as he stared at me and peered around the room with his big dark eyes.

He was the *cutest* thing. Even though he was skinny, he was nearly beagle-sized—I'd always been surprised at how much animal could fit all folded up inside an egg—and was covered in dark scales that caught the light with an iridescent shimmer and big, droopy wings. He already had teeth, and claws and horns, being a perfect, smaller replica of his parents. I say his, because while I don't have a ton of experience sexing reptiles, the bulge behind the baby's cloaca was a pretty clear indicator that I was dealing with a male. And he was going to get *big*—quickly. He was skinny now, sure, but from what I could tell, he was one of the species of lesser dragons and would eventually end up being about the size of my apartment—a far cry smaller than the bigger species of greater dragons, but he was going to be a *big boy*.

He'd been quiet for the first few days. We'd bought one of those used playpen things for kids and stuck it in the living room area to keep him contained, but he hadn't moved much. I draped a blanket over the top of it so it would be dark and warm, and to lessen his habituation to us as much as possible. It went against all my instincts to just leave him alone and let him rest, because baby birds needed 'round-the-clock care and feeding and most of my experience was with them. But reptiles often didn't eat for a few days after they hatched, and just needed a warm, dark place to rest while they got their bearings and prepared for the first shedding of their skin. The only time he moved was when I left the room for something and Josh wasn't in there with him. He'd thrash and claw until one of us ran over to reassure him, afraid he was going to rip through the fabric of the playpen.

But now I wanted him to eat, and he wasn't having it. I had a plethora of foods for him to try, everything from a dead rat, to fish, to chicken hearts, but he wouldn't take anything. I was back on the kitchen floor again, this time trying to restrain a large, winged reptile, with him pinned between my legs so he couldn't bludgeon me with his wings and trying to pry his mouth open at the same time. Sometimes, if you could just get food into an animal's mouth, then they'd eat it, but he kept waiting until I released him and then he'd push it back out with his tongue.

My brother leaned over the edge of the counter. "We should name it."

"Shut up, Josh. We're not naming him." I was struggling to hold the dragon's mouth shut around the chicken heart I'd just snuck in there, but blood was making my hands slippery.

"We could name him Onyx, since he's black."

"We can't name him. He's going to be released back into the wild. You don't name things that aren't pets." I wanted to get at least three meals into him before we released him, to prove he was thriving, but that might take a while since carnivorous reptiles didn't eat every day. The wildlife refuge still hadn't contacted me either.

"What about Spot?" Josh mused, completely ignoring me.

I slowly let go of the dragon's mouth, holding my breath in the hopes that he'd swallow. The chicken heart popped out onto the floor. I slumped in defeat.

"You should cook it," Josh said. I turned my head and blinked at him. "This book you got says they like their food cooked." He pointed down at the counter, where I'd left a stack of books on dragons.

"They like it cooked," I repeated in a mocking tone. "Because they cook their food in their big dragon kitchens."

Josh squinted at me. "They breathe fire." *Okay, fair.*

I picked up the dead rat, wondering how I could cook it. *Maybe I should start with the fish.*

"Wait, I've got the perfect name," Josh said proudly. "Humphry Herbert Hucklebee, the Fierce."

"I'm not naming it that."

MY WHOLE APARTMENT SMELLED like burnt rat.

The dragon did end up showing more interest in the cooked foods, but I'm not a great cook, so it was by a happy accident that we found out that what he *really* prefers is burnt foods. Which was great; he ended up eating quite a bit. But now my whole house reeked of burned rat fur.

It made it impossible to sleep. Between the acrid smell and my own general restlessness, I'd been tossing and turning for a few hours already, and the little dragon wasn't helping. He was in my room because I couldn't get him to stay out. If I wasn't home, he was fine being left with one of my brothers, but if he knew I was here, he would scratch and huff until I let him in. Which was cute, but he was making it hard for me to sleep. Every couple of minutes, he'd worm his way up onto my bed, down near my feet. I'd pick him back up and haul him back to the floor, but every time I did, he'd make that same squeaky noise that he made in the shell, and it'd make my heart clench.

I wasn't trying to be mean to him, he just wasn't a pet. Dragons *aren't domesticated*. He was a wild animal, and he needed to be able to return to the wild. It made me nervous for him that he was already this interested in people. He could end up being the size of a small house someday, and he needed to be up in the mountains doing his own thing and hunting his own bigger-than-a-rat-sized food before he did. What was I going to do? Roast him a cow?

He crept to the edge of the bed and laid his head on the mattress again, peering at me to see if I was going to react. When I didn't, he flapped his wings to give himself a boost and clambered up the side and onto the bed.

I sighed. "You are relentless," I said to the darkness.

He took that as permission and plopped down on my blankets, but he kept twitching and moving. Eventually, he rolled over and wormed his way up against my leg.

As I laid there, staring at the ceiling in the darkness, Elara's words came back to me from a few days ago. *And he's normally so playful and friendly, but he doesn't act like that around you.* What the hell? So, *what*? He was still the same normal, friendly Jordan to everyone else but not to me? Why did I get the cold, glaring, asshole Jordan and everyone else got playful, fun Jordan? What did I do to him? It had been bugging me ever since she'd said it.

When I'd walked into his apartment the first time, he'd gotten up and left without saying a word to me. I kept smelling his cigarettes around town—with a distinct note of vampire mixed in—but he was never there. Then he took the heat for the guys I roughed up at the warehouse, but he spoke one sentence to me the whole time, and even Elara noticed he was acting weird that day. None of it made sense.

The longer I lay there, the madder I got, something ugly twisting at my stomach. If Elara had been telling me this, I would have told her that her feelings were hurt, but that couldn't be the case here. I don't care what people think of me. I just didn't like not understanding something.

When the dragon twitched again, I got up out of bed. I was too restless to sleep. Jordan was being weird, and I didn't know why. But I could find out. I was going to make him talk to me. He needed his boat rocked a little bit anyway.

Chapter 6

I WAS BLAMING LACK of sleep for all my faulty decision making as I circled above Jordan's apartment at midnight. His bedroom light peeked through the crack in his curtains, and from the way they billowed, his window was open. I circled one extra time to double check, because shifters heal fast, but I didn't think I'd survive a broken neck.

Then—because I know how to make an entrance—I hit that crack in his curtains at a million miles an hour, bursting into his bedroom in an explosion of feathers and billowing fabric.

"What the—" Jordan was propped up in his bed, reading a textbook by the light of a lamp on his nightstand. He was wearing nothing but boxers, with the book propped on his bent knee and the other leg sprawled haphazardly on the bed. And oh, my word, he looked *good*. I shifted forms and landed at the foot of his bed while he was still talking and did my best to ignore his gorgeous thighs. I wasn't here to ogle him.

Much.

"I want to know what your deal is," I said, tossing my hair out of my face. I glanced around his room—total bachelor-pad, no scent of a woman anywhere. I'd never find a hair tie in here. I hated not having a hair tie.

"Oh sure, come on in. Window's always open. Where are your *clothes* at?" he groused.

"I can't carry them in my *beak*, Jordan." I raised my chin and cast him a haughty look before turning and stalking over to his closet. Hanging on the closet door was an embroidery hoop with some pale fabric and the words, "Home is where the vampire is," stitched so poorly a five-year-old could have done better. *Levi.* I pushed the door open.

"What are you doing?" Jordan asked, giving me a side-eye.

"I'm getting *dressed*." I flipped through the clothes on his hangers. Everything looked expensive and tailored. I pulled a white dress shirt out.

"I mean, you don't have to get dressed on my account," he replied, and when I glowered at him over my shoulder, he was staring at my ass.

"It sure sounded like you were complaining about me not wearing clothes, so I'm putting on clothes."

I put the shirt on and fastened the bottom three buttons, while he mumbled something like, "I wasn't complaining."

I ignored him, briefly considering raiding his dresser for some boxers, but whatever. My bits were covered. When I marched back to his bed to stand at the end of it, his eyes were locked on my tits, so maybe my bits weren't *that* covered. I raised my chin. "What's your deal?" I repeated.

Jordan slowly closed his textbook and set it down beside him. He raised an eyebrow as he leaned his head back against the high wooden headboard and draped his arm over his bent knee. It was hard not to watch his muscles flex as he moved. His chest and shoulders were nicely muscled, even with the oddly pale vampire skin. He toyed with his pack of cigarettes in his other hand, turning it around and around in his fingers as he stared at me. *Still not answering my question.*

I tried another one. "Since when do you smoke?" I asked, gesturing at the pack with my chin while I started to braid my hair out of my face.

He circled the pack in his fingers a few more times before answering. "It helps with the smell."

I frowned at him while I finished my braid. Since I didn't have a band, I jerked out a strand of hair and tied the end off with that. I didn't have any idea what he was talking about.

He sighed before explaining further, "It makes it so I can't smell so much. Why? You want one?" He lifted the pack.

"Smoke is bad for bird lungs." I scrunched my nose at him. "And it stinks."

Jordan considered me for a second with his haughty eyes. He had the most gorgeous, arrogant-looking face. Everything he did looked imperious and vain. He slowly raised his hand higher in the air, glanced to the right, and flicked the package off his fingers. It landed with a thump in the trash can next to his bed. It was my turn to raise an eyebrow.

"What are you doing here?" he asked, his voice low.

"Do you want me to leave?"

He was quiet for a long moment before he said, "Do whatever you want."

I adjusted the shirt and his eyes dropped to my chest again. I'd been a gangly, knobby kid until I'd had my glow up as a teen. I'd liked the attention from guys sometimes, but mostly I was just proud of how physically capable I'd become. That said, I certainly wasn't against Jordan looking at me. He could look all he wanted.

"I already told you what I'm doing here. I want to know why you're acting like you don't know me. Why you got pissed and left the other night, and yet, you've been stalking me around Dry Gulch." I crossed my arms under my breasts, forcing them up higher.

Jordan narrowed his eyes at me. "I'm not stalking you."

I narrowed my eyes back. *Then why can I smell you following me?* I wanted to ask, but his shoulders had gotten tense. In fact, as I watched him, his whole body was getting tense.

I thought for a moment while letting my eyes linger on his sprawled legs and his black boxer briefs—which did great things for his... *bulge*—a little longer. He wasn't the hulking, burly type of guy I normally went for. He was lean, and sturdy, and pretty, while still being masculine and a little menacing. Something about him just did it for me. Laid out as he currently was, he looked like a feast, and I was starting to feel hungry. I wondered what his skin tasted like. I had an impish impulse to find out, and I had terrible impulse control. "I'm curious about something," I said, placing my knee on the end of his bed. His eyes widened slightly as I prowled toward him with mischief in my eyes.

"Sidney, I don't know what you're doing, but this isn't a good idea," he said as I settled between his legs. I stopped where I was as he lifted a hand to stay my approach, but his eyes were still transfixed on my tits.

I tried not to grin. "I love bad ideas."

He huffed a laugh, but it wasn't humorous. "You don't get it. I could really hurt you. I get in trouble with the guys all the time for breaking stuff. I don't know how to control it even after several years." He shook his head. "This isn't safe, Sid." He cast a quick glance at his closed bedroom door.

Well, that was a challenge if I ever heard one.

Maybe I liked to be hurt a little. He didn't know my life. I squinted at him, considering. Vampires did have their own set of complications… and Jordan had always had a quick temper and not a lot of control, but in the end, I decided, "I'm a big girl. And I'm completely capable of deciding what I should and shouldn't be doing. Of course, if you want me to stop, I will. So, let's play a game." I leaned forward again, halting once more when he tensed.

"I think what we need… is a safe word," I said. I'd stumbled over the word "we" almost saying "you", but I didn't want to point out his obvious nervousness. And if I had been entirely honest with myself, as I looked at his tense muscles and remembered the strange glow his eyes got sometimes, I might have wanted one too.

"A safe word?" he repeated, his voice sounding unimpressed. He was trying to scowl, but I caught the slightest lift at the corner of his mouth.

"Yes," I said with mock brightness as I made myself comfortable on my knees. I cast my gaze around the room, looking for inspiration, and my eyes landed on the embroidery hoop. "My safe word is 'cross stitch'. If at any point, I say the words 'cross stitch', I want you to stop what you're doing immediately."

His fingers were clenched in the sheets next to him. I reached forward slowly, keeping my eyes on him and his reactions, before taking his wrists in my hands and directing them upwards. "This will be your 'safe word'," I said, wrapping his fingers around the top of his wooden headboard. "If you take your hands off the headboard, or break something, I'm done and I leave."

"What?" The word was completely flat, and I almost laughed.

"We're going to work on your self-control," I said, placing my finger in the center of his chest and trailing it lightly down to the top of his boxers. He shivered and shifted his gaze between my finger and my face, as if he wasn't sure where to focus. "You complain about your strength, but it's your lack of self-control that's the problem, not your strength."

"What?" His brain was stuck, and he tightened his grip on the bed.

I could tell his mind was having trouble focusing on my words, so I paused and looked at his face. "I could tie you up, but I suspect you're too strong for that, aren't you?" I glanced pointedly at his hands. "So, you're going to have to be your own restraint. Consider it character building."

Every time I'd leaned forward so far, he'd tensed or flinched, like he was cringing away from me, but he was fine with me being between his legs. He just didn't want me near his face. I wondered if maybe he had some hang-ups about his new fangs. I could work with that.

I let my gaze drift down his figure, from his tense but interested expression, to the tendons standing out on his forearms, to his loosely sprawled shape lying on the bed in front of me. *Delicious.* I decided I liked him like this.

I chose to start with what I thought might be an insecurity first, reaching slowly when he turned his head away a fraction, and tapped his chin. "So, what have we got going on in here?" I asked casually and pulled down his bottom lip with my thumb. He flinched again, and I pulled my hand back when I saw the hint of panic flicker in his eyes. But we were going to talk about it, so that he knew I wasn't scared. Maybe I should be, but we were going to talk about the fangs, get it out of the way, and then it wouldn't be an issue anymore.

I heard him swallow roughly and his arms started to tense again, so I decided he needed some incentive to talk it through. "Can I touch you here?" I asked, setting my hands lightly on the inside of his thighs. He took a deep breath and gave the briefest nod, so I slid my hands up to his rock-hard erection and rubbed.

"Oh, Sid," I heard him breathe, and even biting my lip couldn't stop my grin. His cheeks flushed the lightest shade of pink and he shifted his eyes to focus on my mouth, and then my neck, before letting his gaze drift down to my breasts. His pupils had completely swallowed up the pretty amber flecks in his brown irises, and I couldn't help but mentally preen at his reaction.

"Focus," I reminded him, reaching up to tap his chin again. "How does this work?" I pushed his head back gently and peered into his mouth, like someone might when checking out a docile pet's teeth. Like I did this every day. No big deal. Nothing to be afraid of here. He turned his face away again, so I went back to rubbing his erection through his boxers, smirking mentally when he shivered. *Interesting... Face, no... dick, yes. He's got some strange boundaries.*

Seemingly lulled by my casual charade, he finally answered. "Venom sacs, in the back of my mouth, up in the soft palate."

I massaged the base of his erection a little harder—a reward. His breathing hitched. "Huh. Like a snake?" I tried to look in his mouth again, but he stuttered out an agreement, so I relented and focused on his eyes instead. "So, even if you bit someone, you wouldn't actually turn them unless you meant to?"

"Right," he gasped, and I increased the pressure again.

I studied his face, trying to understand the issue. "Then what's the problem?"

"I just don't like people in my *space*," he growled quietly, clenching his teeth, and staring at the ceiling. *Huh.* "And they look ridiculous." He suddenly bared his sharp teeth at me.

I blinked at him. "I don't think they look ridiculous at all." My voice was matter of fact. And I didn't. It made him look a little feral maybe, kind of vicious, but I counted that in the plus column, personally. I slid my hands up to the waistband of his boxers and gripped it in my fingertips, enjoying the way his abdominal muscles flexed and twitched.

"What... what are you doing?" he rasped out. I bit my lip so hard to keep from laughing. What did he think I was doing? Poor, sweet Jordan. This was going to be so fun. His abs flexed again as I curled my fingers around his waistband and tugged. His breathing was already a little rough, but it sped up as his mental gears started turning. He lifted his hips enough to help me get the material down, and then I jerked it the rest of the way off, gleefully tossing it over my shoulder when it was free.

I couldn't help the pleased sound that escaped me as I felt a Cheshire grin spread across my face. He had a nice figure—even if he was a little lean compared to what I tended to drool over most often. *Had I really thought I was only attracted to burly men?* I'd even say Jordan had a nice-looking dick, and I hadn't really thought such a thing was truly possible. But what I hadn't been expecting were his *thighs*.

What on earth had he been doing to develop thigh muscles like that? First of all, *yes please*, and secondly, I kind of hoped he didn't crush me with these beauties. I raised my eyes to meet his and let my pleased disbelief show clearly on my face as I prowled back up between his legs.

"Someone doesn't skip leg day." I trailed my middle finger lightly down his thigh, from his hip to his knee. If I could have been purring, I would have been.

"Didn't," Jordan choked out. "I was still playing hooks every day before the change. It doesn't matter what I do now though."

"Hm." *Interesting.* "Venom sacs, pointy fangs, muscle retention... what else should I know?" I trailed my fingers back up his leg toward his groin, stopping an inch or two before I got there. He was hyper-focused on my hand. "Jordan?" I prompted.

"Are you going to take the shirt off?" he asked my chest.

"Maybe." I shrugged one shoulder, looking between his eyes. "Are you going to answer my question?" I knew he heard me. I wasn't above bargaining.

"What else do you want to know?" he bit out. "I can't get or carry diseases. I have a stupid diet, and I can't age—or die unless somebody kills me. Sunlight hurts like a bitch, and I get tired during the daytime. What else? Oh, and I probably can't get anyone pregnant now."

I'd been unbuttoning my borrowed shirt but paused with my fingers on the last button. His eyes were locked on my bare skin. "You can't have kids?" I'd known that was a probability for him, being a vampire now, but hearing it confirmed still felt like a punch in the gut. I felt my eyebrows draw together.

His jaw clenched, and he shook his head. "They tried to freeze some sperm as soon as I got to the hospital, but it was already ruined. They said the chances of me ever having kids were practically zero. I'm basically dead now anyway—it's not something I'd want to pass on."

I paused a beat to think before continuing with the buttons. I wanted to know more about him going to the hospital and how he'd ended up becoming a vampire in the first place, but I figured I was pushing him enough as it was. This wasn't the time for that conversation.

I pulled my shirt off and tsked at him. "You're not *dead*." Or maybe he was. He was completely frozen, had stopped breathing, head back against the headboard, mouth a little open, eyes on my tits. I glanced down. I couldn't really blame him. I had great tits. He was great for my ego though—there was no denying that. I felt my nipples tighten under his stare.

I grasped his shaft, which was so hard that the skin was already pulled back, and felt hot desire tighten in my own core. He sucked in a breath, letting his eyes flutter closed as I stroked him. It was a beautiful sight, but I was curious to see what he looked like coming apart at the seams, so I leaned down to lick the slit in the head of his cock. His whole body flinched, and I grinned, licking him again and again until he cursed, and his breath started trembling out of him. Taking him in my mouth and sucking the rounded head, running my tongue along the underside of his shaft, had him tightening his grip on the headboard and panting. He looked helpless and vulnerable, delirious with pleasure.

I increased my suction until he was growling and groaning, his muscles tensing and releasing as he fought his desire to thrust deeper into my mouth. I rewarded him by relaxing my throat and taking him to the root. His shouted cursing was pure gravel, and when I pulled up to the tip, his face was strained with pleasure.

The bed creaked with movement as I bobbed on him, taking him into my throat each time, and began to set a rhythm. I debated with myself whether I was going to make good on my promise to leave if he broke the bed, acknowledging that it would be incredibly difficult to peel myself away from this. His jerky, minute thrusting. The way his abs and biceps flexed as he lost himself to his pleasure. The gasping, groaning noises he made when I added suction. I found myself utterly entranced. I loved it. This might be my new favorite thing. I was so turned on I was practically throbbing.

"Oh, god. Sid… Sidney," he gasped. It was a warning I didn't need. I could already feel his shaft swelling and his balls drawing up. But as I pulled up to the tip to prepare to swallow, I realized I might have gotten a little more than I bargained for. His jaw clenched, and he bared his teeth as he came, his muscles contracting and flexing as his orgasm wracked his body. The headboard cracked under his right hand and his pupils shrank to pinpoints, his irises changing from their beautiful amber brown to looking like lit coals as the monster underneath showed through.

I sat up as a thrill of terror stole through me, forgetting his seed spilling between us as it landed on my chest and his lap, but quickly suppressed my reaction when I realized he hadn't let go of the bed.

His eyes were still wild, his irises glowing as I backed away from him slightly. He kept his jaw clenched tight with obvious effort, the muscles ticking as he tried to calm his breathing. I raised an eyebrow at the dented, cracked wood under his right hand.

"Gonna have to try a little harder than that next time," I said flippantly. If there was a next time. The broken headboard as a "safe word" was a perfect excuse to escape, so there was no need to upset him. He was already touchy enough about his changes. I stood and grabbed his shirt from the bed to wipe his spend from my chest and stomach, noticing that it was clear instead of milky. *Huh. I guess he was right.*

I blew Jordan a kiss with a wink as he watched me with a ferocious glare. Not even the prickling sensation on the back of my neck would make me show my fear of him. And then I shifted forms and was out his window without a backwards glance.

I never did get my answers.

Chapter 7

"So let me see if I got this right. You burst into Jordan's room, gave him a blowjob, and then ran away?" I couldn't tell if Elara sounded more scandalized or disbelieving. It was early the next morning, and I was slumped across my desk at work, my face firmly pressed to the wood. I was exhausted.

"That's not exactly how I would have phrased it, personally. But yeah, that's basically correct."

"But, *why?* I thought you guys didn't even *like* each other. Every time you're anywhere near him, you're practically bristling with irritation."

"I don't know." I shrugged slightly and pondered the haughty way Jordan always looked at me. "You ever just see a hot guy, all buttoned-up and straight-laced and want to muss him up a little? Mess his hair up and pull his tie askew? Play his flute and see what sounds he makes?" Elara choked on her morning tea. "No? Just me then." I shrugged one shoulder. "I guess I think he's cute."

Elara was coughing hard enough that I turned my face to watch her, wondering if I needed to whack her on the back to help clear her lungs.

"I'm fine." She waved me off, continuing to cough into her hand. I probably should have waited until she was done with her drink before throwing in that "flute" line. "I'm just surprised, is all," she continued. "I never would have pegged him for your type."

"He's not," I said to the wood.

She was quiet for a beat. "But you like him?" she asked in a smaller voice that made me feel guilty for my grumpiness.

I sat up and sighed. "It wouldn't matter if I liked him. There's nothing between us." She eyed me doubtfully. "He's a vampire, so he's immortal, right? Am I just supposed to grow old with some ageless hottie? That'd be weird. I'm not interested in becoming a vampire, so we'd always be unequal. Blood is disgusting, and I love sunshine. I'm not going to change who I am." I refused to admit how long these thoughts had been circling through my head, but they just kept pouring out once I'd opened the floodgates. "Plus, he can't have kids, and you know how my mom is about wanting a billion grandkids." I flopped backwards over the backrest of my chair and dangled my arms to the sides, feeling restless.

If I just stuck to listing out the facts, I wouldn't have to think about annoying things like *feelings*.

Elara studied me for a long moment, and I peeked at her out of the corner of my eye. "But do *you* want children?" she asked thoughtfully. *Ugh.*

"I guess?" I shrugged again. "I've never really thought about it all that much. But I've always assumed I'd have kids someday." I loved kids. I had to fight every day to keep from mothering everyone around me. My mom always told me I was basically born to be a mother. Not *now*, obviously, but someday, sure. Elara was still staring at me, and I didn't like whatever wheels were turning in her head.

"It doesn't matter anyway," I insisted. "We were just messing around. There's nothing there." Yes, he was hot as Hades—that was true—but feelings? He didn't have any feelings for me. Navel gazing about whatever feelings I had for him wasn't going to do any good.

"If you say so," she finally relented, but I could tell she was still curious. "You look really tired though, Sid. Maybe you should go home and rest."

"Can't. It smells like burnt rat," I grumbled, kicking off and spinning slowly in my chair.

"What?"

I waved her off. "Did they finalize the table decorations for the wedding?"

Her parents had objected to her eloping with Levi and re-quested they be allowed to throw her a formal wedding, which was a big deal in elvish society. She hated being the center of attention and wasn't a huge fan of the planning stage either, so her mom was doing most of that. But I'd taken over where I could, hoping to take some pressure off of Elara.

"What else is left to do? I only get to be your Maid-of-Honor twice, so I'm going to do it right," I joked, with my head dangling over the back of the chair as the ceiling spun slowly in circles above me. There were only a few days left until the big event, which she was low-key dreading, but I was more excited than I wanted to let on. This was the closest I would ever come to attending something like a royal ball. I could do this. One day at a time.

MAYBE I COULDN'T DO this.

We'd switched to burning fish for the baby dragon, but I wasn't sure the smell was an improvement over burnt rat. He definitely preferred the rat.

It was a good thing shifters healed quickly, because I was con-stantly covered in rapidly healing bruises and scratches. This adorable little guy was a *wild thing*. My house was in shambles because he kept getting into everything. We had to keep a strict eye on him every second because he was literally climbing the walls. He'd easily destroyed the playpen, shredded the sofa, and tried to eat part of a couch cushion. Then last night he crashed through the bathroom door trying to get to me while I peed because, apparently, we'd adopted the Kool-Aid guy.

And I know baby animals—and people—don't sleep well, but I wouldn't have thought that applied to reptiles, even magical ones. The real problem was, I couldn't handle his cries. Every time he squeaked or moved at night, I'd wake up in a panic, with my skin feeling too tight. Something about his squeaky little sounds just sent my heart hammering into overdrive and made me need to fix whatever he was upset about. Some of the books I'd read said dragons can affect those around them with their magic, but it sounded like there was some kind of bonding process necessary for that to happen. I didn't know what was going on, but I was way more attached to this dragon than I had ever been to any other animal in my care. Just a few more days and we could take him back to the rescue center, where they'd give him a "soft release" with the other dragons in a large enclosure built to mimic their natural environment. Then, after they'd proved they could hunt effectively, they'd all be taken up into the mountains for a proper release. That was the game plan anyway. I hoped I could handle letting him go.

So, when I walked into our apartment after another day of work and helping Elara finish more of her wedding stuff, I felt like I'd entered the twilight zone. "What are you doing?" I asked my brother. The house was destroyed, but that was normal at this point.

Josh was sitting on the couch watching something on his calling stones, but he had the dragon strapped to his chest using a weird buckle and harness contraption. And I'm pretty sure he was feeding it chips.

"Are you feeding that dragon *Doritos*?" I could already feel the vein in my forehead bulging.

"As a matter of fact—ow! Hey, ow! Calm down!" The dragon flapped his wings, battering Josh in the face as he fought to wrap his arms around them to contain it. "As a matter of fact, yes. Humphrey Herbert Hucklebee, the Fierce, *loves* Doritos. We've been having a great time watching baking shows." The dragon gave a happy sounding trill.

"Do you think Doritos are a natural part of a dragon's *diet*, Josh?"

"I don't think Doritos are a natural part of anyone's diet, *Sidney*. But it makes him happy."

"It's not *healthy, Joshua.* You don't feed a baby reptile chips! You don't feed a baby *anything* chips. And what are you *wearing*?"

Josh was completely unconcerned with my tirade. "This," he said smugly, "is a baby carrier. Aaron went on a Void-run today and brought us back snacks and this thing called a Baby Björn. I had to cut some extra holes for his tail and his wings, and it took a while to figure out all the buckles and straps, but he's been contained all day and hasn't destroyed any more of my plants." He looked so proud of himself.

My brothers had about two brain cells to rub together between the three of them, and today obviously wasn't Josh's day to use the brain cells.

I took a deep breath and let it out as slowly as I could. Josh smiled at me and fed the dragon another chip. I lunged for his throat.

I WAS UP FOR another evening of bandaging knuckles at a boxing match and making sure my oldest brother, Sam, didn't get his face smashed in too badly. Sam had always been into mixed martial arts and had been backroom brawling for cash for as long as I could remember. My mother *hated* it. Now that he was over thirty, I wasn't sure how many years he had left in him for this, but I was looking forward to making a good chunk of change from the bookies tonight, at least. My brother was a beast in a fight, and yet people still placed bets on the orcs or trolls who fought him because they were bigger.

The fights were always held in some abandoned warehouse on the outskirts of town, so I was ducking through seedy back alleys and side-streets when I caught a whiff of vampire on the damp night air. I stopped in my tracks because that wasn't just any vampire, it was Jordan-vampire. There wasn't any cigarette smoke mixed in with it, I noted with puzzled amusement. Had he really quit smoking just because I didn't like it?

I turned on my heel, casting my gaze around the alleyway and up to the rooftops where his scent was drifting from. *What is he up to? Literally.*

A dumpster on the far side of the alley caught my attention, and I climbed on top so I could see the roof. There was no point in bothering with stealth or trying to be quiet. Vampires could hear better than anyone I knew. He would have heard me creeping around from three blocks away. I landed on the lid of the dumpster with a bang. The scuff of a shoe from the rooftop told me he was on the move, and by the time I hauled myself up to the gutter, he was gone.

I half-considered shifting forms to chase him down as a bird, but I was too lazy to get dressed again and I was already late to meet with my brother. *Stupid, sexy vampire.* I hopped down to continue on with my trek, but my mind kept drifting back to the way Jordan had looked at me as I'd kneeled between his legs.

Chapter 8

I'D FINALLY GOTTEN A lead. Three nights ago, I'd spotted Rowdy in a crowded saloon called "The Salty Wench" and cornered him, demanding to know if he was in on the egg smuggling that I'd uncovered in the Void. He was the one that told Bane about the warehouse in the first place, after all. Rowdy denied it, of course, but promised he'd ask around with his crew and find out which supply lines the eggs had come in on.

Last night, he'd come back with some answers for me. Phantoms were responsible for the dragon egg smuggling, and while the two guys I'd stuffed in a closet weren't officially part of the gang, they worked with them, and the Phantoms weren't happy about them ending up in the clink. Luckily, they didn't know who I was, but they were *pissed* about their missing eggs, and they had my description, so I had a tenuous target painted on my back. I wasn't happy about it, but I also didn't regret my actions. It didn't really change anything anyway. They'd already made me angry by coming after Elara. Now I just had more incentive to ferret out where they were and what they were up to.

And Rowdy had come through. His crew had given him multiple new locations where they'd seen what was left of the Phantom network frequenting. It was go time.

I wasn't looking to start a fight. Yet. I just wanted to poke around and see what was going on. I'd winged my way through several of the areas Rowdy's crew had described already this evening and not found much of note, but at least now I had some ideas of where to keep an eye out. I landed in my feathered form on the tallest building in the industrial part of Dry Gulch, looking for the last place he told me about. Trying to stay low, I worked my way from rooftop to rooftop until I found an old two-story building that matched his description. This one had some activity, guys moving crates in and out of an alleyway in the back.

No sooner had I landed than another bird landed on the gutter beside me, one I recognized. I tried to ignore him, but he wasn't going to let me. I don't know where he came from, or how he knew me, or why he followed me, but this pigeon made a nuisance of himself every time he found me in bird form around Dry Gulch.

Pigeons get a bad rap. They have this reputation for being dirty, or unintelligent, but they're just as clean as most birds and can be surprisingly smart. Not this particular bird though. Just like there are variations among any population, there are certain birds that just don't have much going on upstairs, and this pigeon had rocks for brains.

"Go away." I tried to send him on his way with a quick jab from my beak, but he misinterpreted my violence as "mutual grooming" and immediately began to "display" for me.

"Pidgy, get out of here." I raised my wings and opened my beak: a threat display.

"*Coo. Coo.*" He bowed and preened, bowed and preened.

Ugh! Pigeons are comparatively quiet birds, so I wasn't worried too much about him drawing attention with his mating displays, but it was hard to see what was happening below. He was right up in my face with his mating dance.

I grabbed his shoulder with a clawed foot and shoved him away from me. "Personal space, dork!" A loud "caw" in his face sent him fluttering away, but it also made the people in the alley way glance up at me, so I fluttered away too. *Just a bird, doing bird things, nothing to see here people.*

But as I flew away, I caught a glimpse of a familiar face on another rooftop, watching the same scene below from behind a low wall. As I doubled back, it didn't escape my notice that

I was behaving disturbingly like Pidgy, but this *wasn't the same thing*. Jordan was stalking *me*. He was crouched on the rooftop wearing the same black leather outfit I'd seen him in the day we found the eggs, with the same thick hooded cowl, but no helmet. I squinted at the setting sun. *Maybe the rays are weak enough to not bother him as much now.*

I gained altitude and watched until the people in the alleyway had cleared out, waiting for the perfect moment to strike. When they finally went inside, I tucked my wings and dove for the vampire from behind. He was just starting to stand up when I shifted forms and landed on his back with full momentum. But *holy shit-snacks* Jordan was fast! And strong. I'd grown up scrapping and fighting with my brothers, and even spent some time cage fighting on the weekends in college for quick cash, so I was completely comfortable grappling with people bigger than me. But I had no chance in Jordan's grip. He launched me over his shoulder before I could get a hold on him, only to haul me around and pin me with my back to his chest. A spike of fear hit me at being handled so easily.

"It's raining naked shifters," he said, breathing hard against my neck and sounding strained. "Do you not own any clothes?" He pulled one of the long ends of his cowl from around his neck and draped it around my body, which I appreciated because it was chilly up here without feathers.

"We've been over this, Jordan. I guess I could carry a tiny little bird backpack, but it wouldn't fit anything large enough for me to wear in this form," I gritted out. I've always known I have a few screws loose, and as the spike of adrenaline from his capture of me began to fade, I was reminded of those loose screws by the heat building between my legs. Apparently, being pinned by a much stronger, much faster male—whom I already thought was hot, even if he was a little bit scary—was a turn on for me. *Who knew?* I squeezed my thighs together, knowing he would be able to smell it.

He recognized it immediately, and his deep chuckle sounded positively wicked. "You like this, do you?" he asked, his grip on me still firm and unyielding. His body responded too. I felt a distinct bulge in his groin pressing into my backside, making the muscles in my lower abdomen clench.

I tried to shake it off. "Shut up, Jordan. You're following me again." I wasn't going to be distracted by how turned on he made me this time, so I tried to ignore the way his hardness felt pressed against my rump. I completely and utterly failed. I gave in and tried to arch into him for more pressure.

His breath hissed out of him as he held me still. "What are you talking about?" It sounded like he was speaking through clenched teeth. "I didn't even know you were here."

"Then what are you doing here?" I growled.

"I could ask you the same thing." His grip hadn't loosened at all. It was really annoying how hot this was making me, and I was starting to get mad.

"I'm keeping tabs on the Phantoms," I said as quietly and icily as I could, knowing he could hear me. He didn't respond, and I started to shiver. He was warm, but his scarf wasn't enough this high up in the wind. Suddenly, his hands were as warm as heating pads and I could feel extra heat penetrating through his jacket. Him being a fire elementalist was certainly turning out to have its benefits.

"Why?" he asked.

"Because they've been after Elara," I hissed, "and now I'm told they're blaming me for the financial loss of the dragon eggs and snitching on their operation." I had to hope against hope that Levi wouldn't be friends with Jordan if he wasn't trustworthy. "So, answer my question."

"I thought you knew what I do," he said, his words sounding clipped. "I got hired on to a special Enforcement team and our current assignment is taking down Phantom groups."

I felt my forehead wrinkle. I guess it was true that every time I'd smelled him around was when I'd been looking for Phantoms in their old stomping grounds. "Have you not been able to find them until now either?" Him having me pinned like this was making me crazy. I wanted to either strip his clothes off of him or throw him on the ground. My brain couldn't make up its mind.

"Not until a few days ago," he said. "I made the mistake of mentioning to the sparks where their last hideout was and that they'd been harassing Elara, who was helping out their fairy cousins." I felt him smile against the back of my neck, and it made my skin prickle. "My bad. Now they're scattered to the winds, and we've been having trouble tracking where their new meeting places are."

"On the plus side, it does seem that their numbers are drastically reduced," I muttered.

"Oh, yeah, they're dead," he said with a dark chuckle that made my heart race.

My adrenaline spiked again, and I acted on impulse, feeling panic flare with him at my back. I gripped his arm and reached around for his neck, intending to flip him in front of me, and *he lost his mind.* Before I could blink, he had me on my knees with his weight pressing me down, snarling in my ear like a predator. I couldn't move, though I briefly considered smashing his face with the back of my head and dismissed it. I couldn't fight Jordan—he was just too quick, which wasn't something I was used to—and I feared angering him further could tip him over the edge. I crouched there, in the heavy silence, with Jordan wrapped around me like a cage. The only sounds were his rapid breaths and my own heart hammering in my chest until, eventually, his breathing slowed and he spoke through a clenched jaw.

"Don't. Touch. My neck."

My eyebrows shot into my hairline. I hadn't been expecting that reaction. "Your neck?"

"Sidney, I'm warning you. I killed the last girl who did."

I felt ice slide down my spine at the casual way he said the words, and I imagined a hundred scenarios for how that could have happened. I needed to get out of here. "Let me go," I said, and he did instantly, standing and stepping back from me with a wary eye. A quick glance at the alleyway below showed it was still empty, so I hopped up onto the low wall we'd been hiding behind and threw him a glare.

Jordan's eyes went wide. "Sidney, what—"

I did a backflip off the side of the building and shifted forms mid-air. I had the information I came for.

Chapter 9

MY DREAMS WERE PLAGUED by a sultry vampire with high cheek-bones and pretty eyes. This time, I wasn't afraid of the sounds of snarling and the feeling of sharp teeth lurking just beside my ear. I was confused and disoriented when I woke up to a dark room with an uneasy feeling in my chest and my heart racing. I lay in my bed panting, listening in the dark, trying to figure out what had woken me. Huck, the baby dragon—I'd tried refusing to name him, but even if I gave in, I *definitely* wasn't calling him that monstrosity of a name my brother did—fidgeted next to me on top of my covers.

I waited for my heart to calm, and he snuggled closer, rooting around in the covers until he finally came to rest with his head on my chest. I sighed, rubbing the scales between the spikes on his head. His chest thrummed, and it almost felt like he was purring. But then he opened his mouth and made a clicking sound that gave me the same primal feeling I'd had upon waking and made me freeze. It sounded like one stone clacking against another, but from deep inside his throat. I couldn't pinpoint what about it made me nervous until he opened his mouth again and clicked, and I saw a light flicker in the back of his mouth.

"No!" I grabbed his snout and clamped it shut with my hands. He coughed and sputtered through his closed muzzle, and his breath had the familiar pungent smell of lighter fluid. "No, baby, no. Don't start that yet! You're too young to make fire." *Right?* Otherwise, a two-week-old dragon the size of a full grown Corgi was going to set my bed on fire. Not good.

I scrambled up to look for some tape. "Joshua!" I yelled for my brother, pulling open drawers and searching cluttered tabletops. My room looked exactly like a magpie lived here. I had interesting sticks and rocks and jewelry and glass bottles placed artfully—and sometimes not-so-artfully—atop my dresser, and it wasn't hard to find seashells tucked away in random drawers. It made it hard to find anything else in a hurry, though.

Josh came stumbling sleepily through my door. "What?" He was bleary-eyed but had an urgency that meant he'd clearly taken notice of the panicked note in my voice.

"I need tape!"

"You need tape… at—" He looked at his watch. "—four o'clock in the morning?"

"He is making sparks in his throat!" I pointed an accusing finger at Huck, who blinked his giant dark eyes at us from his comfortable spot on my bed.

My brother stared at me like I had two heads.

"He could burn the apartment down, Josh! This isn't a joke." The smell of lighter fluid still lingered in the air.

"So, you're going to… tape him?" Josh asked, frowning.

"I'm going to tape his *mouth shut*. People do it all the time with alligators!" Josh continued to stare at me. "Do you happen to have a better idea? I don't have a baby dragon size muzzle on me now, so unless you want to take him out on a tour of the desert where he can't light anyone on fire, I need you to help me find some tape."

Josh left, then stumbled back through the door a few minutes later, holding a roll of sports tape and paging through one of my borrowed dragon books. I snatched the roll from his hand and stalked toward Huck, who edged away from me on the bed. When I peeled up the edge of the tape, he launched himself off the bed and scrambled underneath it. He'd gotten wary of me tackling him when I first tried to wrestle food into him and now I was paying the price.

"What's that smell?" Josh asked.

"It's his breath. It smells flammable, right? Freaks me out. Heeere dragon, dragon." I crouched to peer under the bed and found him against the far wall where I couldn't reach him.

"Try calling him by his name," Josh said distractedly.

"Here, Huck," I tried, keeping my voice soft and sweet.

"Use his full name."

"I'm not calling him that." I could barely fit if I turned my head sideways, but I couldn't quite reach him.

"It's Humphrey Herbert Hucklebee, the Fierce."

"Shut up, Josh. Help me get him out; I can't reach him."

"Just go in the other room," he muttered. "He'll follow you out."

I squinted at Huck. That wasn't a bad plan, but I didn't trust him not to start sparking under the bed. After clambering back out, I grabbed the underside of the bed and started to pull. "Help me out, dork." Why was he letting me do all the work?

Josh reached out to pull on the bed with one hand, still reading the book. "Looks like they have a gland under their tongue that squirts flammable liquid. They create the spark in their throat and breathe out, and they can shoot flames the same length as they are."

"Oh, god." Huck was already three feet long, including his tail. "So, I guess a greater dragon could roast an entire mountainside in one go." I knuckled down and pulled, dragging the bed several feet with a loud squeal across the hardwood. Huck tried to scurry under the bed again, but I dove across it and latched onto his tail. "No, you don't! Josh, put the book down and help me with the tape," I said, straddling the dragon and trying not to squish him. "I'll hold him, and you wrap it around his jaws to keep his mouth shut. Make sure it's not too tight. This'll have to do until the stores open and we can find him a real muzzle."

"CAN'T YOU JUST TAKE him to the wildlife rehabbers today?" Elara asked, shooting a puzzled look at Huck. He was giving us all the stink-eye from the nest of blankets I'd made for him in the corner of the room. Josh had picked up a properly sized muzzle as soon as the pet shops had opened, and Huck seemed even less happy about it than the tape, for some reason. "We can always finalize the last of this wedding stuff another time, Sidney. Does it really matter if the flowers match the cake?" She was probably just trying to get out of event planning.

I tried to ignore how the thought of taking Huck somewhere and leaving him made my skin feel itchy. It was the right thing to do for all of us. "I can't yet," I said, rubbing my face with both hands. "They're not open for drop-offs today." Today was Saturday, and the intake clinic was only open on weekdays, even though there were people there every day to care for the animals.

Levi squatted on the floor next to Huck and stroked the scales on the top of his wings. "He's so *cute*. I'm petting a baby dragon! How cool is that?" He'd been making baby talk at Huck all morning.

"Super cool, until he burns the apartment building down with all my neighbors in it," I grumbled. Levi sounded just like my brother.

"Aww, he's only making sparks so far. But yeah, don't burn the house down, little buddy. People could die!" Still in the ridiculous baby talk. His enchantment was stronger than usual too. He must be really enamored with Huck. I ignored him, trying not to feel possessive of my dragon, and he stood and paced to the kitchen window.

"If you're hoping for a repeat of last time, it's not going to happen," I said. "Delores hauled those boys to their mothers by their ears. They haven't stepped foot near her rose bushes ever since."

Levi broke into a wide grin. Why was watching kids getting caught doing ludicrous stuff always so fun?

"Why don't you ask Jordan for help?" Elara asked, and I tensed. She narrowed her eyes at my reaction.

"Why would I call Jordan?"

"Because he's fireproof and you're not," she said, like it was obvious. Maybe it was, but I still wasn't having an unstable vampire in my house. Even if he was ridiculously and unfairly hot.

"Hm, I'll pass."

"Why? I thought you liked him now. Did something happen?" She was instantly suspicious.

I hunched in my chair. I wasn't *afraid* of him per se, but I wasn't *not afraid* of him either. "Jordan's kind of psycho," I grumbled. "Granted, I'm *also* kind of psycho. But putting two psychos together just seems like a bad idea, you know?"

Levi huffed from behind me. "Jordan's not a psycho. He's just like a prickly pet cat who only comes out of hiding when there's no company around. And only wants to be touched on his terms. And has a very specific diet," he said lightly.

So, what he was saying was that Jordan had personal *boundaries*. And I was admittedly terrible at respecting boundaries. We were obviously not fit to be in each other's presence. Besides, I was more of a dog person anyway. Or maybe a dragon person. I cast a glance at Huck, who was sulking in the corner. He probably didn't feel like I was a dragon person either.

No, I definitely wasn't calling in a vampire who said he'd killed a girl just for touching his neck.

Chapter 10

Several hours after dawn, there was a knock at the door. A peek through the peephole showed a black helmet and leather clothes, and my heart jumped in my chest. I jerked the door open with a glare, trying to keep my arm wrapped around the dragon. Jordan didn't say anything, just stood staring at me and Huck while the dragon squirmed in my arm.

"Is someone at the door?" Josh yelled sleepily from his bedroom.

Jordan immediately stiffened and stepped to the side like a skittish horse, like he was going to head back the way he came.

"Just a package," I yelled back to my brother and turned to shove Huck back through the door before pulling it shut behind me. He was wearing his muzzle, so he should be fine for a few seconds. Josh could deal with him. "What do you want?" I asked Jordan, turning to face him and crossing my arms in front of me.

He looked back at the door for a long moment before reaching up to pull his helmet off. His eyes were flat and guarded, his posture tense as he considered me. He seemed even more withdrawn than usual, or maybe now it was just more noticeable. His hair was a mess that left him looking a little wild, and his pale skin was still a shock when I was expecting the healthy, tanned color he'd always had before. He ran a hand through his mussed hair, trying to straighten it and push it out of his face.

"The wildlife refuge reported a break in tonight," he said stiffly, "and the news just made it to my unit. The two juvenile dragons that hatched from the clutch you found were reported missing, as well as the other four unhatched eggs."

I blinked at him. *Well, that sucks.* "So, you're... wanting me to help find them?" I couldn't piece together why he was here.

He squinted at me. "No... My unit is assigned to the case. I just wanted to check that you were safe and find out if anyone knows you have a hatchling. Whoever broke in might come after you too."

I bristled at the implication that I needed protecting or that I'd been naïve enough to flaunt an extremely valuable exotic animal in a town full of thieves. "No one knows but Elara and Levi, and your own team. I'm not sure why you'd care if we're safe since you already threatened to kill me," I said with narrowed eyes. I couldn't help but needle him. *Why am I like this? Just tell him you're fine and send him on his way, idiot.*

Jordan huffed and looked down his nose at me. "Is that what you think?" His voice was so quiet I had to strain to hear it.

I didn't respond. Of course that was what I thought; that was what he'd said. Wasn't it?

He narrowed his gaze further. "Did I scare you?"

I was practically vibrating with the desire to punt his arrogant, imperious, gorgeous rump down the hallway. *Dick.* Was he getting some kind of kick out of this? "I think anyone who wasn't mildly scared of your unhinged ass would fall into the 'too stupid to live' category."

He was quiet for a beat before taking a deep breath and releasing it. "I see," he said with a nod, glaring at me and obviously struggling with himself. I eyed him, considering his reaction. Had he somehow not realized that his actions had been intimidating? I wasn't sure if that was better or worse. "You should be afraid of me," he said quietly, almost gently, "but I regret that my actions caused it."

"You regret that your actions—? *Yes, Jordan,* killing a girl just for touching your *neck,* and implying you'd do the same to me, will generally make someone afraid of you," I said flippantly. Not to mention his *physical* reaction.

The muscles in his jaw flexed as his irises took on that otherworldly orange tinge that always made chills slide up my spine. "That's not what I *said*, Sidney. And you attacked me. *Twice*. I can't help my defensiveness."

I mean, yeah, that was a fair point. I did attack him twice. But I wasn't trying to *kill him*. He was practically looming over me now, but I stood my ground, straightening my shoulders and refusing to cower. I tried to calculate how much force I'd need to kick him through the wall on the other side of the hallway.

"And if I'm unhinged, she made me this way," he said through gritted teeth. "I killed her in *self-defense*—which the courts agreed with—because she turned me into this." He gestured with an angry, slashing motion at his bared teeth. "And I'd do it again, because she *hurt* me. She caused me *immeasurable* pain. It was torture. And she *took* from me. She took everything I'd ever worked toward. She took my family from me. She took my friends. She took my future. I can never have children because of her. I will never enjoy a simple meal again. I will never exist within mortal society again because of what she did to me, and I regret *nothing*. And yes, because of all that, I have different reactions now. I cannot control my defensive reactions. She *hurt me*, and I can't help reacting to every intrusion of my space like it's a similar threat." He paused and took several heaving, angry breaths. "I can't help it. I wasn't threatening you, Sidney. I was trying to warn you about what I've become."

It was the most he'd ever spoken to me at once, and I felt like the air had been sucked from the room. The longer I stood there processing what he'd said, the more I was filled with a wild, overwhelming mixture of grief, anger, despair, and... heartache. I worked quickly to stamp out that last one—because it wasn't about me—but it was hard. I wasn't sure whether I wanted to scream in rage or wrap him up in the tightest hug that ever existed, but obviously he wouldn't want that if he didn't like people near him.

I didn't respond—*I couldn't.* I just stood there staring at him like a jackass. It was like I was trapped inside my body, and I couldn't make my mouth say *words* because my brain didn't even know which way was up. All I could make sense of was the hollow feeling in my chest as I watched him struggle to regain his shuttered expression.

"I hate who I've become," he said quietly, "and I'm sorry I scared you. I'm sorry I panicked and reacted defensively when you grabbed me." Jordan took a deep breath, let it out in a shuddering rush, and then turned his back on me and headed back down the hallway.

When he reached the end, I finally got my mouth to work. "Jordan." He froze mid step and slowly looked over his shoulder at me. "I'm glad she's dead," I whispered, knowing he could hear me.

He gave me the smallest nod and then continued on into the stairwell. I watched him go, with the unwelcome sting of tears behind my eyes and a disturbing feeling in the pit of my stomach.

I STILL HADN'T MADE any sense of my feelings. I didn't even know how to process what Jordan had revealed, and I couldn't discuss it with Elara because it felt like a breach of trust for me to share what he said. Grief and rage at what had happened to him, and how he had struggled in response to it, were at the forefront. How was *he* processing it? Was he getting professional help? Was he close enough to his roommates to trust them with his trauma? He said he had no family or friends left, and he seemed absolutely miserable. I didn't know what to think anymore.

Having him around still seemed like a bad idea, but now that I understood his responses to my provocations better, I was less skittish about him. It didn't make him any less dangerous to me—or anyone else—but I felt like I understood him better. I wasn't sure if that was a good thing or not though.

"Yes, that's a much better fit." The diminutive elvish employee interrupted my thoughts as the goblin tailor finished pinning the back of the dress that Elara's mother had picked out as my bridesmaid gown. They'd introduced themselves by name when we arrived at the boutique this morning, but I couldn't remember them for the life of me.

I tried to recenter myself in the moment and turned to face the mirror in the fitting room. The girl staring back at me in the glass looked like a frickin' princess. Elara's parents had spared no expense on her wedding, and as their daughter's Maid-of-Honor, they'd gone *all out* on my dress. It was a light-blue ballgown that matched my eyes, and it was the most expensive thing I'd ever owned. Large swathes of white gemstones decorated the bodice, and a big poufy skirt flared out from my waist. While I didn't normally spend a ton of mental energy on clothes or fashion—I liked them well enough, but I was lazy—I made exceptions for costumes, lingerie, and *incredibly expensive ballgowns*. I'd been so excited when I selected it from the options I'd been presented with, and I'd been downright giddy about the fitting today. But now, after my interaction with Jordan this morning, my heart just wasn't in it. It was beautiful. I *looked beautiful*. But all I could see in my mind's eye was some faceless woman injuring Jordan so profoundly that his whole life was ruined.

"Do you like it, Miss?" asked the employee.

I tried to force my face into some semblance of a smile. "Yes, it's perfect, thank you." She beamed at me with pride and my smile became a little more genuine.

"I'm so glad. Your friend is ready. Would you like to see?" The elvish woman pulled back the curtain to the next dressing room and my heart nearly melted on the spot. If I looked like a princess, Elara looked like a queen. Her dress was gorgeous white gauze with gold accents and a backless bodice. Thin gold chains draped over her shoulders and down her back. She stood in front of her own mirror, with tailors kneeling all around her feet to pin up her hem, looking every bit the imperious empress her husband teased her about being.

I just wanted to pick her up and squish her and shout, "You're getting married!" but she was technically already married, so that would be weird. Not the picking up and squishing part—I did that all the time. I'd had to learn to tone down my physical affections a little bit with her over the years, but she put up with a lot of my nonsense. *See? I could learn boundaries... occasionally.* "Elara, you look stunning," I breathed.

She turned to me with a decidedly unsure expression on her face. "It's gorgeous, but are you sure it's not too much?" she asked.

"Honey, there's no such thing. This is going to be the biggest party of your life. Embrace it." That was clearly the wrong thing to say by the way her face paled, but I pasted on the biggest, bravest smile I could muster. I loved Elara, and I really wanted her to enjoy this, so I forced all my tangled emotions into the background. "The dress is perfect for you. Just focus on how taken Levi's going to be with it." And he would. That guy went moon-eyed over Elara every time she stepped into the room and their wedding ceremony would blow his mind. That approach landed better, and her face softened as she turned to face the mirror again and smoothed the dress against her thighs with her palms.

"Deep breaths, honey. It's going to be great," I encouraged her, and she gave a small smile into the mirror that became more and more genuine as she looked at me in the reflection. One step at a time. We could do this.

Chapter 11

EVERYTHING ABOUT THIS FELT viscerally wrong to me, but logic said my feelings were what was wrong. I was trying to keep a lid on my crazy emotions.

"You okay, Sid? You look a little pale," my brother said as the train slowed to a halt outside of the town called Redrock. He shifted the weight of the cage that rested across his lap to prepare to stand, causing Huck to thrash against the already bent wire walls of it. A blanket draped over the top obscured the dragon from view of the other railcar passengers, who were eyeing the covered cage with apprehension.

"I'm not pale," I grumbled. To the closest passenger I said, "It's fine, Fluffy just doesn't know his own strength," and nodded until the older dwarvish man gave me a confused nod in return. I patted the top of the cage—causing Huck to thrash and hiss again—and stood to make my way off the train. It was amazing that the cage was still holding together, considering the way he was crashing around in there.

Josh groaned as he stood, heaving the cage to chest height and wrapping his arms around it. "I feel like he's gained weight. What have you been eating, little dude?"

"Burned rats," I answered dryly as I stepped off and scanned for the street we needed. The refuge was supposed to be located on the outskirts of town, down toward the south, so I headed that direction.

"This is the right thing to do, Sid. You were the one who kept saying from the beginning that he was a wild animal and needed to be returned to the wild," Josh said for the third time since we left the house this morning.

"I know that." The streets were hard-packed dirt with a thin layer of sand, and the town wasn't much to speak of. It smelled like dry earth, and most of the buildings here were made of sunbaked brick, just like they were in Dry Gulch. These old mining and cattle stops were like little glimpses into the past as we wandered farther and farther from the bustle of the train station.

"He's going to get so big, Sidney. Like as big as that whole saloon," he reminded me, nodding toward a building with a sign advertising liquor down the road.

"I know that, Josh."

"Then why do you look so sad?"

"I'm not sad," I said, and I wasn't—I was panicking. The thought of leaving Huck's fate to someone else terrified me. What if he wasn't okay? What if he got killed? What if he was scared? Even now, I tried to block out the little sounds he made as he shuffled around in his temporary travel cage. He kept making this soft little whimper-cry sound, and it ripped my heart out every time he did it. And honestly, I had no idea why my brain was spiraling like this. I'd raised and released dozens of baby birds, and while it always hurt a little to say goodbye and wish them well in life, I didn't have this feeling like my skin was too tight or my magic was out of whack just at the thought of it. Maybe it was because their instincts were screaming at them to fly free. Maybe it was because they were comfortable around me, maybe even saw me as a mother figure, but they weren't *attached* to me like Huck was—they were primed and ready to strike out on their own long before I was ready to set them free. But Huck seemed just as reticent about this whole "parting ways" thing as I was. That's probably why this felt more like abandonment and less like returning him to where he belonged.

"He's gonna be fine, sis."

"I know." I tried to ignore my overly helpful brother as we rounded a corner and the front of the refuge came into view.

It was a typical square mud building with large front windows no one could see through due to the thick coating of reddish dust. A large sign declaring it the Redrock Wildlife Refuge was barely legible, also due to the aforementioned dust. Hazards of desert living. I eyed the sprawling metal fences that sectioned off areas to keep animals separated to the sides of the building and probably behind it too. Was that really enough to contain a growing dragon?

Josh clearly sensed my growing apprehension. "This way he'll be free to live his happy dragon life roasting all the rats he wants, and he won't burn us and our neighbors to crispy bits."

"Joshua, I may look calm right now, but in my head I've already punched you three times."

"You just wake up every day and choose violence."

"Every day," I agreed, heading for the door. I propped it open with one foot and then grabbed the cage to help back it in, since trying to get it through the door long-ways was a two-person job. We set it on the floor in front of the intake counter while the large ogre receptionist looked on with wide eyes.

"Can I help you?" she asked politely.

I took a deep breath and pasted a smile on my face. "Hi, I'm Sidney Anvindr, the one who took in the last of the eggs that were brought in from the Void." Her eyes widened further, and before I could even state why I was there, she was giving me the stiffest little head shakes in the world.

"You don't want to bring it here," she whispered, leaning closer. Josh made a dismayed sound behind me.

"I don't?" I asked, bewildered. She was right, I didn't, but how did she know that?

The nice ogre lady, with light green skin and her hair pulled back into a ponytail of small braids, looked around like there might be someone else in the small lobby area, and then leaned back to look through a door into an adjoining office. Once satisfied, she turned to us and hunched closer to me to whisper some more. Her whispers were like an average person's speaking volume. "The rest of the dragon eggs and the two that hatched from that clutch got stolen two nights ago."

I nodded because I'd heard that from Jordan.

"And the owners still haven't gotten our security straightened out," she continued. "I'll get in trouble for telling you this, but I wouldn't leave any animal here until they get that fixed. You know what I mean? They've got no one watching this place at night and think they can leave rare, expensive animals behind a simple padlock?" She made a face. "Don't do it. I'm telling you; he'll get snatched up just like the others."

My heart was beating a mile a minute, and I felt like I had ants crawling on my skin, because I'd figured they would have fixed that *immediately*. Time to get the hell out of dodge before the owners caught sight of us. I gave her a sloppy salute and said, "Message received, ma'am. Good day."

Josh made a pained sound and hissed frantically at me about how we couldn't take the "bonfire baby" back to the apartment while I bent to haul the cage up off the floor again. He was right, this little guy had gained some weight. I gave my brother the "get your shit together and open that door or so help me..." look, and he threw his head back to whine for a few more seconds before obeying. I cast a last frantic look at the receptionist before we heaved the cage back out the front door, and she nodded as if to reassure me that this was the right choice.

"Sidney, we can't do this!" Josh continued to hiss at me as we made our way back toward the road.

"What do you want to do, Joshua? Let him get stolen by gangsters again?" I hissed back. I'd carry the cage all the way back by myself if I had to, even though I was half his size.

"Something that doesn't involve us accidentally killing our neighbors!"

"Then we can move into a stone house with stone furniture and stone bedding that he can't set on fire!"

"Oh, my god!" Josh threw his head back again and flailed his arms like a child.

I jerked the cage away from him and marched up the road in the direction of the train station. "I'm not allowing them to take him again."

"I'm not fireproof, Sidney!"

"We'll get you some leather clothes and stock up on fire extinguishers."

He let out an obnoxious groan that sounded like a moose in heat and stomped up the road behind me. "Give me that," he said, taking the cage back. We headed back to the train station in silence, and even Huck seemed to sense that things were tense because he kept the hissing and thrashing to a minimum.

We didn't say a word to each other as we took our seats on the train back to Dry Gulch, and all I could think about was how terrible an idea this was. *He's gonna burn our frickin' house down.*

Chapter 12

I WENT TO WORK and left my brother in charge of the dragon, which—in hindsight—was probably the worst of all my recent bad decisions. As soon as I entered the Boundlands after work, I had a frantic message waiting with a spectral messenger from my brother. It was completely unintelligible, but I hustled home as fast as I could to find the living room in even more disarray than usual. Huck had already made several large tears in the sofa, but now Josh's potted plant was laying uprooted on the floor surrounded by an explosion of dirt. A disemboweled cushion was strewn about in the middle of it all. Josh was shouting something from his bedroom when suddenly Huck came bursting out of his room with a shoe in his mouth and galloped across the living room and into my bedroom.

Josh came thundering out of his bedroom with murder written on his face. "He's got my shoe! I've just gotten those perfectly broken in!" he yelled as he blew past me into my bedroom. Claws scrabbling on the hardwood in my room preceded Huck sprinting back out and blasting past me into Josh's room with his head thrown back and the stolen shoe on proud display. Even his little wings quivered with excitement as he ran.

"Uh, which part of the mess do you want me to tackle first?" I asked my brother as he turned around and doubled back across the living room.

"Get my shoe!" he answered angrily. *Well, ok then.*

"What happened in here?" I asked as I followed them into his room. "Look, dude, first step... shut the door," I said, pushing the door shut. "It becomes a much smaller game of keep-away when he only has access to one room."

"What do you *think* happened in here?" Josh shouted as he wrestled on the floor with a small dragon who did *not* want to give up the shoe. His blankets were in a tangled mess all over the floor. The mattress was shoved off the bed and standing on one side. Every single item that had been stored in his closet was pulled out and strewn across the floor. One of his shelves had been emptied, all the contents laying broken or tossed about on the floor.

"Well, I'm assuming Huck happened, but I'm morbidly curious about the specifics."

Josh pried his shoe out of Huck's mouth with a crow of triumph. "Ha! Got it. He was making a little nest in my bed at first, which was cute, so I let him," he panted as he collapsed onto the floor with the shoe clutched to his chest. "But then, he got tangled up in all the blankets and started to panic and was thrashing around, knocking stuff down, and shredding my sheets. So, I got him out, right? But then he was all scared and ran and hid in my closet." I eyed the chaos of his room, wondering where this was going. "And he stayed holed up in there for a while, which was fine. I figured he was just enjoying some quiet time in a dark place."

I cringed at that. There was no such thing as "quiet time" for this animal.

"But he stayed in there for a long time, so I went in to check on him. Sidney, he had peed *all over* the floor and all my stuff in there. And all my missing socks were stockpiled behind a box back in there!"

"They are known to hoard things," I said with a nod.

"All my missing socks, Sidney!"

"And the mattress?"

"When I pulled him out of my closet, he grabbed my shoe and ran under the bed with it. I couldn't reach him, so I pulled the bed apart."

That still didn't answer what had happened in the living room. I heaved a sigh and then lunged for Huck, because he already had the twin to Josh's shoe in his mouth.

"Did he do it again?" Josh yelled from the floor.

I shook the pungent smelling dragon drool from the toe of his shoe. "Yes. Why don't you have his muzzle on him?" I asked as I opened the door to his bedroom. Huck pranced out of the room in front of me and started to chase his tail through the mess of dirt in the living room as I headed to the kitchen to look for our broom.

"He seemed like he wanted a drink," came Josh's voice from his room.

"Well, get up off the floor and put it back on him." I pulled the broom out of the closet and set to work in the living room, listening as Josh entered the room and crouched in front of Huck to replace his muzzle. We'd been doing this so often that he was pretty good about tolerating it now, so I wasn't paying attention until I heard something that sounded like, "Hic-FOOM," and turned around to find my brother's shirt on fire.

"Josh!" I dove over Huck to beat out the flames on the front of his shirt. "What the hell?"

Josh just blinked at me, still clutching the muzzle that was tightly fitted around Huck's jaws with the buckle half-fastened around the back of his head. "I think he hiccupped," he said, sounding dazed.

"Well, go put some ice on that," I ordered, pulling the dragon away from him and taking over finishing the buckle that would hold the muzzle in place.

I'd barely gotten it buckled when he hiccupped again and sprayed fire onto the couch. It was just a short blast, but everywhere flame touched, it took hold. I dropped Huck and ran for the fire extinguisher, grabbing it up, pulling the pin, and unloading foam until the flames went out. Josh just stood staring at the scene from the kitchen while I panted with wide eyes, clutching the extinguisher for dear life. "His muzzle is still on,"

I said incredulously. Flames had just shot out the tiny crevice of his closed mouth anyway.

"It was on when he *torched me*," Josh said.

"I don't know what to do if the muzzle doesn't stop him from flaming."

He hiccupped again and spit fire on the rug, which I promptly put out with the extinguisher while Josh sprinted over and grabbed Huck. "I don't know! Take him outside?" He swung the dragon up in his arms while it continued to hiccup repeatedly, fire arcing across my face, up into the air, and across the ceiling. Huck's eyes were so wide I could see the whites around the outside.

"Watch where you're aiming that thing! And I can't take him outside while it's daylight! Someone will see him! Now, put him down. You're scaring him."

"He's scaring *me*, Sidney! He's *setting the house on fire*!"

I was trying to put the couch out again, but just as he said that, the fire extinguisher ran out. I grabbed the scorched rug and used it to beat out the rest of the flames.

"Go stand with him in the shower until his hiccups stop," I said.

"You need to call someone!"

"Who am I going to call?" I yelled. I knew who I *needed* to call, but I didn't want to do it.

"I don't care who you call, just call someone!" Josh yelled back as he carried the dragon into our bathroom. I followed behind, frantically smothering the flames he trailed behind him with the burned-up rug. "He can't stay here, Sidney! I'm serious!"

"I know that!" I rubbed my stinging eyes and dug out my calling stones. For the second time today, a panicked message left our apartment with a spectral, this time headed for Elara's house. We would still have to wait for nightfall, but I could pack a bag in the meantime. I didn't want help from the vampire who was emotionally unstable and—justifiably—angry at me, but I was out of ideas.

THE KNOCK THAT CAME as soon as night fell sounded like both my salvation and my doom. I tried not to glare as I opened the door, but I'm not sure how successful I was. Jordan didn't say anything, just stood there surveying the damage. I had multiple burns that had already begun healing, but the worst ones would take a few more days. My hair smelled like smoke, and I had bags under my eyes. What was left of the couch was a charred mess, and there were scorch marks up the wall behind me. We were never going to get our deposit back on the apartment.

"Why does it smell like burned hair?" Jordan asked quietly. He pulled off his helmet and raked his eyes over my face and hair, like he was searching for singed spots.

"That's probably the rats we feed the dragon," I grumbled, but Jordan shook his head.

"No, this is mixed with the scent of human skin."

"Oh, right. Yeah. The dragon decided my little brother needed some… personal grooming."

"He burned off my *chest hair!*" Josh shrieked from his bedroom.

"I said I was sorry!" I hollered back. It felt like Jordan's eyes were drilling into the side of my head as he stared at me, and I hunched my shoulders in an ineffective effort to shrink away from him. "It's fine. We heal fast, and he's got an ice pack," I said to Jordan.

"It's *not fine*, Sidney!" Josh bellowed. He *would* be fine, but he was super cranky because burns hurt like the devil until they healed. Also, we found out that dragons hate getting wet, and Josh was blaming me for all the new claw marks. All the more reason for us to high tail it out of here.

I squinted at Jordan. "You *are* actually fireproof, right?"

"Yes?" he answered like it was a question.

"I need your help," I admitted through gritted teeth.

Jordan's eyes were still flitting over the damage to the living room as he answered me distractedly, "That's what Levi said, yes."

I hauled the dragon out from behind the door where he was hiding and shoved him at Jordan. "Take this." He stuffed his helmet under his arm and awkwardly took Huck in his hands. "He started flaming this weekend, and then he got the hiccups this afternoon and couldn't control it. The refuge can't take him while their security is still compromised, and we have to get him out of here. I'm packing a bag so we can go hang out in the desert where he can't set anything else on fire."

"Take the baby carrier! Humphrey Herbert Hucklebee, the Fierce, loves his baby carrier!" my brother yelled from his bedroom.

"That's *not his name*!" I screamed back, but a mischievous image of Jordan wearing the baby carrier popped into my brain, so I grabbed it as I crammed a few more items into my backpack. Jordan looked entirely confused as he stood in the doorway holding a squirming dragon as big as a medium-sized dog. "Let's go," I said, and I pushed past Jordan and headed for the stairwell.

I heard him stuff his helmet back on his head as he trailed behind me, and his voice was muffled when he asked, "What, exactly, is your plan here?"

I didn't have a plan, so I ignored his question as we stepped outside of the building. "Here, give me the dragon."

Jordan handed me the baby as it whacked him on the helmet with its flapping wings. "What did your brother say its name was?"

"Huck." I passed him the baby carrier. "I need you to put this on." I used every ounce of mental strength I possessed to keep my face straight.

"It was definitely a longer name than that." He held the carrier up by one of the straps. "I don't know what this is. Why do I have to wear it?"

I did my best to shove the loops over his arms with one hand while keeping a grip on the dragon with my other arm. "Because you're fireproof, and I'm not. He keeps trying to turn me into birdie-barbeque. I can't buckle it with my hands full. You need to buckle those two straps hanging at your waist behind your back."

Jordan obeyed as if he were on autopilot, or just too confused to argue, but either one was fine with me. "The refuge still hasn't fixed their security?" he asked as he snapped the buckle into place.

I held up Huck and then dropped him down into the pouch on Jordan's chest, cringing to the side as I did in case he decided to torch me in the face again. It was sheer luck that I still had my eyebrows right now. We threaded his tail through the hole my brother cut in the bottom and tucked his wings through the side openings. He was going to be too big for it soon with how quickly he was growing. I gave it a few tugs to test that he was firmly in place while hanging from Jordan's chest. Huck gave a happy sounding trill. *Okay, they do look kind of adorable like that.*

"No, their employee told me on the down-low that their security isn't fixed, and they're still relying on simple padlocks at night to protect their animals," I said as I walked around to snap the last buckle into place behind his shoulders. Jordan flinched when it clicked into place. "Sorry," I said, jerking my hands off the buckle.

He didn't respond.

"Has your team figured out who broke in yet?" I asked, skittishly waving him forward to walk with me. I was only half afraid he would turn around and snarl at me. We were going to have to figure out how to exist in each other's presence somehow, if only just to get me out of this weird dragon situation.

"We don't have proof yet," he said in a rough voice, "but we figured it was Phantoms trying to recoup their loss. The refuge is the most likely place for Enforcement to take wild animals, so it wouldn't be hard for them to figure out where they went."

Ugh. "Do you have any ideas where to find the ones that were stolen?" I asked.

"Not yet, but my team has eyes on all the locations we've found them working out of so far."

"And they won't need you for tonight?" I shot him a look, wondering if I was majorly inconveniencing him with this.

"Nah, I'm the new guy. I try to help with scouting, but they hired me for literal firepower. They can call me in if they find them." The word "scouting" filled me with a wave of nostalgia for a time I'd never known. For thousands of years, long before I'd been born, my people had been scouts and spies within the shifter tribes. Something ancient and primal called to me about it and made me wish for half a second that I could help with that. Until I remembered that I already had a job that I liked very much. I blinked it away with a wistful sort of longing.

There weren't many people around as we paced down the dirty sidewalks, which was a little unusual for this time of night. It took me a few blocks to realize I was focusing so intently on Jordan and his every movement that I'd failed to notice the sound of beating drums in the distance. "Ooh! The desert people are here!"

Chapter 13

I CUT LEFT ONTO the next street and had to restrain myself to keep from running with excitement. This was one of my favorite occasions in Dry Gulch. Every year the People of the Sand—nomadic villagers who lived in the desert mountains—would come down to the city once or twice to gather extra water and trade goods with the locals. They also sold bootleg liquor that would peel the paint off the side of a building. Not that any buildings in Dry Gulch had much paint.

They'd been traveling back and forth for time immemorial and would set up camp for a week or so for each visit. Originally, desert people were made up of tribes of naga, the snake people, but these days they'd diversified a little and there were families of harpies and goblins that lived and traveled with them. By the time we made it to the outskirts of the city, I was practically skipping with excitement. Jordan followed behind at a sedate pace, clearly not in the hurry I was.

Multiple bonfires lit the night sky and large tents were erected on the desert sands. There were blankets laid out with people already bartering, and a large group dancing and playing music around the fires. A naga man with gray skin and black scales on his coiled snake-like tail was yelling at passersby about the wares laid out on his blanket. Maybe I could find something fun for Elara's shop since that girl couldn't tell a cutlass from a bowie knife.

"Lots of things for pretty ladies," he said as I approached to crouch at his blanket, and he gestured at some shoddily made jewelry. "And I have ancient elven artifacts! Sourced from deep in the mountain caves of Ardac."

I flipped over a ceramic bowl and raised my eyebrow at the vendor before plunking it back down.

"Hey! Careful with the artifacts, lady!" he groused as I stood, obviously offended by my handling.

"Your ancient artifacts say, 'Made in Korea,'" I grumbled back at him as I moved on down the row.

A small, pasty, pale goblin with thinning gray hair who was set up farther down the line had some interesting shiny rocks that I decided I wanted. "Is that a dragon?" he asked as I dug around in my backpack looking for some drahk—the popular currency in this part of the Boundlands.

I turned to look at Jordan, who was waiting dutifully for me off to the edge of the encampment, unwilling to venture into the chaotic mess of people. "No. It's just a winged lizard," I said dismissively. There were no such things as winged lizards, but he probably didn't know that. "How much drahk do you want for the rocks?"

"Don't want drahk."

I squinted at him. "But you can take the drahk into the city—" I gestured at the buildings in the distance with both hands. "—and get whatever you *do* want."

He just stared at me.

I huffed in irritation and dug out a fleecy hat with kitty ears on it. "Here," I said, setting it on the blanket between us with my hand still on it.

The goblin scowled at the hat and lifted his lip in a sneer. I glared back at him without blinking. "Fine, give me," he muttered, snatching the kitty hat out from under my hand. I grabbed up the shiny rocks and made my way back to Jordan with my prize, dodging around revelers and hawkers of all sizes. Huck had been watching the bonfires but started flapping his wings when he saw I was coming back, causing Jordan to have to pin them down again.

"Not in the mood to haggle?" I asked when I reached them.

"Too many people," Jordan muttered.

"Want to dance around the bonfires wearing nothing but our birthday suits?" I waggled my eyebrows at him.

"I'm honestly surprised you're not already doing that. This is the longest I've seen you wear clothes recently." I glowered at him, but he turned toward the open desert, so I had to hustle to stay with him.

"I wear clothes sometimes," I said, feeling mildly indignant. "What's with yours, anyway? I thought they were meant to block out sunlight, but it's dark out." I hefted my backpack higher onto my shoulders and trudged toward the cliffs in the distance. Maybe we could find a good cave to hang out in. There wasn't anywhere else out here to go, just sand and rocks and an occasional shrub. It was a perfect place for a baby dragon who was still learning to control his fire. I glanced at Huck to see how he was doing, but he was just looking around with wide eyes, taking everything in.

"It's dark out now, but it won't stay that way. And I didn't know who was going to be at your apartment when I came."

I frowned at him. "Were you expecting a shootout?"

He huffed a laugh that sounded bitter. "No. I don't want people to recognize me."

"Whyyy?" I drew the word out as my frown deepened.

He was quiet for a long time as we walked, but I stubbornly stared at the side of his helmet, waiting for him to answer. "I don't want to deal with people who knew me from before," he finally said. "It's awful, and I hate the reaction every time. Plus, your older brother knows my family, and I don't want word getting back to them about where I am. I'd appreciate it if you kept our... friendship... to yourself."

I looked over at Jordan with big doe-eyes and my most innocent expression. "Do all your friends know what your dick tastes like?"

Jordan stumbled on the sand, causing Huck to squawk and bash him with his wings again.

I reached back and grabbed my water bottle from the pouch on my bag. "What's wrong with your family, anyway?" I asked before cringing and taking a swig of my drink to hide it. That hadn't come out right, but why wouldn't he want them to know where he was?

He huffed a breath, and I didn't think he was going to answer until he said, "My parents were particularly awful toward me after my change and blamed me for all of it. I don't have any desire to talk to them anymore."

"I'm sorry." He didn't respond. I had a million questions, but I didn't want to push him. *Too much.* "Is that why you left the first time you saw me?"

"Yes." His answer was flat.

"So, it wasn't about *me* specifically? It wasn't personal?"

"No."

I clutched my hands around my water bottle and held it under my chin, tilting my head to give Jordan a cutesy, sarcastic look. "Aw, Jordan, *you love me*! My heart just grew three whole sizes!"

Jordan didn't respond at all other than to turn his head toward me as we walked. I couldn't see through the visor, but I could feel his glare, so I beamed at him. I don't know why it made me feel better that he wasn't furious with me personally, but I couldn't help but ham it up a little bit, even if it didn't really mean anything.

We were getting pretty close to the cliffs now, but I figured we didn't need to head into the caves just yet, since sunlight was a long way off. "We could just park it here for a few hours and watch the stars since it's a clear night," I suggested.

He stopped and looked down at Huck hanging from his chest. "What do I do with him?" he asked.

"We could let him go," I said with a shrug. "He can't really get into too much trouble out here, and if he runs away, well, then I guess he's released himself back into the wild. I can unbuckle your straps if you'll let me." I waited, trying—for maybe the first time in my life—to be respectful of his space.

"Yeah, go ahead." He sounded hesitant.

"Okay, coming in," I said, making sure my movements were slow and he could anticipate them. I grasped the buckle behind his shoulders and pinched, and the instant Huck heard the buckle click, he exploded out of the carrier, smacking Jordan on the helmet with his wings and flailing around in the air.

"Ah, sh—" Jordan slapped him away from his head while I scrambled to grab Huck and get his wings pinned again. So much for not getting into trouble.

"Sorry!" I yelled, my body tensing at Jordan's reaction to the ruckus. I was apologizing a lot today, which wasn't my favorite thing. Huck squirmed in my arms while Jordan stood a few paces off, breathing heavily, with his arms braced on his knees. "You good?" I asked him. I knew he wasn't hurt. He was wearing a full helmet and vampires healed faster than any race I knew of, but I felt bad for startling him again.

"I'm fine, just wasn't expecting it," he said.

I wasn't sure what to do. Should I risk spooking him again, or should I wait for his nerves to settle? When I remained frozen with my scaly captive clawing at my arms, Jordan raised his head.

"I said I'm fine, Sidney. Let him go."

"If you say so," I muttered. "Let's try this again, okay, little guy? Be chill." I lowered us both to the ground and kept my hands around his wings until I was ready to back away. Getting clubbed by a wing bone repeatedly did not feel good, even from a smaller animal. Pigeons were much smaller and could still dish out a slap that hurt. My voice seemed to do something for Huck though, because I felt his muscles loosen when I spoke to him. "That's right, buddy. Nice and easy," I crooned. Letting go and backing away in one smooth movement, I tensed for flailing, but Huck had a much calmer posture now. "Okay, well, that was anticlimactic," I said, taking a seat on the sand.

I pulled my backpack in front of me, digging through it for some toiletries. A wet wipe and a hairbrush felt like a godsend right now since I'd never gotten the chance to clean up after Huck's... debacle. I scrubbed my face with the wipe and then pulled out my loose braid to redo it. Two tight braids seemed like a good option around fire.

Jordan stood where he was, watching Huck as he sniffed around in the sand, eventually getting bored and beginning to chase his tail again. "What's he doing?" Jordan asked.

"His best." I gave him a shrug and stuffed everything back in my pack, pulling it behind me and flopping back to use it as a pillow. "Nobody ever said dragons were geniuses," I said. There were few clouds tonight in the rapidly darkening sky, I noted as I fixed my eyes above me. "You gonna stand there all night, or come look at the stars with me?" I asked Jordan. I didn't necessarily want him *right* near me—*yes, I did*—but having him just standing there staring felt weird. The scuff of a boot told me he was moving, and I tried not to flinch. Why was I always so conflicted with him?

He dropped onto the sand next to me and his helmeted head hit the sand with a thud as he lay down. After a few minutes of fidgeting, I finally managed to get comfortable on the warm sand, focusing on the sky, with the stars so visible and close here in the desert. The two moons hung near the horizon, and clusters of pink and white nebulas smattered among the twinkling stars looked almost close enough to touch. Except for the sounds of Huck snuffling around, doing whatever he was doing in the sand, and a few insects chirping, everything was quiet. And yet... there was nothing I was more aware of in that moment than the person next to me. I was staring at the sky, but every ounce of me was hyper-focused on Jordan, no matter how much I tried to wrest my attention away from him.

His smell had changed so drastically since I'd known him, with the scent of vampire nearly overwhelming the underlying smell of *him*. He'd always smelled warm and masculine, like low burning coals and summer forest. It was hard to describe the scent of vampire in his blood. Like sharp spice and challenge, an unspoken danger that put me on edge. But if I searched for it, if I was patient with it, I could tease out the notes of him, the Jordan that I'd always known, underneath it all. I tried to center myself, breathing deeply and savoring the hidden notes of campfire and man deep in my lungs.

Huck thrashed in the sand, jumping and pouncing and jumping again, and Jordan twitched. "What's he doing now?" he asked, sounding concerned.

I glanced at Huck, watching him play for a bit. "He's chasing crickets." That was a good sign. He needed to be able to hunt on his own, so it pleased me to see he had the instincts for it. "He's just playing. Are you scared of him?"

"No… I just don't know what to expect from him." Jordan lifted his head to stare at Huck, and then let it drop back onto the sand with a thud.

"He can't hurt you," I said matter-of-factly. "Just think of him as a dinosaur toddler. That breathes fire. Since fire can't hurt you, you don't have anything to worry about."

"If he was a toddler, I probably wouldn't be okay with him eating sand."

I shot up off the ground and lunged for Huck to find that he *was indeed* eating sand. Tackling him and wiping the sand out of his mouth made him fuss, but I held his jaws open and made sure all the little grains were out. "Don't eat sand, dingus." I crawled back to my backpack and collapsed on my side, facing Jordan. "I don't remember the last time I got a full night's sleep. For precisely this reason," I grumbled. "You should take off your helmet. There are still many long hours of night you can enjoy, and no one is around to see you but me." I was totally just concerned with his comfort and not at all obsessed with his pretty face. I took another deep breath, just to pull his smell deep into my lungs again, separating out the different layers of scent in my mind and letting myself get used to the changes.

"I'm not sure you can enjoy night," Jordan said with a quiet rasp, but he pulled his helmet off anyway and dumped it beside him. He pulled his arm behind his head to rest on. My heart squished at his tone, but my frustration sparked at his stubbornness.

"Of course you can enjoy night. Nighttime is lovely. The air is cool and soft. The darkness is like being all wrapped up in your favorite blanket. Like something cozy to hide in. The most interesting creatures come out at night. And the stars and cosmos are more beautiful than anything in the daytime."

Jordan didn't respond, just took in my words and the stars above. His hair was still a mess and the thick covering he wore around his shoulders was bunched around his neck. His breaths were deep and even, but other than that, the only thing that moved was his eyes as he scanned the night sky. He really was handsome, his face all hard angles and flat planes, except for his lips that looked soft and kissable. *Sigh.* It occurred to me I was being rather silly, watching him as he watched the stars, but I couldn't think of anything else I'd rather be looking at right now.

"Night," he began quietly, startling me from my reverie, "is only half of the equation. Being confined to it is a half existence. It makes me feel half alive. The future stretches on forever, and yet, I have no real future."

I huffed at him. "Okay, I get it that nobody likes to have their choices taken away. I don't condone what that girl did to you, *at all*, and I'm sorry it happened. But you have a whole new hand of cards you've been dealt. You have *new* choices. There's *so many* cool things you can do when you *can't die.*"

Jordan squinted his eyes just the tiniest amount as he continued to watch the stars.

"Do you even need to breathe air?" I asked, as a thought occurred to me.

He took a beat to answer, like he was actually thinking over the answer. "Not really, no. It's uncomfortable not to."

"You can go to *space!*" I hollered in excitement. Huck squawked and hiccup-flamed where he sat. "Sorry, Huck." I guess that was the baby dragon equivalent of a puppy peeing when it got startled. "Okay, hear me out. You don't even need a space suit. You can explore anywhere you want, just launch yourself into space and you can go see what's inside the gas giants or drift around looking at the sights for eternity."

He turned his head to stare at me like I was insane. "Just because I'm not aging and I can't die of natural causes doesn't mean I can't be *killed*. Or feel pain. I'd imagine being crushed by the gravity of a gas giant would still kill me."

"Oh." Lame. "I guess that blows my next idea."

He turned his face back to the sky and grumbled, "Do I even want to know?"

"Scuba vampires," I blurted. He looked at me out of the side of his eye and made a "you're ridiculous" face. Which was fair. "Just imagine getting to walk around in the deepest trenches in the oceans, and since you don't need an air tank, you could go anywhere you wanted. Scuba vampires would be the most metal thing."

"Except for that whole crushing pressure thing," he said. But then he gave me the world's smallest smile and said, "Or getting eaten by a shark." And my heart fluttered in my chest at getting to make this man crack a smile. My own smile was so delighted I couldn't possibly hide it.

Chapter 14

SOMETHING WARMED IN JORDAN'S eyes as he watched my grin spread. They looked nearly ink black in the darkness, even with the light of the moons, but the intensity in them made my breath catch. I let my gaze trail over the stark lines of his eyebrows, the strong angle of his nose, the scruff he wore on the sharp line of his jaw. But then he seemed to withdraw, his expression shuttering and becoming something brittle.

"As much as I would love to get eaten by a shark or crushed by the overwhelming gravity at the bottom of the sea, it's not just about what I can *do*. It's about—" he paused briefly to swallow, searching my face for something he didn't seem to find, before continuing, "not having anyone to share it with. What good is any experience when you have no family or partner to experience it with you?" he asked in a murmur.

My stomach twisted uncomfortably at the thought. My brothers, Josh especially, were part of who I was. My parents—as frustrating as they could be sometimes—were my backbone and my safety net, the people I was most excited to share my achievements and my accomplishments with. I loved them all fiercely. I couldn't imagine the pain it would cause me if they turned their backs on me. But then I thought about Elara, who was practically a sister to me, who I shared a kind of comfortable kinship with that even my brothers couldn't fulfill. She was family to me too, just in a different kind of way. "If you don't have a family anymore, you should make one," I said.

Jordan shifted on the sand, his gaze cutting to me in the darkness.

"Friends can be just as important and valid a family unit as blood relatives," I insisted. "And you actually get to choose them instead of just making do with what you have."

I didn't want to press him too much, so when he turned his attention back to Huck, I did as well, watching as he pounced after a tiny cricket in the sand. After a few frustrating misses, he clacked the stones in his throat and huffed out a flame in frustration, torching the cricket from three feet away. He stared at it in stunned silence, and I could practically see the little gears turning in his walnut sized brain, before dashing forward to gobble up the charred bug. I was so glad we'd left the house.

"And then what?" Jordan asked, interrupting my thoughts. I let my confusion show on my face. "So I make friends, and then what? They just grow old and die and I go on living forever?"

I shrugged at him, feeling uncomfortable with the notion of my own mortality. "Just because a person has an end date, does that mean we're not worth knowing? People and animals die all the time, and we still make connections with them. Think about all the people who keep pets for their companionship knowing they'll live less than a decade in most cases." Not that I wanted to compare mortals with pets, per se, but the idea of an immortal keeping a bunch of mortal people around like pets was kind of an amusing yet disturbing idea. He really was separated from mortal society now that I thought about it.

I didn't really want to bring up making friends with other vampires and make it seem like I was suggesting he segregate himself, but then a mischievous thought crossed my mind. "You could partner up with Grim," I said, a wicked smile spreading across my face. "He's immortal too, right?"

Jordan rolled his eyes and gave an exaggerated shiver, surprising a quick laugh from me. "I don't think Grim swings that way. I'm convinced reapers reproduce via binary fission."

I sputtered. "What, like a starfish?"

A short burst of laughter from Jordan was so shocking to me that I almost missed when he said, "Absolutely. I bet he just divides himself in half and creates a clone of himself. Or maybe he cuts off a toe and just grows a whole new reaper." We both burst out laughing, and *my heart...* Oh, man, my heart couldn't handle the silly mischief written all over his face. This was the Jordan I remembered. The one that joked, and played, and rough-housed with his friends as he fought for a goal on the field. Who had a quick wit and a smart mouth that was just as likely to get him in trouble during practice as his temper.

I wanted to prolong the moment, to watch his smile for a little longer, so I said, "Nah, he seems more spider-like. I bet he has an ovipositor."

Jordan wrinkled his nose as he chuckled, and I let the warm feelings settle into my bones. "Wouldn't that be for a female?" he asked.

I just shrugged. I wasn't an expert in spider anatomy. Huck had found a new cricket to stalk and flamed it as soon as he spotted it. He was getting better at it already. "It seems like you've got some good friends in your roommates, at least?" I asked Jordan. Not that I'd seen them interact much, but Levi seemed to care about him, and Grim... I dunno, Grim seemed like a decent guy from my interactions with him, even if he did give me the heebie jeebies.

He shrugged back at me. "Yeah, I guess. They're good guys. But it's not really the same as a life partner."

"But it could be," I said obstinately. Found family was just as valid as blood family. "Which one of them keeps leaving all the weird stuff in your room, anyway?"

He sighed. "I'll give you one guess."

Levi.

Huck tried to flame another bug, but this time he missed and a scraggly looking bush about two feet tall caught on fire. The resin in the wood burned fast, shooting flames much higher than the limbs of the bush. "That's the second plant you've murdered today, you little plant-murderer."

"I wonder if it'll talk to us," Jordan mumbled.

"What?"

"The burning bush."

Why would a burning bush talk to us? I dragged us back on topic as the flames quickly died down to a much more reasonable level. "Why don't you take it down?"

"The bush?" he asked, sounding bewildered.

"No, you goof, the stuff in your room." What was his deal with the bush?

Jordan huffed, sounding exasperated. "That's his love language."

That made me chuckle. "Yeah, I guess that fits. Levi plays pranks on everyone he cares about." And probably random unsuspecting people as well.

He shrugged again. "It's his version of affection, his way of including me in the group. So I take it for what it is. If he wants to hang Twilight posters in my room and give me a pillow with my face on it 'since I can't see myself in the mirror and I might forget what I look like' then he can go for it."

I reared back and blinked at him. "You can't see yourself in a mirror?"

"No, I can, but he likes to pretend I can't since it's an old vampire myth among humans."

I thought back, trying to remember seeing this pillow he spoke of in his room. "I don't think I saw that pillow, which is disappointing because that's kind of hilarious."

"Pretty sure he moved it into Grim's room. He said it would be funny to have my face be the first thing Grim sees when he wakes up in the morning, but I'm not sure Grim actually sleeps. I haven't seen it since."

That made me cackle. "Okay, but the real question is, do you speak his love language back to him?"

Jordan slid his gaze over to me with a disgruntled expression. "I don't think I speak that language," he muttered.

Welp, my time to shine. "Then I can teach you." I rolled forward to sitting and dragged my bag around in front of me again, opening the top and digging through it. "Perfection," I said, pulling out an old copy of "Space Raptor Butt Invasion" by Chuck Tingle. It was a great book, but I didn't mind donating it to the cause. I slapped it into Jordan's hand, and he took it from me reflexively. "Hide that in one of the boxes in Levi's room," I told him. According to Elara, he'd boxed up most of his stuff, but hadn't moved all of it into her house yet.

Jordan studied the cover, obviously perplexed by the badly photoshopped half-naked man and the dinosaur in an astronaut suit. "What in the world are you reading?" he asked haltingly.

"Don't kink shame me," I said primly. I didn't really have any kinks for butt invasions or space raptors, but I loved Chuck Tingle. "That man is a literary treasure."

"I'm not kink *shaming*. I'm just kink *asking-why*."

I ignored him. "Wait! I've got more." I knew I'd find a use for this! Zipping open a side pocket, I dug out a roll of stickers that said "FOR ANAL USE ONLY" in bold, black letters, which my brother had stolen during his last visit to the medics and I, in turn, had stolen from him. Being a magpie who hoarded random interesting things came in handy sometimes. I tossed it to Jordan. "Slap those babies on everything Levi owns. His shampoo, his toothbrush, his guitar case, everything." I resituated my bag and settled back into the soft sand, feeling smug.

"Why is it all butt stuff?" he asked.

"Because butt stuff is funny." Yes, I realized I had the sense of humor of a twelve-year-old, but so did my brothers, so I fit right in with them. "Levi will love it," I insisted.

We lay staring at the stars and talking about nothing while the fire in the bush died down to low coals and Huck frolicked in the sand, chasing beetles and other bugs, but always sticking close by. There was a lull in the conversation as we listened to the night sounds—crickets and toads calling to each other in the dark—until Jordan suddenly asked, "So... what is your love language?"

My gaze shot to his face to find him staring at me in the dark. "Violence," I said, giving him a flippant answer to try to fend off the way my stomach swooped and tightened when he looked at me.

He snorted. "No."

"What do you mean, no? You don't get to decide what someone else's love language is."

"Yes, I do. Violence isn't a love language," he answered just as flippantly.

"Fine. Nice sticks."

"... What?"

"Yeah. You know how it goes," I explained. "A daddy bird loves a mommy bird very much, so he goes and finds her a nice stick." I could feel the mischief dancing in my eyes.

He gave me a completely skeptical look in response, as if he didn't know if I might be telling the truth or not since I was a shifter. When I didn't comment, he narrowed his eyes at me further.

I smiled innocently. And then I sighed because my stomach started to rumble, making me realize I hadn't eaten dinner tonight even though it was well past bedtime. A granola bar or three from my bag would have to do. "Do you need to eat?" I asked as I dug them out and tore into one. "Not that I'm offering, just so we're clear." No need to give the vampire the wrong idea about whether my own blood was "on the table", so to speak.

I turned to find his glower had deepened. "I don't need to eat, thank you," he said, but the "thank you" didn't sound genuine.

"How often do you need to eat now?" I was infinitely curious about what his life was like after the change.

The breath that gusted out of him was heavy. "I usually eat once every few days or so, but I can eat more or less often. I could go for weeks without if I needed to. Are you going to need to sleep?" he asked.

"I'm pretty tired, yeah. I doubt I'll make it through the night without it, considering how little sleep I've gotten lately." I was getting to the point in my exhaustion that I was beginning to feel nauseated.

"You could try to head home if you want, and I can hang out here with the dragon. You'd just need to come back to tag in before daylight."

I was already shaking my head before he finished. "Won't work. If I leave, he'll follow me. Watch." I stood and made it ten steps back toward town before Huck squawked and shuffle-flapped his way after me, calling out with his little baby dragon cry until he caught up to me. With a sigh, I scooped him up with both arms and hauled him back to Jordan, plopping back down in the sand next to him.

"Huh. Can you sleep out here?" He sat up and looked around doubtfully.

"It's a little too exposed," I said with a shrug. "Why don't we look for a small cave in the cliffs?"

"Somewhere with a little more privacy would be nice," he said, and I tried to stifle the unintended flame the thought of privacy with Jordan lit inside me.

"Yeah," I answered, sounding a little breathless to my own ears. "Let's go see what we can find."

Chapter 15

WE HIKED UP INTO the cliffs and I got to enjoy seeing Huck climbing around and exploring in a natural environment. His curiosity and enthusiasm for being outside was infectious, and even Jordan seemed to find his antics amusing. It was such a relief to have him out here in nature, where he could just be himself and not cooped up in a house destroying everything. He would find a rock, or a stick, or a leaf that he liked and carry it along with us in his jaws until he came upon something else he liked better, and then trade it out for the newer, better object. He'd cycled through six different random items so far as he followed along beside us at a jaunty little trot. When he stopped again to inspect a new stone, he tried to fit it into his mouth along with the one that was already in there but couldn't manage it.

"Sorry, bud," I told him, rubbing the scales between his little nubby horns. "I know how it feels to be excited about trinkets and not be able to carry them all." I picked up one of his stones and tossed it higher up the path, causing him to scramble off after it.

"That's one way to get him moving, I guess," Jordan mumbled. "Which one of these do you want to use?" He bent down to peer under an overhang of rock in the cliff face. The whole side of the cliff was riddled with openings, some large enough to crawl into.

"Whichever one is large enough to lie down in and has the least amount of bugs." I was starting to not care at this point, as tired as I was.

"This one looks defensible," Jordan said after checking out a few more openings. He only had to bend at the waist to enter, and when I followed him in, we could both nearly stand. The back was closed and there was enough room to spread out in, with a layer of sand covering the floor.

"Are you planning to be attacked?" I asked, dropping my sack on the floor and laying down on it again. Normally, I wouldn't have been able to sleep this close to a vampire, even if it was Jordan, but I was so tired I would probably drift right off. I probably wouldn't even feel it if he tried to eat me. Even as I lay there wondering if I could trust him, guilt chewed at me when I acknowledged that he was doing me a massive favor to help with Huck and let me have a chance to rest.

Jordan frowned down at me. "Don't you have a blanket or something to lie on?"

"No. I'm trying to be as un-flammable as possible. Not all of us are fireproof." Just to punctuate my point, Huck bounded into the little cave and torched a spider on the wall before gobbling it up like he was starving.

Jordan's frown deepened as his gaze transferred from Huck and his spider snack back to me. "Get up."

"What? I'm fine." Sleeping in the dirt wasn't on my list of concerns at the moment.

"Get up, Sidney," he insisted, dropping his helmet on the ground and unwinding the heavy cloth he kept wrapped around his shoulders. I hauled my exhausted bones up off the ground and stared as he draped the thick material across the ground where I'd been laying and over my pack. "It's wool. He'd have to work really hard to catch that on fire, and I won't let him."

"Thanks," I said, feeling humbled by the weirdly chivalrous gesture. The fabric was soft, but dense, and certainly felt better than the cold ground that hadn't been warmed by the sun's rays like the sand in the open desert had. As I settled onto it, I tried not to be obvious about huffing his scent, but I wanted to stuff my face in it. I lay on my side instead and tucked my arms around myself as Jordan settled against the wall across from me.

"Wouldn't you be more comfortable sleeping in your other form?" he asked after a few minutes.

I'd thought about that already. "We've been feeding Huck small animals," I muttered, turning my head to watch the dragon as he tried to pull a larger branch he'd found—*god knows where*—into the cave. It looked like he'd dragged in a whole dead bush. "I'm mildly concerned he'd mistake me for food." My magpie form was a little larger than a real black-billed magpie, but it wasn't worth the risk to my feathers. My body healed quickly, but feathers took longer to repair.

Closing my eyes was so nice that blinking felt almost rapturous. "Are you sure you don't mind me dropping off for a little bit?" I felt bad leaving him to do all the dragon-sitting alone.

Jordan shook his head. "What do I need to do for him?" he asked gruffly.

"Try to make sure he doesn't eat sand. Don't let him set me on fire. If he takes off somewhere, that's fine. Just don't let him head into the city. Use your best judgment." It was babysitting an incendiary dinosaur toddler, not rocket science. Not that we had rockets here in the Boundlands, but my point stands. They would be fine.

"Sleep," Jordan told me. "I'll take care of him."

I pulled a deep breath of his scent into my lungs and closed my eyes, searching for the notes of his familiar smell underneath the stronger vampire scent. Savoring it when I found it, I held it for a moment and released it, using it to remind myself that he was still the same Jordan underneath all his changes. But when sleep pulled me under, I felt uncomfortable for a completely different reason.

The crowd around me seemed endless, stretching out in every direction. I couldn't remember what I was searching for until I spied Jordan's face in a gap between people. What were they all doing here? Why wouldn't Jordan wait for me? I pushed through the milling crowd, trying to follow him, feeling like I was losing the battle against the surge of bodies as they all pressed in around me, intent on their own destination.

Several times I caught sight of his face, only to lose him again when my brother or my mom or some cousin passed between us and blocked my view. Every time they moved out of the way, Jordan was gone, and a deep unease filled me as I had to start my search all over again. My frustration spiked when someone big cut me off *yet again*, and I glanced up to see that it was my goofy older brother Aaron.

"Stop getting in my way!" I yelled at him, and he looked at me with confusion written plainly on his face. He turned to hand me a bundle he carried in his arms, wrapped in cloth like a swaddled baby. I took it carefully and startled when it began to cry like an infant, but when I lifted the cloth, Huck's snout poked out at me. I looked up at my brother, but he was gone. The faceless crowd continued to push past me, and I clutched the baby dragon to my chest. I felt lost.

IT WAS STILL DARK when I woke. My back felt like I'd lost a fight in the ring, and I made a noise that sounded embarrassingly like a whimper. The rasp of paper scraping against paper cut through the darkness and relief swamped me when I opened my eyes to find Jordan propped against the cave wall in the same spot he'd been when I fell asleep. The last vestiges of my dream hadn't quite left me, and I sucked in a deep breath, using his scent to try to dissipate the feeling of panic I felt from not being able to find him in the crowd. Why had I been so upset in the odd dream? A few more breaths and my heart rate finally began to even out into something reasonable. I was still tired, but the nap had helped relieve some of the worst of my nausea and exhaustion.

The sound of paper scraping again made my gaze shoot back to Jordan. He was reading the book I'd given him earlier, seemingly having no trouble in the dark. "How is it?" I asked, my voice sounding scratchy and thick.

"I have no idea what this is," he said dryly.

"It's a space raptor butt invasion. It says it right there on the tin." I made a sound like a wounded elephant as I rolled onto my knees and opened my bag again. It was cold now, and my joints were stiff. "Where's Huck?" I asked, looking around.

"He's outside trying to dig something out of the ground," Jordan answered without lifting his eyes from the page.

"Were you out there with him?" I frowned and shot a look outside but couldn't see anything. My night vision was sadly average.

"No. I can hear him."

I held still and strained my hearing for any sounds but couldn't make out anything other than crickets and a gentle breeze. Vampires were so overpowered. "How long was I out?" I asked.

"Most of the night, it will be dawn soon," he answered quietly, still focused on the book.

I smirked at him. "Have you heard anything from your team?" I asked as I pulled out a toothbrush and some other toiletries.

He lifted a shoulder and let it drop. "They checked in earlier, but there's nothing new. They're grateful for the work you've done, keeping the dragon safe and healthy."

"Aww. That's nice." I hadn't done it for anyone's approval, but it was nice to be acknowledged sometimes. "I'll be right back. I know you can hear a pin drop from a mile away, but do me a favor and don't listen to me pee."

Moonlight blanketed the desert floor, highlighting sand and rock peppered in black scorch marks that hadn't been there when we'd arrived. Huck was digging and prying industriously at a rock wedged in the ground that was far too large for him to carry. He gave a happy trill and scampered over to greet me as I exited the cave. "Come on buddy, let's go get me cleaned up."

When I returned to the cave, the faintest fingers of light had begun to stretch over the horizon. I shook the dirt out of Jordan's wrap and smoothed it out, handing it back to him so he could wind it around his shoulders and neck again. "Should you head home so you're out of the sunlight?" I asked him. I tried to ignore the pang of panic that sparked in me at the thought of him leaving. It would just be boring out here all alone, that was all.

"I'm fine," he said, but he did replace his helmet. "I won't be able to stay awake though." He already sounded tired, and my heart tugged at the sleepiness in his voice.

"You should rest," I told him. "I really appreciate you giving me a break from Huck and letting me sleep."

He was quiet for a moment, until he said, "I won't be able to keep you safe though."

I paused while I was putting away my gear to squint at him. "I don't need protection. I'll be okay." At least, I didn't need protection from anyone except Huck and his hiccups.

Jordan grumbled something I didn't catch and stared at the entrance to the cave, watching the sunlight brighten along the horizon. After a few minutes, he laid down on the dirt and stretched out on his side. "Don't let anyone touch my neck," he said quietly.

My hands froze on the zipper of my bag, and I shot him a look, noting how bundled up against the world he looked. My heart squished at how vulnerable he sounded. "I'll keep you safe," I promised him.

Chapter 16

Turns out it was nearly as boring with him asleep as it would have been if he was gone, but I still felt better that he was here for some reason. I sat on my side of the cave watching Huck as he scurried in and out, bringing in dozens of little rocks one at a time. He piled them behind a larger rock in the back of the cave, stacking them in a little pile, diligently re-piling them every time the mound grew too tall and toppled.

"Hm. I'll give you points for quantity, but your quality sucks, buddy. Try to find some shiny ones," I murmured to him, not sure how much sound would disturb Jordan. I learned a few minutes later that it probably wouldn't matter if a bomb went off in here—Jordan still wouldn't wake up. Huck was making one of his runs to the back of the cave when he decided it would be a good idea to climb *over* Jordan's sleeping body, so I jumped up to drag him off, concerned about Jordan getting startled again and hurting him. But Jordan didn't even flinch.

The tussle shifted his clothing so that two inches of skin were exposed where his coat and shirt rode up. *Shit.* I glanced at the entrance of the cave, noting that the sun was shining in, but hadn't quite reached his body. How much sunlight was too much? Sunlight reflected off the moon obviously didn't hurt him, but I didn't want to risk him getting injured on my watch. I also didn't want to touch him when he was vulnerable like this and liable to lash out. *Ugh!*

I crept forward, staying low to the ground, and reached out with one hand, watching my fingers shake as they closed on the hem of his jacket. If he woke up and attacked me for trying to help him, I was going to kick his ass. Slowly—*gently*—I tugged his coat down so that it overlapped his pants by several inches. And then I backed away.

I turned my death glare on Huck. "Don't touch him while he's sleeping," I breathed.

Huck replied with a happy sounding trill, as usual, and went back to piling his rocks.

My stomach was rumbling again, so I dug out an apple and another granola bar and settled in. Once I'd eaten, I rebraided my hair and dug out some knives from my bag that I could work on sharpening. I was the type of person that always needed to be doing something productive or I'd get fidgety. Sitting and guarding Huck and Jordan was productive, but it didn't *feel* productive, so I was getting itchy. By midday Huck was slowing down and so was I. He curled up around his rock pile in the back of the cave and decided to take a catnap, and after sitting there twitching for another half hour, I decided that wasn't a bad idea. Jordan hadn't moved all day—he'd slept like the dead. I knew we should probably stay on opposite schedules, but at least I would wake up if something went wrong.

I stretched out next to him as best I could without bumping him or getting too close, but there wasn't a ton of room to keep my distance. He'd probably be irked if he found out I'd slept in the dirt again after all the trouble he'd gone to last night to keep me clean, but I didn't really have it in me to care. He was sleeping in the dirt—so could I. It didn't take me long to drift off, even though it had only been a handful of hours since I'd woken. Being sleep deprived for several weeks was going to take a while to fix.

This time, I dreamed I was fighting: fighting as a child to defend my little brother from bullies on the playground at school, fighting to protect Elara from Phantoms who were stalking her from the shadows, fighting to keep Huck safe from people who wanted to keep him as a showpiece or sell him for parts. And I just kept failing. It was never enough. *I* wasn't enough. No matter how fast I moved or how hard I punched, I wasn't enough to save the people I loved.

I woke up panting for air, only to feel a spike of panic as the fog of sleep cleared and I realized I was *firmly* wrapped around Jordan. "Oh shit!" I rolled away, flinging myself across the small space to the other side of the cave. With eyes as wide as saucers, I looked back to see that he hadn't moved at all. I should have known better than to sleep next to him. I turn into a total octopus when I sleep, always waking up clutching something like a pillow or, lately, even Huck.

It didn't seem like my heart would ever slow down, but eventually it did as I lay there cursing my grabby tendencies and my own subconscious's desire to mess with me lately. I cleaned myself up and propped myself back against the rock wall. Judging by the fading daylight, Jordan still had a bit to sleep, so I pulled out another book I had stuffed into the bottom of my bag and got comfortable. This one was about a bunch of human women who get lost on an ice planet and rescued by a tribe of purring blue aliens. I wasn't willing to donate this book for a prank.

I'd made it a few chapters in when Jordan suddenly exploded off the floor in a fit of hisses and snarling, crouched in the middle of the cave with his hands curled into claws. It was all I could do to stay in my skin and not sprout wings and bolt. I kept my butt glued to the dirt while he calmed himself, heaving huge breaths and looking around as if he were confused. He still had his helmet on, so I couldn't see his face, but I imagined he looked as startled as I felt.

"Do you want to talk about it?" I asked, after he'd been crouching there holding his pose for a long moment. He turned his head toward me, and I made a big show of turning the page and *not* looking at him. I knew what it felt like to wake up scared.

He took another deep breath and pulled his helmet off, dropping it on the floor beside him. He froze when he was straightening up, sniffing at his jacket right where I'd had my arm wrapped around him. *Dang it!* I'd hoped he'd just assume my scent was from when I slept on his scarf. His expression was confused when he looked at me.

"I didn't mean to! I took a nap while you were sleeping and woke up next to you."

He raised an eyebrow.

"Hugging you," I admitted grumpily. There was no need to call me out like that. "But I didn't touch your neck."

Jordan ignored my pouting and plopped down against the far wall, facing me. His throat worked a few times before he asked, "What's the plan?" in a scratchy voice.

I shrugged. "You gotta stop asking me that. I never have a plan. We could check in with your team and take Huck for a walk." Time for another granola bar.

Jordan grimaced as I pulled one out. "Don't you need more nutrition than that? I haven't been off food long enough to not know granola bars aren't healthy for three meals in a row."

"I'm hungry. I had an apple earlier. Call your team." Why was he fussing over me so much? He didn't even like me.

While I ate, he sent a message to his boss with a spectral, but didn't get a response right away. Huck woke up and slunk to the front of the cave to sniff around, and after he decided it was safe enough, started stretching his wings and legs. Eventually, he stood and stretched as tall as he could, beating his wings in the air and flinging sand and dirt every which direction. I was glad I'd finished my food already.

"What's he doing now?" Jordan asked with a frown, clearly not a fan of the miniature sandstorm.

"He's building muscle," I explained, shaking dirt from my book and replacing it in my backpack. "Winged animals aren't born strong enough to fly. They have to work at building up muscles while still on the ground for a while before they're ready for lift off." He'd been doing it on my bed every night for a week already. I preferred that to the dirt shower.

When I went to stand and groaned like an old man, Jordan shot me a concerned look. "You should shift," he said.

"I already told you I don't want to be dragon food." It was unfortunate that I didn't feel safe taking his suggestion, because my back was going to be jacked up for at least another hour. I counted my lucky stars for shifter genes, knowing most people would take much longer than that to heal, and checked the worst burn on my arm. Almost gone. It itched like crazy though.

"Sidney, do you trust me?" His voice was exasperated, but the way he said my name made me shiver anyway.

I gritted my teeth and squinted at him, because how did he want me to answer that? Was Jordan a decent person? Absolutely. Would he kill me if I spooked him and startled him too much? Probably. Jordan had made it abundantly clear that he wasn't *tame*.

He sighed. "I'm not going to let anything hurt you, Sid. I'm doing my best to control my reactions around you, and I'm not going to let Huck hurt you either. I want you to shift so we can see his reactions to your other form. I'll keep you safe."

I frowned at him, thinking of all the damage that could come to my feathers. I'd been working extra hard not to give in to my startle response and shift, lest Huck decide to turn me into charcoal, and if even one piece of plumage got charred, we were going to throw hands. "If you're just trying to see my boobs again, all you have to do is ask," I grumbled.

Chapter 17

Jordan made a scoffing sound and shook his head like I was
ridiculous, but he did look up at me with mischief in his eyes
when I pulled my shirt off. "Why do I need to do this?" I asked.
"Huck's either going back to the refuge or he'll take off into the
wilds on his own after he gets his bearings. I can just wait to shift
until he's gone!" I was doing what he asked but that didn't mean
I wasn't going to gripe about it. His eyes were firmly glued to my
boobs as I tossed my shirt and bra onto my bag and stepped out
of my boots.

"Because you're not always in control of when you shift—"

"Hey, I stayed in my skin today when you came out of sleep
like some kind of hell hound."

"—and I intend to make sure you're safe if that happens. Not
to mention, it would be more comfortable for you to sleep
and eat this way. You can scavenge for smaller portions of food
instead of living on granola bars."

"I'm not going to eat roadkill just because I'm a bird, Jordan."
I knew he meant nuts and berries, but I was nervous about shifting around Huck and anxiety made me grouchy. My pants went
on top of the shirt, and then I stepped out of my underwear.
"Just so we're clear—" I turned to him to find he had *no* shame
about where his naughty eyes were pointed. "—if my feathers
get ruined, I will *end you*."

His eyes finally flicked to mine, but he looked frustratingly
patient. And amused.

I pulled the fire of change up my limbs and into my middle, triggering an explosion of magic and energy as my form

snapped and shifted faster than any eye could follow. My wings shot out, pumping once to keep me aloft before Huck swiveled his neck to turn and look at me.

"To me." Jordan's whisper was urgent, like he hadn't expected Huck to notice so quickly. I dove for his open arms. He covered my whole body, clutching me to his chest as Huck bounded over and snuffled at me through the gaps in his arms. *I swear I'm going to kill them both if he flames me!*

"Back up, Huck." He sounded calmer and certainly more confident than I felt. His arm lifted off of my back, and I heard Huck shuffle backwards unsteadily. Jordan had pushed him backward. "Give her some space." He picked me up and turned my body so that my head was visible to Huck. The dragon immediately started sniffing at me again, getting his nose as deep in my feathers as he could. I pecked his nose—*hard*—and he jerked his head back.

"Easy on the feathers, bud," I squawked. Talking took more effort and my voice wasn't perfect in this form, but I was grateful my ancestors had ended up with an animal that could speak. Huck seemed to recognize my voice, even as tinny as it sounded, and his stare grew more intense.

And then Jordan did the *weirdest* thing. He *stroked* me. Just picked his hand up and petted me like I was an actual animal. He kept talking to Huck as he did it, so I'm not even sure if it was an intentional action or just an impulsive thing, like petting a cat, but I basically went limp in his lap. I am nothing if not a sucker for petting in either form. He seemed totally at ease with me being this close to him, and come to think of it, he hadn't flinched at all when I'd flown into his lap. Maybe he was less reactive to animal forms?

"There, see? He's calming down." His tone was soothing, but his hand froze on my back like he'd just realized what he was doing.

"It's all fun and games until I move, and his prey drive kicks in." I bonked his hand with my head, trying to get him to start petting again. He didn't.

"Maybe I should restrain him, and you can fly around. We'll just see what he does."

That sounded a lot less fun than being petted.

Jordan reached out to pull Huck toward him and wrapped his arm around his torso and wings. I hopped down and put some distance in between us, bouncing across the dirt floor to the front of the cave. Bird legs were so much better for bouncing than human legs. I cocked my head at Jordan and squinted one eye at him. "You better not let him slip."

"I've got him." He tightened his hold around his wings.

ARGH! I jumped into the air and fluttered over to the opening of the cave, watching intently for Huck's reaction. His legs flailed in the air as he tried to scramble free, but he appeared more excited than predatory. I landed and hopped a little closer, trying to stay out of his flame-range, and he trilled happily.

"Head outside," Jordan said. "I'll let him go now, and that way you can fly away if you need to."

He didn't have to tell me twice. I bolted for the opening and spread my wings to head for the open sky. This was glorious. The dry desert air pushed me higher as the heat from the warmed sand rose into the cooling night sky. I circled back and watched the cave entrance as Huck tumbled out onto the desert sand in his excitement. Jordan was close behind him, ready to pounce if need be. His protective mother-henning made me want to laugh, even though I appreciated his readiness. I swooped closer and closer, still careful to keep out of fire range, as Huck beat his wings furiously in the air.

"I think he just wants to join you," Jordan called over all the flapping.

Maybe so, but I still didn't trust him not to torch me yet.

I stayed low enough to be close, but still out of reach, and Huck followed me around in the sand in a happy trot while working his wings. *Maybe this could work*, I thought, as I headed back for Jordan. Normally I would have aimed for his shoulder—or the top of his head if I was feeling mischievous—but since I was trying to be respectful of his space issues, I came in for a slow landing on his forearm.

"What should we do?" he asked, sounding almost pleased as he watched Huck frolic around in the sand.

"Get drunk and terrorize the neighborhood."

He made a disapproving sound. "I can't get drunk."

"Then stay sober and terrorize the neighborhood," I amended.

"Hmm… Well, there're no neighborhoods here, so we'll take a little walk-about. Come on, Huck!" he called, but Huck was stuck in a bush, so he couldn't come. Several minutes of Jordan cursing and trying not to get scratched later, we were on our way into the wilderness. We made our way around the cliff face to a rocky area that was a little more sheltered from the elements. I flew from one bush to another, waiting for Huck to catch up, while Jordan trailed behind, bringing up the rear. It looked like he was picking things up occasionally and tearing old branches off the scrubby bushes as he passed them. Huck, for once, wasn't trying to carry half the landscape in his mouth. He was more focused on trying to follow me, flapping his little wings the whole way. There weren't any large trees out here for him to climb, but maybe I could teach him to scale rocks and glide down.

We circled among boulders and brush under the moons for over an hour, with Huck plodding along, trying to catch me and Jordan watching from a spot against a boulder. He was fiddling with whatever he was holding the whole time, but he still managed to keep a sharp eye on Huck, just in case he torched me. It didn't happen though, and it seemed my anxiety was unfounded. After a while, I hopped closer to him and showed him how to scale a decent sized boulder, one that he could catch a little air from on the way down. I jumped off several times and held my wings out stiffly so he could see how it was done, but he just watched with big eyes from the top of the rock. He seemed like he desperately wanted to jump but was hesitant to try. So I stood like a dutiful mama bird on the ground below and called to him, mimicking the little cry he used when he was searching for me—or trying to break through the bathroom door.

After several false starts, he *finally leapt!* And promptly plummeted straight into the sand below… "You have to flap your wings, bud." He popped back up and shook himself like a dog, no worse for the wear. Several more practice jumps convinced me he wasn't ready to fly yet. I had a pretty good handle on the timelines for when baby birds developed flight muscles and feathers, but I had no idea about dragons. "Keep working those wing muscles and it'll happen. Someday." Worst pep talk ever.

I'd just started making my way back toward Jordan when I heard a sound that sent a spike of fear up my spine. I shifted back into my "human" form immediately, and Huck shot out a flame so hard he knocked himself over. "Sorry!" We were practically made for each other, with how easily we both startled. I continued the trek back toward Jordan on foot.

"Why are you naked again?" His tone was amused, and he bit down on his bottom lip as I drew closer.

"Owls."

Jordan tugged his cloth wrap off and handed it to me, his eyes scanning my body hungrily the whole time. He looked a little disappointed when I pulled the wrap around me and sat down. "Why are owls a problem? Should we get Huck?" he asked distractedly.

I shook my head, only to be irritated by the fact that my hair was loose again, and I didn't have any way to tie it back. "Huck's fine. He's too big for an owl to take. As for me, it probably wouldn't kill me, but I'd prefer not to deal with a talon through my body cavity." I scratched at the healing burn on my arm; it was itchy from being stretched repeatedly. "Owls are sneaky gits," I grumbled.

Jordan huffed a disbelieving laugh. "Owls?"

"I'm of the opinion that all birds are secretly some kind of fae. Nothing else makes sense," I said, doing my best to sit like a lady—which wasn't great. "I don't know how they would have made it into the Void, but just think about it," I continued. "The weird songs, the noise mimicry, the incredibly complicated weaving abilities that *no one teaches them!* They just grow up and automatically know how to do it. Sometimes it's even real, actual sewing, using their *beaks* as a needle. And the insane migratory birds with unfailing compasses who can travel thousands of miles to an old nest site. *And people leave food out for them!* Just like the old stories of the fairies in the Void!" I squinted, trying—and failing—to make out the owl in the dark. "And if birds are like fairies, owls and hawks are the malevolent ones."

"What? Owls are awesome. Everybody loves owls," Jordan argued.

"Nah. Birds that murder other birds are *not* my kind of people."

Jordan squinted at me. "Do you actually think birds are fae?"

I laughed. "No. But you have to admit, they're weird creatures." I still loved them though. As long as they weren't cannibals. *No thanks* on the cannibalism. *Not* a fan.

"Sidney, *you're* a weird creature," Jordan mumbled. Huck bounded up to us and Jordan picked up a stick from a little pile he'd made beside himself and chucked it as hard as he could throw. Huck's little head whipped around so fast it was a blur as he took off after it. I guess he *was* kind of dog-like sometimes, but I wouldn't have thought to throw a stick for him.

"But you still love me, so what does that say about you?" I asked with every ounce of sass he deserved.

"Maybe I do," he answered in a whisper so quiet it might have been a breath.

He wasn't looking at me when he said it—he was staring down at his little stick pile—but my breath caught in my chest. Every one of the intense feelings I'd had for him throughout my childhood and teenage years, all the feelings I'd been shoving down, down, down, since I'd first walked into Levi's apartment, came surging forward. It was so strong that I couldn't speak, and I didn't know whether to be angry and tell him not to tease me or to cry because I was so overwhelmed. I was leaning toward angry, because how dare he make me feel this way?

But then he turned slowly, with a stick in his hand as if he were studying it, and raised his eyes to meet mine. "Is this a nice stick?"

Everything stopped. My heart stopped. My lungs stopped. My thoughts stopped. His hand drifted toward me with the stick held aloft, his eyes bright with curiosity. He was joking—*he had to be*—about my declared love language being nice sticks. But I hadn't been. He had no way of knowing this—he couldn't have—but a proffered stick, a nice one, was the magpie equivalent to a marriage proposal. I watched my hand lift of its own accord and grasp the stick, taking it from his hand. My bird brain was doing an end zone victory dance, even as my rational side was telling me there was no way he meant it. Bird brain didn't care. He'd just proposed.

Chapter 18

"I WAS LYING! STICKS aren't really my love language!" My voice was pitched several octaves too high as I clutched the stick to my chest. Jordan narrowed his eyes at me. He couldn't have known, *could he?* That a stick, a good stick, delivered to a prospective mate meant, "*We can use this to build a nest. Let's build a life together.*" I wasn't *actually* a bird, of course, but shifters took on many qualities of the animals we shifted into. And black-billed magpies, like all corvids, mated for life. My brain was *screaming* because I'd just accepted his offer.

His curious gaze flickered back and forth between my eyes and the tightly clutched stick I held in a vise grip. "Hm. If that's the case, you'd be okay with me taking it back, then?"

I held it tighter. "No, you gave it to me. It's mine."

The corner of his mouth twitched with the barest flicker of movement. "Oh, I see. And I guess that means you also don't want—" He flipped another stick from his pile up into his fingers, so that it stood balancing on end, one tip pinched between his thumb and forefinger. "—this stick?"

I stared at it for a long moment, not seeing the stick at all, but what it meant. A life together, building a home and family with this man who couldn't have children, who was rejected by society, who would outlive me by millennia, who was prickly and stubborn and flighty. Who I'd pined after for *years* without his notice. Who I *still* pined after without his notice. Who didn't even know what he was offering. I snatched that stick from his grip too, adding it to my other one. "Sticks aren't my love language," I squeaked, the lie ringing hollow in my high-pitched protest.

He was studying my expression with all the intensity that a predator studies its prey, and try as I might, I couldn't scrape the emotions off my face. "Is that so?" he asked, his voice barely a whisper.

I nodded my head far too wildly to be believable.

His lip twitched again before he schooled it and leaned forward just enough to be in my space. My heart was racing. The sharp scent of vampire overwhelmed the subtle smell of the desert around us. "Then what *is* your love language, Sidney?" The quiet words were colored with a hint of menace and a larger dose of mischief.

"Kissing," I blurted. It was a dare, and he would know it. There's no way he'd let me get that close to his face, and if he did, well... then we'd have a little fun.

He narrowed his eyes into a haughty glower. "Who have you been kissing?"

"Hot boys." *Why am I this way?*

He bared his fangs in a wicked grin, hearing the bluff for what it was, but it was there and gone in an instant. "You think I can't kiss you?"

I was practically panting as I glanced at his mouth and then made myself lock eyes with him. I didn't dare answer him, afraid I might push him too far, but I let the challenge show in my eyes. *Can you?* I really didn't know.

"I can kiss you," he said, and the arrogance of his tone almost made me believe him until I heard the shakiness of his breath. He leaned closer, and I held my own breath, letting my gaze flicker from his mouth to his eyes and back again. But he hesitated, as if he were just as unsure of himself. Slowly, he lifted his hand and wrapped it around my jaw, gently but firmly pinning me in place. The pressure of his grip on my face nearly made my eyes roll back in my head at how obscene it felt. If he hadn't been holding me up, I would have melted into a puddle of short-circuited goo. Those loose screws in my brain were rattling away as he closed the distance between us so slowly. I could have died from want.

I was nearly startled when his lips finally brushed mine, as satiny and pillowed as I'd imagined them to be. "Is this okay?" he whispered against my mouth, hot breath fanning my face with the scent of him.

"Mm-hm." I didn't feel coherent.

"Sidney, I need a yes or no." Was that amusement?

"Jordan, shut up and kiss me." I couldn't move my head to kiss him first, but I darted my tongue out to lick a playful line between his lips.

His quick intake of breath and the way he grabbed my upper arm told me he hadn't been expecting that. He hauled me closer, angling my chin and molding his lips to mine almost hungrily. When I opened my mouth again, he met my tongue with his own, the hot slide of his mouth sending need spiraling into my core. I tried to press closer still, but his hands gripped me so tightly I couldn't move. My hands found their way into his jacket, and I fisted his shirt, pulling him to me instead. His breaths were ragged, panting, as his tongue teased me, promising me things I intended to cash in on. I moaned into his mouth, and he nipped my lip gently, making heat spike between my thighs.

"You smell so good," he groaned, chest heaving, clutching me against him.

I was too busy to breathe, personally, and stars started to light faintly behind my eyes. I pulled away just as I was starting to feel dizzy, just in time to smell smoke and hear the crackle of burning wood nearby. *Very* nearby.

"Shit." Jordan snatched up the flaming stick Huck had dropped an inch from my lap and launched it into the night again, Huck bolting after it with glee. Little tufts of grass that had sprouted in the hard-pan soil next to me smoked and popped with small flares of fire.

I stared at Jordan as he watched to make sure Huck found the stick and that it didn't catch anything else on fire, heaving oxygen into my lungs as I debated what to do next. One side of me screamed that I should jump his bones right here. He'd even proposed to me, so I was his mate now, whether he knew it or not. The other couldn't believe how insane I was for making out with a vampire and knew that a nice stick didn't mean anything to him. I wanted to punch the second side in the face. Why was I so conflicted about him? Why couldn't things be easy?

He turned to look at me, his bedroom eyes pulling me firmly into *"do what I want and worry about the rest later"* territory. I was promptly interrupted by a spectral messenger flickering into a wispy existence in front of Jordan's face. He slipped his hand into a jacket pocket to feed some magic into a calling stone and a deep voice reached us from the aether. "We've found some intel. I'll fill you in next time you're in." The messenger disappeared, and all was dark and quiet.

"Come on," Jordan murmured. "Your stomach is rumbling again. We can find out what they learned and get you some real food at the same time."

I stuck my bottom lip out in a pout, causing him to huff a laugh and brush his thumb across my jaw. I nearly melted on the spot. "Do you think Huck will follow us back?" I asked as I stood up, wrapping his cowl around me more tightly. I felt a weird pang at the thought of him deciding he was happy out here all alone, but I shrugged it off. We would do what was best for him.

"I guess we'll see," Jordan answered, casting a glance at the dragon as he stood.

Chapter 19

I DIDN'T WANT TO walk back to the cave barefoot, so I shifted forms and rode on Jordan's arm instead, carrying my sticks in my beak the whole way. To my confused relief, Huck did follow us back, and after a momentary internal debate—I'm assuming, because he was just staring at the carrier silently—Jordan decided to wear the baby carrier. He put it on all wrong the first try, but I didn't correct him because it was hilarious watching him try to figure out the straps and buckles. He finally got frustrated and asked for help.

"You've got it on inside out and upside down," I squawked, scratching the back of my head with my foot. Nobody ever talks about how itchy feathers can be.

He spun the contraption around and held it out in front of himself. "Like this?"

"Yeah. Now put your arms in those loops. Buckle that big bottom thingy behind you." I hoped he was flexible enough to reach the shoulder buckles because I wasn't shifting again tonight. I'd decided on the ride back that I was the Queen of Bad Decisions, and I couldn't be trusted around Jordan at all. Even in this form, I wanted to plaster myself against him and rub his scent all over me, but at least that wasn't as bad as making out with him. *I think*.

"Okay, now what?" he asked.

I cocked my head and stared at Huck. "Grab the munchkin." I'll admit, I was hoping Huck would run so Jordan would chase him in circles like a cartoon character, but Huck recognized the carrier and was excited about it. The little traitor. His wings were quivering with excitement as Jordan picked him up.

Jordan grunted at him. "Huh. He's getting kind of big for this, isn't he? How much longer is he going to fit in here?" He stared at the pouch of the carrier while Huck dangled in the air from his hands, apparently stumped on how to get him in.

"Tail first, face out," I instructed him. "Probably not much longer. He's definitely on the large side for it, and he's growing faster than I expected for a reptile." It made sense, I guess, considering *how big* dragons actually got—even the lesser dragons like Huck—but they were practically immortal, so they had a *very* long time to get that size.

Jordan finally got them both situated, and all the buckles closed. "If I run, will you be able to keep up?"

"Probably not." Vampire speed was legendary for a reason. "But if Huck stress-poops in the baby carrier because you freak him out, I'm not helping you clean it up."

"Fair point," Jordan muttered, looking down at the top of Huck's little horns. He bent to stuff my folded clothes and his two sticks into my backpack, making Huck flap his wings as he was jostled.

"What are you doing?" I asked.

"I'll ask if we can sleep at the office. I don't like you having to sleep in the dirt like this," he said as he slung my bag onto his back and grabbed his helmet.

"Why do you care where I sleep? I'm fine."

He ignored my question and left the cave, starting down the trail into the open desert without me. "Come on, Sid," he called.

I flapped along after him and caught up to land on his left forearm, which he had wrapped around his helmet. "Fine, but I'm not taking the blame if he burns your office down."

"It's made of mud, like all the other buildings around here. It's not going to burn," Jordan muttered as he lifted my body and placed me on his shoulder. I scooted closer to his arm, trying to keep away from his neck.

"Thank you," he said gruffly, and then took off into the desert at a slow jog toward the far end of the city. Huck flapped his wings the whole way, imagining he was flying as far as I could tell—*what a cute little doofus*—and I clung to Jordan's jacket as he ran, feeling as happy as I could remember feeling in a long time.

He took us into a section of town filled with office buildings, each one like the next, big adobe constructions full of dust coated windows, and the street carts were empty, all the vendors gone home for the night or off to revel with the desert people alongside the rest of the city. The building he stopped in front of was as boring as the rest of them, no signage or anything to set it apart. He pulled the front door open and stepped into an unlit hallway with a solid door at the other end. A spectral flickered in front of him and disappeared. He waited several seconds before it appeared again. "Let me in, assholes. They're with me," he said, irritation plain in his voice.

"You some kinda woodland princess now, Houjin?" a booming voice answered through the spectral. "What's with all the wildlife?"

"Piss off, Tobias. Cyrus, open the door."

The sounds of chuckling echoed through the spectral before the door clicked open. Jordan pushed through into a maze of hallways and doorways and climbed a set of stairs to the second floor, which opened into a room lit with the dim glow of conjured lights. Several people looked our way as Jordan stepped into the room. There was an enormous mountain of a man—he had to be at least part giant, I didn't even know how he could have gotten in here unless he squeezed in the doorways like a snake—with fair skin and short brown hair hunched over a relatively smaller elvish man. The elf was a dark-elf like Elara's dad, with the same graphite colored skin and white hair, and he controlled an astounding number of spectral images from calling stones on the desk in front of him. Both men wore wicked looking grins and the overwhelming smell of vampire made me puff up my feathers. It hadn't even occurred to me that he worked on a team of vampires and visiting his office would mean being surrounded by them. I wondered if any of the windows were open, and I could bail out.

An orcish lady with short spiky hair and a lorelei man—I'd noticed it seemed like the merman-orc hybrids often got along well with their orcish cousins—sat at another desk, poring over a file full of papers, and a second elvish man stood against a wall in the back of the room talking through his own spectral messenger. They all reeked of vampire, making my adrenaline spike and my heart pound in my chest. The orc and the lorelei had both tusks *and* fangs, which was just *way* too many poky teeth if you asked me. The desire to shift forms and start kicking everything within reach had never felt stronger than it did this second.

"Whatever you're thinking about, don't do it," Jordan said under his breath, reaching up casually to run his fingers down my back. I flattened myself further against his shoulder and tried to focus on enjoying the pets.

"Dude, what are you wearing?" asked the giant. It was the same booming voice that had spoken through the spectral at the door.

"Is that a *baby carrier?* Wait, you found one of the dragons?" squealed the orc lady, jostling the lorelei man as she scrambled up to get a better look at Huck.

"The rookie brought pets!" said the giant.

"Shut up, Tobias. You're still the rookie. You'll always be the rookie," said the lorelei. He had dark, mottled skin with even darker hair, and his eyes looked positively devilish with their slitted yellow irises.

Tobias, the giant, frowned at him. "I've been on the team for *fifty years* now. Houjin got hired on months ago. He's the rookie."

"You're still the rookie," said the lorelei, going back to his paperwork.

"He comes in here with a dragon in a baby carrier and a bird on his shoulder like this is his normal Tuesday and no one but me bats an eyelash?" asked Tobias incredulously.

"Tobias, listen to me. We are vampires. When was the last time one of us had a normal Tuesday? Maybe this is what the youth are into these days." The lorelei didn't even bother to look up as he spoke.

"This isn't normal," insisted Tobias.

"Watch out, Allie," Jordan said, motioning the orc back. "He spits fire." Allie pouted, which was strangely adorable on a big, burly orc woman.

"Perfect pet for you, I guess," she muttered wryly, giving a little smile to Huck, and making kissy noises at him. He flapped his wings. "You look so *cuuuutte*," she said, dragging out the word in a squeal.

"They're not *pets*," Jordan said flatly. "This is Sidney, the shifter who found the dragon eggs in the Void." He gestured to me. "And this is the dragon hatchling that she was caring for, not one of the missing ones. Sidney, this is Alejandra," he gestured at the orc.

"You can call me Allie," she said with a bright smile. She looked like she could break me in half, even in my human form.

"That's Lucas," he said, pointing at the lorelei. Lucas raised his clawed finger in a lazy wave. "The guy with the big mouth is Tobias."

"It's not just my mouth that's big," said the giant with an eyebrow waggle. I liked him already, even if his neck was bigger around than my human torso.

"Gross. And that's Cyrus," Jordan said, gesturing toward the seated elvish man with all the calling stones. "He does our surveillance. Cyrus and Lucas were both at the Void site with us, along with Augustus." I wasn't going to be able to keep all of these people straight. He looked toward Allie. "He said you guys had new info?" he asked, glancing at the man standing at the back of the room.

"Yeah, we've narrowed it down some. Let me know if you need a break from dragon-sitting duty," she said, moving back to her desk.

"You're not fireproof," Jordan responded as he made his way to the back of the room.

"Eh, but I heal fast," I heard Allie mutter from behind us as we walked past.

The elvish man leaning against the back wall wasn't a dark-elf like Cyrus and Elara's father, but he was every bit as debonaire and noble-looking. He had the same light-colored hair, but his skin was a light green color that reminded me of my sylvan friend, Solandis. He glanced at me, and the dragon hanging from Jordan's chest, and shut his calling stone down with a delighted expression. "Jordan!"

"Augustus," Jordan returned, his tone more reserved. "You remember Sidney," he said as he gestured toward me. "Although not in this form."

The man nodded toward me. "Pleasure." I eyed his fangs, which were a little more prominent on Augustus than they were on Jordan. He studied the dragon in the baby carrier for a moment. "What an interesting contraption! I suppose that is the safest place for it currently, all things considered. Team Six has relayed that they've been approached by known Phantom operatives who were looking to find a buyer for some exotic animals. While pretending to be interested, they were able to ascertain that the animals were dragon hatchlings. So now that we know for sure who we're dealing with, we can focus on narrowing down their location." Augustus had a predatory kind of gleam in his eye that made my skin prickle. "Once we find our area, I'll send you out with Lucas to scout around, yes?"

"Sounds good. Is it okay if we crash here for now?" Jordan asked as Huck wiggled in his carrier.

"You know the sleeping quarters are always open for your use," Augustus answered, sounding like some old-world butler. Who was this guy?

"Yeah, well, I wanted to try things her way first." He pointed a thumb at me. "Do we have any real-people food?" Jordan asked. I squawked at his inference that he wasn't a real person. He placed his hand over my whole head to shush me.

Augustus watched our interplay with interest. "We do not, but I would be delighted to place an order for you. What would you like?"

Jordan turned his head to me, apparently waiting for me to answer.

"Uh, a burger? Noodles? I don't care," I croaked. "And a burnt rat, but that's not for me." Huck didn't actually need to eat, but it would be funny to see this stuffy looking guy try to procure a burned rat.

Augustus simply blinked at me. "As you wish." A short nod and then he smiled at Jordan. "The VAC made a blood drop earlier this evening, as well."

"Fantastic." Jordan was already on the move. *A blood drop?* He walked down a hall and into a kitchen, pulling open a cooler with the words "Vampire Advocacy Committee" stamped onto the side. He rifled through the blood bags inside while Huck looked on curiously until he found one that was apparently more pleasing than the others and pulled it out. The whole bag went into a pot of water he brought to a simmer on the stove. "Bottle warmers are definitely easier," he muttered. Whatever that meant. Huck was getting antsy and flapping too much for my comfort, so I fluttered over to the back of a chair at a nearby table and perched on the back.

"You don't have to watch me eat this. I can take you to one of the sleeping quarters to rest while you wait for your food."

Was he embarrassed about the blood? I mean, it was gross, but it wasn't that bad. I squinted at him. "I'm good." If he could eat it, I could watch.

Jordan just sighed. "Suit yourself, I guess." He pulled the blood bag out and felt it, shaking up the contents gently and then piercing the top with his fangs. He drank straight from the bag, looking just like a kid with a juice box. I was glad I couldn't involuntarily smile with a beak.

"Does this Committee have a body farm where they drain people on the regular?" I had a hard time imagining that the government would be cool with that, but what did I know?

Jordan's expression melted into a glower as he drained the rest of the bag. "They bring us unusable donated blood from the medical centers." I guess that made more sense. "Come on, let's find an open room so we can let this guy down to roam."

That was a terrible idea.

Chapter 20

I followed Jordan down the maze of hallways to one of the last doors at the end. He stepped in and to the side, revealing a simple bedroom with a double bed, a wooden desk and chair, cabinet, rug, and private bathroom. I hopped into the room and fluttered up onto the dark gray bed sheets that smelled faintly of him. "You saw what he did to my house," I said to Jordan, cocking my head to watch him as he lifted my backpack from his shoulders and set it down with more care than I ever have.

"Sid, please trust me. I'll keep you safe." He waited until I made eye contact with him and then set his helmet on the bed. He carefully wrapped his arm around Huck, bracing him while he reached behind his head with his other hand to unclip the buckle. The dragon bucked twice and then calmed. "Hah, see? I learn fast, little guy."

I huffed a laugh at Jordan's smug attitude.

He wrapped his hands around Huck's torso, careful to keep his wings pinned, and lifted him from the carrier to set him carefully on the floor. Huck immediately scuttled under the bed.

"He's gonna pee under there," I grumbled.

"Then I'll clean it up." He reached out to run his fingers down my feathers—*oh, heck yes*—and then unclipped the rest of the carrier and draped it over my backpack. I gave a disgruntled chirp at the cessation of petting, but he didn't notice. Instead, he bent to roll up the rug and gathered it and the desk chair to carry out of the room. He came back several seconds later for the desk and lifted it with ease to haul from the room as well. When he came back, he eyed the cabinet and then dismissed it. "I'm not taking the cabinet out, but now he can't damage the other flammable things. The bedding was made for me specifically, so it's wool."

I blinked at him. "You have your own sleeping quarters?" I'd have figured they were just for whoever was working, but they did smell like him.

"Yes."

"Then why don't you just live here?" I asked.

"I don't want to live at work."

That's fair. "Is this where you came when you left your apartment after I showed up?"

He hesitated a beat before answering. "Yes." He turned to the door. "I'm going to go check on your food and see if we have a uniform in your size."

That gave me pause. "Why do I need a uniform?"

"They're fireproof. It'll protect you better," he said as he walked out, leaving me alone with the chaos demon that was Huck.

Since I didn't want to risk getting eaten by the dragon toddler while we were alone and the private bathroom was calling my name, I decided it was worth the energy drain to shift forms again. The mattress creaked quietly under my added weight, and I crawled off the bed to peek at Huck. He was curled up in a little ball with his tail wrapped around him and a wing draped over his head, peeking out at me from underneath it. Poor buddy was stressed out. I decided to leave him to decompress and shut the bedroom door to keep him from slipping out while I made use of the facilities.

The bathroom was pretty spartan, but the water from the shower reached an appropriately scalding temperature, so I wasn't going to complain. I stood in the water far longer than I needed to before finally bothering to look around for shampoo and soap. It just felt so nice after hanging out in all the dusty sand with nothing but wet wipes. The soap didn't smell like anything I'd scented on Jordan before, so it must not have been something he used often. I tried not to think about why that felt disappointing or why I wanted to coat myself in something that smelled like him in the first place, focusing instead on getting clean.

A knock sounded at the door with Jordan's brisk, "Food's here," so I cut the shower and wrung the water from my hair. There were no towels in here. Nothing on the towel racks and nothing under the sink. I jerked the door open. "Where are the towels?"

Jordan turned to look at me and stared for far too long without answering, his eyes trailing up and down my dripping wet body. I raised an eyebrow, causing his mouth to twitch. He stepped sideways to the cabinet, opening it without breaking eye contact and pulling a folded towel from one of the shelves, moving as slowly as a turtle. Instead of immediately handing me the towel, he held it aloft, a haughty smirk on his face, clearly enjoying himself.

I rolled my eyes. "I told you if you want to stare at my boobs, you can just ask. Can we play this game when I'm not soaking wet and cold?"

Jordan's cheekbones flushed pink, and his amusement crumpled instantly. "I'm sorry, Sid," he murmured. "Are you cold?" He wrapped his hands around the towel as he eyed my goose-bumped skin. Then he shook the towel out and stepped into my space, wrapping it around my shoulders and dragging it down my arms. The towel was toasty warm, as if it had just been pulled from a dryer. He was instantly forgiven, because this was lovely, but he stepped even closer, his body several degrees warmer than it usually was as he worked to warm me up. He dragged the towel up my sides and back, using it to grip my hair gently and squeeze the water from it, working his way up to my scalp, massaging the whole way.

I think my eyes rolled back in my head, but I know I slumped forward against his chest. His chuckle was deep and rumbly, and it made butterflies swirl in my stomach. I pressed my face against his chest and huffed his scent as he draped the towel over my shoulders and rubbed a hand down my back. "How do you smell so good after laying in the dirt for a day and a half?"

His laughter grew a little incredulous. "I don't, you little weirdo."

I raised my chin until my mouth was a few inches from his own and narrowed my eyes at him playfully, daring him to kiss me again. He was the one in my space, the one who'd approached me, who'd wrapped me up in his towel and his own warmth. "I say you do," I whispered, the words coming out breathier than I intended.

He didn't pull away like I half expected, his eyes locked on my mouth as he considered me, something that looked like hot need passing behind them. I stood stock still, barely breathing, knowing he would have to be the one to come the rest of the way. The menace of his presence wasn't *forgotten*, exactly, but I still had to restrain myself from wanting to seize control and take what I wanted the way I usually did. The heat of him radiated over my skin as he leaned closer, brushing his lips against mine and retreating, possibly still unsure of himself. I watched him through slitted eyelids, my heart thundering in my chest, full of empathy for his fears and his struggles as his breathing increased. I could be patient for him. If I had to be.

He reached up with both hands, achingly slowly, placing one on my shoulder and wrapping the other under my jaw. Locking me in place again. Waiting for my reaction. I gave him none, simply continuing to watch him in return. Willing him to act. His gaze shifted restlessly between my eyes. I wished I knew what he was so desperately searching for so I could give it to him. It occurred to me that I would probably give this man anything he asked for, and I couldn't even tell you why. Why did I care so much? What was it about him that took me out at the knees so thoroughly?

His lips finally met mine, and I decided it didn't matter *why* I cared. I just *did*. With the smell of him rampaging through my brain and the taste of him on my tongue, I felt voracious. I kissed him hungrily, daring him to return my passion, my want, my need. His lips were satin pillows that I delighted in. I wanted them all over my body. His breaths were ragged gasps as I trailed my fingertips down the bumps of his abs. The pressure of his hand on my jawline felt like something I needed, and I didn't care if that was wrong. It felt strangely comforting to be trapped, to be held so securely like this. I liked it and I grinned against his mouth to let him know it.

He met every kiss with just as much hunger as I gave him, gripping me tightly, hauling my body against his. My skin flushed warmer everywhere we touched, but whether from him purposely trying to warm me or from arousal, I couldn't tell. His hand was scorching as it slid from my shoulder down my arm, then his knuckles dragged up my stomach to caress the underside of my breast. I arched my back, pressing myself into his hand. He took full advantage, turning his hand to palm my breast, kneading it gently until my nipple was a hard point against his palm. Warmth spiked in my core, twisting and growing with each kiss and caress until I was moaning deliriously against his lips.

Jordan broke our kiss and, before I was even aware we'd moved, spun me around so that my back was pressed against his front and his arms were locked around me, trapping the towel between us. He had the side of his face pressed against my shoulder as he heaved for breath behind me, and I couldn't help but arch my back into him like a cat seeking contact. "*Fuck*, Sidney, you're so dangerous right now."

Chapter 21

THE POSITION CHANGE MADE me practically quiver with need. His heat against my back, the pressure of him wrapped around me, the vulnerable feeling of being underneath him all wound me up so tight I was already panting.

"Ah, Sid," he breathed against the back of my neck. "I somehow forgot how much you liked being pinned." He sounded slightly pained. I ignored his muttering, still focused on the last thing he said.

"Jordan, you know by now I would never hurt you." I still was trying to squirm closer to him, but he just lifted me so my feet dangled a few inches off the ground, and I couldn't push off anything. He only managed to press his swollen excitement against my rump. I bit my lip and smiled, trying to stifle my amusement.

He laughed against my back, but there was no humor in it. "I said you were dangerous, sweetheart, but I didn't mean to *me*."

I was loving being pinned against his body, but the lack of friction was starting to annoy me. "That doesn't explain why you think I'm dangerous *right now*." I didn't even have any weapons on me. He might have had my body pinned under him, but my arms were still loose. I shifted just enough to be able to place my hands on his thighs behind me. Sliding them inwards, I dragged them up between his legs until I was palming his hard bulge behind my ass.

Hot breath gusted out of him across my back as he reacted. He had me bent over the bed with my legs dangling off the side and my arms trapped over my head in an instant. *Dang, he's fast.*

He wasn't even that much bigger than me, but with his chest against my back and his hands holding my wrists, I was as solidly pinned as I'd ever been. Those loose screws rattled around in my brain, and I kind of wanted to hate how much I loved this, but I couldn't.

"You're dangerous because if anyone comes in here and gets a whiff of you smelling like this, I'm liable to rip their throat out," he growled.

I couldn't help the delighted laughter that bubbled out of me. "I didn't take you for the jealous type, *Darling.*" I had to turn my face out of the blankets to be able to take a full breath, but I could reach the floor with my toes now. When I arched up against him, the feeling of his hard length against my sex was so delicious it made me even more needy. *Oh yes, I want more of that.*

"I guess you read me wrong," he said darkly as he pressed me down, his hot breath ghosting over my temple.

The sweet image of him eyeing me guardedly with a stick clutched between his fingers, wanting to know if it was something that would please me, made me feel warmly possessive of Jordan. But the juxtaposition of him being possessive of me in return made my brain light up like a bonfire. *Tap, tap, tap,* right on those happy little loose screws.

He trailed his silken lips over the shell of my ear. "Let's play a game," he whispered, echoing my words from all those nights ago. I ceased my wriggling and stilled, trying to soften my excited panting so I could hear his quiet words. "The rules are, this time, we'll *only* be using my hands." His voice was the soft rasp of a knife being pulled from its sheath. He transferred both of my wrists into one hand, and I could already feel him pushing heat into his palm as he leaned up just enough to run his other hand down my back, tugging the towel down to hold me more firmly against the mattress.

Yes, please, I thought with a shiver.

"Your hands stay where I've got them," he stated imperiously. Well, turnabout was fair play, I supposed. The memory of him cracking his headboard while he orgasmed onto my skin sent a shiver down my spine and made my core throb. He left his hand on my lower back and released my wrists, trusting me to do as he said, and then gripped my hips to drag me a few inches off the bed so he could get his lower arm around me. He paused with his fingers on my stomach. "Do you remember your safe word?"

I nodded into the blankets, my heart pounding so hard I could feel it between my legs. Why was I so turned on by this?

"Sidney." He still hadn't moved. I could see him looming over me in my peripheral vision, but more than that, I could *feel* him. He was everywhere. "I need words."

"What kind of *words*, Jordan?" Was that my voice? I wasn't interested in words right now, so I started wriggling again, aiming to get that pressure back on my cleft, but he pulled his hips away just enough that I couldn't reach him.

"Yes? Or no?" he breathed.

"Yes!"

His hand smoothed down my belly, brushing across my skin to my hips and thighs. The pressure disappeared from my back, and he jerked the towel out from between us, only for his hand and solid weight to reappear between my shoulder blades. "This is what you like, isn't it?" It wasn't really a question. It was a tease. His other hand was hot but comfortable as he reached down my leg, caressing the back of my thigh and trailing lightly along the sensitive skin behind my knee. He made his way up the back of my leg and slid his warm fingers briefly through my slit.

"Oh, god," I moaned, and rolled my hips.

He groaned into my back and rewarded me with a hint of more pressure. "Yeah, you like that. I can smell how much you do. You're so wet for me."

I. Was. Riveted. Between his dirty talk and his scorching fingers taking turns circling my clit and dipping inside me—but not providing quite enough pressure—I was already gasping for breath and hyper-focused on everything he was doing. Jordan's chest replaced his hand as the weight on my back, and I could feel his shallow hot breaths against my neck. I surged up against him with my hips, searching for the bulge that I knew would be there. "Take me, Jordan." My words came out husky and hoarse.

His dark laugh turned into another groan. "You want me to rut you like an animal? That's not part of our game." The kiss I felt him press against my temple almost made me orgasm from the sheer shock of it. He shifted against me, and I heard his belt buckle clink and then hit the floor. "But if I don't take these off, you're going to soak right through them." Muffled sounds of him stepping out of his pants preceded a darkly amused, "One quick taste."

I nearly came off the bed when his wet mouth met my opening. My harsh gasp filled the room, and I fought to contain my squeal as he began tonguing my clit, gently at first and then more firmly with each lick. I don't even know what I did with my legs that caused him to laugh and push them down, followed by a soft slap against my rump.

"You're supposed to stay where you are," he said against my shoulder as he took his place over me again. One hand snaked its way under me and grasped my breast, rubbing and groping, rolling my nipple with his fingers. I moaned—realized I'd *been* moaning. I was being embarrassingly loud and there was nothing I could do about it.

His chest was the same temperature as usual, and his arms felt normal too, but his palm on my tit and the fingers he slid into my core from behind felt feverishly warm and made it so I couldn't focus on anything but his hands. He hooked his forefinger around my clit and pushed his thumb inside me, pressing and rubbing at the sensitive flesh behind my clit. My mouth dropped open in a wail as I bucked against him, pressing back against his hand, thrashing beneath him on the bed.

"That's right," he gritted out. "So fucking hot. I'm going to make you come so hard."

I was so out of my mind for this man. When he released my body to gingerly brush back the hair that had fallen in my face, I used my arms for leverage on the mattress and shoved my ass against his groin, grinding on him and trying to get a response out of him. The soft skin of his erection rubbed between my inner thighs so tantalizingly close to where I wanted him. The feeling was so lewd my grin was uncontainable.

"Damnit, Sidney," he hissed. One arm came down beside mine on the bed as he covered me again, giving in and grinding against me. His movements were jerky and short like he was fighting them, but I wriggled harder, daring him to take me, arching my back and presenting myself to him with a secret Cheshire grin. "You're cheating," he growled. Jordan wrapped his arm around my hip to thread his fingers between my legs and over my clit again, before shoving me back into the bed with his body.

"Do it," I dared him. Taunting. Demanding. Pressing. All I could focus on were his fingers milking my clit with their abnormal warmth and the growing heat of his cock as he ground it against my rump. When he shifted and grasped my breast with his hot palm again, I felt myself beginning to crest an orgasm and squealed.

He finally snapped, jerking my hips back and lining himself up. I arched further into him and fought to spread my legs wider as he entered me, gasping and grunting as he pushed his way in. "Is this what you want? You want my cock inside you?" He was so warm that it intensified every sensation, each movement. It was exactly what I wanted, what I needed, and I came apart underneath him, whimpering through my orgasm. I was limp as a rag doll as he continued to thrust into me, languid strokes paired with slow movements of his fingers meant to draw out the final curling contractions of my climax.

"Do you think we're finished?" he asked quietly.

Chapter 22

I GLANCED AT HIM over my shoulder to find an expression of hunger on the haughty lines of his face. His cheeks were flushed, his eyes hooded but sharp, almost daring me to give him sass while he had me pinned to the bed and skewered on his hard length. I opened my mouth to respond, because I will *always* take that bait, but I promptly forgot my retort when he snapped his hips against me *hard*. My jaw went slack at the pressure. He was so deeply inside of me that I lost all semblance of rational thought. I watched him out of the corner of my eye as he straightened, his own gaze trailing down my body while he pumped into me, eventually locking on the place where we were joined. The haziness of ecstasy that flooded his expression told me he liked what he saw, and his motions slowed as he watched himself penetrate me, savoring the moment.

I clenched my core to give him a naughty jolt, and the choked sound he made was *delicious*. He instantly doubled over, giving me his weight again, and began plunging into me like a man starved. His ragged breathing matched my own, and the pressure in my core quickly ramped up to another tipping point. Both my heart and my body felt so full of Jordan, and I realized I wanted to keep him here just like this, inside of me, forever. That was a dangerous thing to want. He seemed to want the same thing, with as deeply as he was sheathing himself. I clenched my core again and heard him wheeze, and the eager grin on my face let him know I'd done it on purpose. He thrust harder, until my body was heaving farther onto the bed with each movement, my nipples scraping the textured, soft wool blankets as I gripped the bed to try to hold myself still.

He slid his fingers into my hair, gripping the strands firmly against my scalp with gentle pressure. "Is this good?" he asked after a second of hesitation. I was too preoccupied with his hips slamming into mine to answer. "Hm." He released my hair and shifted his weight before sliding his other hand up my throat to frame my jaw with a firm squeeze. My shameless squeal told him all he needed to know about my feelings on the erotic act. He gave a brusque chuckle. "Nope, this is what you wanted," he growled into my ear as he continued to pound into me.

My heart was racing as I orgasmed so hard, I think I blacked out. He pumped with rough, shallow strokes on his race toward his own climax, releasing all the intensity that he usually kept so carefully contained, and I loved every ounce of it. I arched my back, allowing him to enter more deeply again. He let go of my chin to bring his hands down on either side of me, white knuckling the sheets as he drove against me to press in as hard as he could. I knew his irises would be glowing like hot coals for the span of a couple of heartbeats before fading back to their beautiful, honeyed amber. My skin prickled, but I trusted him somehow as his muscles contracted with his harsh groans and waves of pleasure pulled him under until he collapsed on my back in exhaustion.

But he didn't grow still like I had, laying limp, and allowing myself to be used for his enjoyment in those last moments. Instead, his fingers curled against my shoulder, tracing soft circles as he painted praises and curse words across my skin with his lips. "You're so beautiful."

I closed my eyes and basked in the afterglow, enjoying the weight of him and the feel of his lips on my back. Eventually, though, he withdrew and started to gather me into his arms, obviously intending to haul me up onto the bed so I wasn't half hanging off like we were. His hand froze on my arm. "Did I hurt you?" he asked, alarm filling his voice.

"No." *Nothing I didn't enjoy anyway,* I thought flippantly.

"Sidney, I've left bruises on you."

Oh, lord, the drama.

"It's fine. They'll be gone in a few minutes anyway." I sounded drunk, my words slurring.

"It's *not* fine," he said, sounding obstinate.

"It was great," I mumbled, still sounding sloshed. "We should do that... at least a few times a week." I stiffened so he couldn't turn me over and—because I was feeling bratty—slid off the side of the bed into a boneless lump on the floor. If he was this upset about a few marks on my skin, there was no way I was letting him see the tops of my thighs.

There was a small problem. "Hey, Jordan?"

"What?" he asked, sounding exasperated as he tried to pick me up off the floor.

"Where is my dragon?"

Jordan let me go and dropped to the floor beside me to look under the bed. "What do you mean, where—" He found the same thing I did, empty dragon-less space beneath the bed, and then stood to scan the room.

A soft knock at the door made me scream and come out of my skin, an explosion of feathers erupting on the floor beneath Jordan who didn't fare much better himself. He hunched over me, snarling like a feral animal.

"Uh, hey, guys? I hate to interrupt, but ya'll need to take your dragon back." Allie's voice was muffled coming through the door, but the scent of burnt orc skin was clear as day. *Oops.*

It took Jordan several seconds to get himself under control, and then another several to put his pants back on. He opened the door with an unhappy glare. Allie stood in the hall, holding Huck out from her body with a disgruntled expression on her face. She had no eyebrows, and her face was marred with soot.

"I know I said I wanted to dragon-sit, but I think I changed my mind."

"Thanks. Sorry," Jordan said gruffly. He took Huck and closed the door in her face, then set him back on the floor while I scrambled to flutter up onto the bed.

"How did he—"

Jordan cut me off. "I must have left the door open on one of my trips into the room while you were in the shower. Sorry. You've got food on the shelf in the cabinet in there, by the way."

That sparked my curiosity. "Did he bring the rat?"

Jordan laughed, dragging his hand down his face and then slumping onto the bed. "No rats to be had at this time of night. Sorry," he said into the pillow. *Dang it. That would have been funny.* Points for trying though, stuffy-vampire-butler-Augustus.

I strutted up toward his pillow on my little bird legs, eyeing his sculpted back as I went. I hadn't even noticed him taking off his shirt, but I was glad he had. *Yum.* As much as I wanted to shift back and see if he'd let me snuggle, I didn't have the energy for another shift right now. He was stuck with bird-Sidney for a little bit. I hopped up onto his pillow and padded around to the back of his head, cocking my own head at him to watch him as he visibly cringed when I got too close. "I'm going to touch your hair," I said to prepare him. When he didn't respond, I gathered some strands in my beak and gave them a gentle tug, sliding them through my beak from root to tip, gathering a new clump and doing it again, and again.

"What—what are you doing? What is this?" he asked.

"Affection." Preening made me happy. I couldn't help it. It was soothing.

"Gross," he muttered, stilling my movements. I narrowed my eyes at his head and considered giving him an irritated peck until he grumbled, "Do it again." And so, we sat, like a couple of weirdos, with me preening his hair and him pretending to not enjoy it. My heart was happy.

Unfortunately, my stomach was not, so after we rested a bit, I shifted back, and Jordan warmed my food up for me. Both a burger *and* noodles. I guess Augustus was trying to make up for the lack of rat. I probably should have felt awkward about someone watching me put away two whole plates of food, but I hadn't eaten much in two days, and I was hungry, so I ignored that impulse. Jordan seemed to relax more as I ate, as though he'd been truly concerned about my lack of nutrition. I tried to ignore that too, because between the stick offering, the sex, and him feeding me, he was already embedded in my little birdy brain. Was he doing this on purpose? I squinted at him, trying to read him, but he was starting to look a little zombie-like. "Is it about that time?" I asked with a mouth full of food.

"Yeah, sun's coming up."

I wiped my mouth and dug some clothes out of my bag to get ready for bed. Huck was curled up in the back corner under the bed again, this time fast asleep. Jordan flopped back onto the bed and scooted against the wall to make room for me when I came back. I gave him a side-eye. "This seems like a bad idea."

"I thought you loved bad ideas," he said tiredly.

"Are you going to come out of sleep like a hound out of hell again?" I asked.

"No," he said, tucking his head into the pillow. "This place smells familiar. The cave didn't, so I didn't know where I was or why someone was next to me."

I eyed the floor, wondering if perhaps it might be a safer lodging. Jordan sighed and took hold of my wrist, pulling me into the bed next to him and turning me so I was facing away with my back tucked against his chest again. I still wasn't sure about this. "Am I the little spoon or a meat shield?" I asked the darkness.

"Go to sleep, Sidney," was his only response before sleep claimed him.

Chapter 23

I stood on the sheer knife-edge of a mountain ridge as the frigid wind buffeted me from every side. My hair whipped about my face, and I knew my skin prickled in the cold, though I couldn't feel it. Above me, the stars shone brightly in the stunning expanse of night sky, and below me was a quiet valley filled with low burning coals. It was nearly a mile down the steep, treacherous sides into the inky blackness, but the glowing embers beckoned me forward. Far, far above, the stars called to me to dance with them in the moonlight as my ancestors had, and their ancestors before them, but I turned to face the valley below. The coals, though dim, had a stronger pull on my soul. I spread my arms and launched myself into the night, easily transforming into my feathered form as I plummeted into the abyss. The sky continued its call, but I didn't hear it. I only heard the fire.

I woke up from a deep sleep in the same position I'd drifted off in. I found that odd because I usually woke up in all kinds of weird positions. Plus, I expected to be glommed onto Jordan like a lonely octopus again. I realized, as I blinked away the final dredges of my strange dream, that I hadn't moved because I physically *couldn't*. Jordan had me locked in the same vice-like spooning hold that we'd been in before falling asleep, only he'd constricted around me even more tightly while we slept. I wondered if that had anything to do with how well I'd slept, but maybe that was just the exhaustion again.

It felt like it wasn't quite night yet, but I really needed to get out of here before he woke up like a cornered beast. Moving his arms proved ineffectual. Good *grief,* he was strong. I could shift, but then I'd be trapped in the blankets and with a much higher probability of getting crushed in his flailing panic. Trying to wriggle free only caused him to tighten his hold and crush me to his chest. His hot breath blowing on my neck through my hair was slow and steady, otherwise I'd have been tempted to think he was messing with me. That and the fact that he hadn't erupted off the bed in a snarling burst to greet the night yet.

I waited for him to relax his grip again, and then tried to slide *slowly* out from under his arms, but I only made it an inch before he tightened his hold again, this time squishing all the air out of my lungs in a rush. "Jordan," I wheezed. "Can't breathe."

The low hiss against the back of my neck made my hair stand up, but he did loosen his grip. "Sorry."

I stayed frozen, not wanting to make any sudden moves. "Are you going to freak out now?"

He pulled his arms back and scooted away from me. "I told you I wasn't going to." Was he... *sulking*?

I turned my head so I could see him out of the corner of my eye. "Is it cool if I roll over?"

"I guess." He was *definitely* sulking.

I rolled slowly onto my back, trying to give him a little space, but also not wanting to at all. Jordan had his arms crossed over his chest and his ears were tinged pink, just like his cheeks. I narrowed my eyes at him. "I'm going to brush my teeth, and then we're going to talk about this."

"About what?" he asked as I heaved myself off the bed.

I flipped my hair over my shoulder and pointed my finger at him, swirling it around in the air to indicate *all of him.* "This," I answered, turning to head for the toothbrush I'd left on his bathroom sink last night after getting ready to sleep. His expression was guarded when I returned. Normally, I would have just flounced into the room and flung myself onto the bed, but this was me *trying* to be considerate.

Jordan still looked pretty tired, so I'd assumed correctly that the sun wasn't quite down yet. I took my time climbing back in next to him, my eyes locked on his grumpy face the whole time to watch how he responded. He gave me nothing, so I—*oh, so slowly*—lowered myself down in front of him and pressed my forehead into his sternum, above his folded arms.

"Pet me."

He barked a surprised laugh. "What?"

"*Pet me*. Anywhere. My hair, my back, wherever."

He gave an amused huff and disentangled his arms, tucking one under his head to make room for me, and reaching the other around awkwardly to pet the hair at my temple. *Whatever. I guess I'll take it.* I snuggled closer as he fell into a slow rhythm, adding more pressure and threading his fingers through the strands. Once I was sufficiently reduced to a puddle of happy goo and Jordan's heart rate had slowed significantly, I asked him why he was being weird.

"Petting a girl's head kind of weird?" he asked dryly. *But it wasn't weird when he was petting my wings?*

"No," I retorted. "Pouting because I expected you to react the same way two days in a row kind of weird."

"Hm." He focused on my hair for several silent minutes, and I wanted to press him about it, but I held my peace. The petting helped. "I told you I'd be fine tonight," he said in a murmur.

"Yeah, but you were pretty worked up *last* night when you woke up, and I take people on their actions, not their words. I'm not *judging you* for waking up ready to fight. I just don't want to be directly in your path before all your neurons are firing at full capacity."

He gave a quiet sigh above my head, and he draped his arm around my head to give me a gentle squeeze. "Thank you.

I'm not... I don't deserve anyone's trust, and yet, I find myself desiring yours," he whispered.

"Why do you believe you don't deserve anyone's trust, Jordan?" I frowned at his chest as a spark of anger flared in me for him.

"I know what I am."

That brought me up short. Because hadn't I had those same thoughts about him? He was dangerous in ways beyond even most of the magical people of the Boundlands, and he'd warned me outright that he couldn't always control his reactions. But he'd also told me he wouldn't hurt me and that he wouldn't let anything else hurt me either. I could take care of myself in most situations, but I acknowledged that sometimes I just wasn't enough. And I knew I wouldn't be enough if I ever had to throw down with Jordan. And yet... and *yet*, perhaps foolishly, I did want to trust him.

Maybe I just needed to better understand him.

"Can we talk about it?" I asked, considering this.

"Me being a vampire?" His voice sounded thick. It made my heart clench in my chest, a cold weight settling in my gut, and I nuzzled my forehead in closer to him.

"Will you tell me how it happened?"

He didn't answer for a long time, and instead began to toy with my hair again, dragging his fingers gently through the strands as he thought.

"Will it change anything?" he asked, finally.

"No." I focused on the tug and pull of his fingers against my scalp. "I just want to know you."

He released an unsteady breath. "I was at a college party with my teammates, celebrating winning a game we hadn't been expected to win."

"Playing hooks?" I asked.

"Yeah, I got a full ride for it."

"Wow." He'd always been a ferocious player, so I guess that didn't surprise me too much, but I was impressed.

Jordan made a noncommittal sound in response, absent-mindedly dropping my strands of hair and trailing his fingers through again. "I had too much to drink that night, and I don't remember most of it. I don't remember leaving the party, or how we got to the girl's place, but my friends confirmed I left with her. The only thing I remember is how much it hurt. This searing, burning pain in my neck that wouldn't go away. The first thing I remember is having some naked girl in my lap, latched onto my neck, and the worst pain I've ever felt in my life blistering through my carotid." He swallowed loudly. "I pushed her off me, but she wouldn't let go of my throat, so I reacted out of instinct. I torched her."

When he fell silent again, I asked him, "Can I hug you?"

He swallowed again before saying, "Yeah." His whispered reply in the darkness felt like it echoed a thousand times in my soul. I laid my arm over his waist and gave him a gentle squeeze. "Someone heard her screaming," he continued hoarsely, "and called for the medics. But when they came, they couldn't save either of us."

Chapter 24

I couldn't help the way my fingers clenched into fists and chills washed over me in reaction to his words. The melancholy way he said, "they couldn't save either of us," as if he had died too, as if he were *lost*, made me physically sick. The idea of him being destroyed like that, being broken, somehow *unsavable*... He was right in a sense; his life wasn't over, but it *was* irrevocably changed. That someone had purposely done this to him was inexcusable. Unforgivable. My own voice sounded hoarse when I admitted, "I'm glad they couldn't save her. I'd want to track her down and kill her myself."

There was no emotion in his voice when he answered. "You wouldn't have gotten the chance. She'd have gone to prison for it and been locked away for at least one lifetime." *A paltry sentence for an immortal.*

"Then I'd just have to survive long enough for her to get out," I grumbled. "How did you manage to kill a vampire, anyway?" *I might need that information against one someday, since blasting one into a gas giant or feeding them to sharks was probably out.* "And why would she go to prison? Assault?" I didn't know how vampire law worked. Biting someone seemed like a pretty natural vampiry thing to do.

I felt him shrug. "Burn someone hot enough and even rapid healing can't compensate." He paused to focus on untangling a knot he'd found in my hair. *He was preening me!* My arms tightened around him as I fought to control my inner-squee of happiness. "They have laws against taking blood from people without conscious consent," he continued, "and they'd have thrown the book at her for changing me while I was under the influence. There's a ton of paperwork that has to be filled out beforehand to prove the one being changed consents and understands the consequences."

Huh. Paperwork and bureaucracy really were everywhere. I felt my forehead scrunch into a frown against his chest. "I don't understand how your parents could blame you for any of that," I said, remembering his comment in the desert about why they didn't get along.

"If I hadn't been drunk, it wouldn't have happened."

"What the hell?" I half-shouted, rearing back to look him in the face. He was dead serious, with a resigned sort of tiredness behind his eyes. "I'll kill them too," I growled angrily. I wouldn't actually kill his parents, but how dare they? *Victim-blaming assholes!*

"Shhhhh," he whispered, blinking sleepily at me before pulling my face back down against his chest. "I'm okay now," he murmured against the top of my head. "I just don't want to be around them anymore." I felt his gentle shrug, and after another moment, his breathing evened out, growing slow and steady as he dropped back off for a few more minutes of sleep.

I lay there wrapped in his arm while he slept, considering how unfair life could be sometimes, and what kind of evil hijinks I could plague his parents with for being so callous toward their own child. Nothing I thought of felt villainous enough. If we were mated, he could just have my parents, who were pretty awesome despite their own flaws. The thought was as startling as it was tempting.

I woke up alone a little while later and realized I must have fallen asleep again as well. The spot where Jordan had lain was cold, so he'd been up for a while. I rolled over and peeked under the bed to find the dragon was gone and half my stuff had been dragged out of my backpack to make a nest in the back corner. Luckily, it didn't smell like pee. My skin felt prickly and tight again, but it was probably just from me not knowing where the boys were. My bag had been righted and a pair of clothes that looked like a smaller version of Jordan's uniform was stacked neatly on top of it, with both of my sticks placed on top. They smelled like dragon drool. *That little brat.*

I set them aside carefully and suited up in the new clothes Jordan had left, since mine were full of dust. The trousers and jacket were black, padded leathers that were loose enough to fight in but tight enough to not get in the way. While leather was already fireproof, there were runes sewn into the insides of both pieces for protection against fire. The high neck wasn't something I would normally have picked for myself, but it was practical and protective, so I wasn't going to turn my nose up at it. I pulled my hair into a high ponytail and then rescued the rest of my belongings from Huck's impromptu nest, tossing it all into my bag with my sticks carefully tucked on top and zipping it shut. I'd need to stop by home tonight and swap out for some clean stuff.

I threw the bag over my shoulder and followed the scent of vampire to the common room, where Allie the orc was poring over another file at the table and the big giant guy was warming up a blood bag on the stove. "Where is my dragon?" I asked, standing in the doorway. I couldn't smell Jordan's or Huck's scent anywhere nearby, and the baby carrier had been missing.

The giant looked at me over his shoulder and did a double take. "Who's that? And why is she wearing our clothes?"

"She's the bird, dummy," Allie answered. "Jordan *told you* she was a shifter."

I wiggled my fingers at him.

"Jordan said to tell you Augustus sent him out scouting and he was taking the little fire-breather with him," she said to me. "I don't know how long he'll be out, but he's always back to check in before daybreak. You're welcome to hang out here if you want."

I was immediately miffed that he'd left without me and wasn't about to sit around twiddling my thumbs if there was no dragon to keep an eye on. "Thanks. I'll be back," I grumbled, heading for the stairs. I did my best to ignore how weird it felt to be without them and decided to take advantage of my dragon-free time.

The *problem* was that it was hard to ignore. I'd been spending so much time with them that I must have just gotten used to it. The farther I got from his workplace, the twitchier I felt. It felt *wrong*.

A quick jaunt home showed that my brother had been busy. The couch was gone and replaced with a newish one—it looked like he'd found it on the side of the road somewhere, but that was fine. That's how we'd gotten our last one. All the remnants of destroyed pillows and plants were also removed. There were cans of primer and paint stacked by the wall, with most of the charred damage already covered in a good coat of primer. He wasn't home, but since he worked in construction, he had no real schedule to speak of, so that wasn't unusual. I restocked my bag and dumped out some dried flowers from a vase on my dresser to replace them with my new sticks, taking a moment to appreciate their structure.

They were nice sticks.

Then it was time to head into Seattle and hope Elara was working late.

It was impossible to concentrate. Every time I started to run the numbers on our accounts to balance the books, my mind would drift back to Jordan. The way he held me. The tremor in his voice when he spoke about his trauma. The shape of the words his mouth brushed across my back. The glint of curiosity in his eye when he held up his stick. The hot weight of his—I huffed out a breath and started angrily punching in the numbers again, feeling Elara's eyes burning into my brain. The ice rattled in her cup, and I turned to find her staring at me owlishly while she sipped on a pink drink from the coffee shop down the street. She was looking healthier—her color was back to normal, and she seemed well rested. But that also meant she was back to being more observant of her surroundings. And she wasn't even trying to hide her staring anymore, which meant a lot coming from her.

"What are you doing?" I asked her.

She blinked at me, managing to look even more owl-like when she did. "What are *you* doing?" she responded dryly, which made me want to laugh but I kept it in check.

"I'm balancing the books."

Her lip twitched the barest amount, but I saw the spark take hold in her eyes. "By staring longingly into space and making lots of huffing sounds? I'm pretty sure you've braided and re-braided your hair five times since you sat down."

I frowned at her and tried to ignore her annoyingly observant remarks. "When is Levi coming back?" He'd been here with her when I arrived but ducked out to his apartment to grab some things.

Elara ignored my question and took another *long* sip of her drink, continuing to watch me as if I were so very interesting. I rolled my eyes and turned back to my desk to start the math from the beginning again. This wasn't difficult, it was just... so hard to focus when all I wanted to do was daydream about the way Jordan smiled and wonder about what he was doing right now.

"UGH!" I dropped my face into my hands and pressed on my head. "This is the *worst*." Elara's ice rattled again as she set her cup down, but she didn't respond. "I think I'm having *feelings* for him," I grit out against my palms.

Elara tutted at me as she scooted her chair over to be within reach. "For... Jordan?" she asked, hesitation clear in her voice. When I nodded against my hands, she reached up to pat my hair with a familiarity that made my heart happy. Only my brothers and parents had ever done that with such confidence, and it made me grateful again for our friendship. "Would that be so bad?" she asked in a small voice. "To have feelings for Jordan?" she clarified, after hesitating again. "I don't really know him that well, but Levi likes him. I'm sure he's... Well, he seems like a lovely man," she continued optimistically.

It made my heart sink. "He *is* lovely, and that *sucks,* because now I'm having all of these obnoxious feelings that I *don't want to have,* because he's immortal and *I'm not,* and because we wouldn't be a good fit anyway. We can't work, Elara." The truth of those words felt raw and jagged as I formed them.

Elara let me stew in my thoughts for a long moment as she comfortingly stroked my hair with one hand, her chin propped heavily on the other. "Does he make you happy, though? When you're with him? Happiness should count for something, I think. You deserve every happiness, Sidney."

But what did happiness matter, in the end, when it couldn't work, and one or both of you would just be left heartbroken and alone?

Chapter 25

MY MOOD WAS DECIDEDLY worse as the night wore on, and after Elara packed up and left with Levi, I headed back into the Boundlands. I wanted to head straight to Jordan's office in the hope that he'd have returned by now, but since my apartment was on the way there, I stopped back in there one more time. With just a few days left until Elara's wedding, I had a bone to pick with my brother.

It was just after midnight when I unlocked the front door and found him standing over the sink with a bowl of cheap noodles, sawdust still in his hair, like he'd been working late as I suspected.

"Hey Sid!" he said, around a mouth full of noodles.

"Hey, *you abominable turd-muffin.* Elara's wedding is literally three days away and you haven't given her mother an RSVP yet. What is wrong with you? I know you have Saturday night free." I crossed my arms and leaned on my backpack against the door since I wasn't staying. If I'd trusted him to not ignore my message, I could have just sent him a spectral for this, but Josh was squirrely and hard to pin down about his schedule sometimes. So here I was making a second pit stop at my house. I glared at him, irritated by his lack of social responsibility to my best friend, who had only ever extended exceedingly gracious kindness to him.

Josh completely ignored my attitude, unfazed as always. Why couldn't I be as scary to my little brother as I was to everyone else in my life? "Where's Huck?" he asked, looking around like

I might have the dog-sized dragon stuffed in a pocket some-where. "And what are you wearing?"

I glanced down at my outfit, distracted by his questions. "Huck's with a friend. These are fireproof clothes," I muttered.

"Cool! I want some," he said as he stuffed more food in his face.

"*Answer me*, dork. You can't just *not RSVP* to an event like this. What is wrong with you?"

Josh frowned at me sulkily, and I cringed at how the sawdust rained down onto the kitchen floor and into his bowl as he shoveled more food into his mouth. *Gross.* "I wasn't sure if I was bringing a plus-one or not."

My expression turned scathing. "So, you can't even let her know if *you're coming?* Do you have any idea how much money these people are spending on this?" I tried to keep my voice down to an angry hiss instead of the banshee-screech I wanted to use, considering the hour.

"I'm sorry!" he said around his food. "I just didn't know how to respond yet."

"Well, it's rude. I told her you were coming and to put you down for a plus-one." I shifted my weight forward to rebalance my backpack and reached for the door handle.

"*What?* Who am I supposed to invite? Why would you do that?" He grabbed a paper towel to hold over his mouth, trying to keep from spraying food everywhere as he spoke.

"I don't *know*, Joshua, just bring whoever you want to. I don't care. Bring a friend, or a date, or that guy you've been secretly crushing on for heaven knows how long. It's going to be the biggest party you've ever seen." From the plans I'd seen for the formal reception, my family had never experienced this kind of bash and likely never would again for as long as we lived. When I said Elara's family was old-money wealthy, I meant *old-money wealthy*. "Just bring someone to enjoy it with."

The panicked look in his eyes made my anger flare hot be-cause only one situation could trigger that reaction regarding this. I *loved* my baby brother, and I would burn the world down if anyone was mean to him about *anything, ever,* but especially about who he loved and what fulfilled him as a person. I took a deep breath and let it out. "Would you enjoy going to the wedding with him, Josh?"

His face visibly paled, and I had to restrain myself from tackling him in a bear hug or punching walls. "Our whole family will be there, Sidney. Everyone would know."

One more deep breath, and then another for good measure. "Do you have *any* idea how apocalyptically I will destroy anyone who says a word to you or makes you uncomfortable about whomever you choose to be with in the future?"

"I don't need you to—" He cut himself off when he glanced at my face, huffing a breath and seeming to take some small comfort in the vehemence written across my features, regardless of what he didn't need. Of course he didn't *need* me, but I would be there for him anyway.

"I'm not trying to make you invite him," I clarified. "Bring whoever you want. I'm just telling you to bring someone who makes you happy," I said as Elara's words ran through my head. Because if anyone deserved happiness, it was my baby brother. "Good job on the walls, by the way," I finished, eyeing the primed scorch marks. I jerked the door open and headed back out into the night.

If I hadn't felt so fidgety, I might have stopped by the bar too, maybe had a shot and poked around for more information about the Phantoms again. I was at loose ends and just wanted to be with Jordan and Huck though, so I went straight back in the hopes that he'd returned.

My heart swelled to find that Jordan sat waiting for me, looking down from the roof of his office while I stared up at him from the street below. He had one leg draped carelessly over the edge of the building and barked a self-deprecating laugh when I crossed my arms over my chest and glared at him. He'd left without me, the jerk.

"I could really use a cigarette," he muttered just loud enough for it to reach my ears on the quiet street.

I frowned at that. "I'm not your mother." I wasn't a fan of the habit myself, but I hadn't asked him to quit for my sake. I could see his wry grin from two stories up as he took in my response. "Where is my dragon?" I asked, and the grin promptly slid off his face.

He pushed off the edge and dropped the two stories to land heavily on the street next to me, before stalking toward the side of the building. *I guess not everyone can land as neatly as a bird.* But I was still impressed with the jump. "He was unhappy about being separated from you." Jordan rounded the corner, and I followed him into the dark alleyway, stopping in front of a rusty, old dumpster.

I glared at him again. "Well, you shouldn't have left without me. I would have come with you."

Jordan just gave me a small shrug. "You needed your sleep. I figured I could take him off your hands for a few more hours and maybe he could help me find his siblings. It was just some preliminary scouting. It did seem like he found some familiar scents after a while, but then we lost the trail and Huck started getting rowdy, so I brought him back. Lucas stayed behind to search some more. This stuff is my job anyway, Sidney, not yours. It can be dangerous."

I rolled my eyes. I was already parenting an incendiary dinosaur toddler. Job descriptions had lost all sense of logical meaning to me. "I'm a big girl, Jordan. You don't get to make decisions for me. We've talked about this." I was very capable of handling myself in most situations. "Why are we staring at a dumpster?"

"He's underneath."

"You couldn't get him out? You're probably strong enough to pick up the whole thing."

I looked at him when he didn't respond, finding his mouth turned down in a disapproving moue. "It's dirty."

I threw my hands in the air, feeling like that was probably a safer option than what I wanted to do with them. *Ugh.* "Huck!" No response. "Huck, come here." Nothing. *Heaven help me if I have to...* I heaved a deep breath and gritted my teeth. "Humphrey Herbert Hucklebee, the Fierce!" Faint scuffling noises sounded from under the dumpster. "Get out here. What are you doing?"

"He was setting the alleyway on fire," Jordan muttered beside me. It was hard to see it in the dark, but now that he mentioned it, there did seem to be some scorch marks here and there. Huck burst out from under the dumpster and scrambled up my leg, using his beating wings to push himself higher so that he could cling to my thigh as his tail whipped around behind him on the ground.

"Jeez dude, watch the claws! I'm here! Everything's cool, okay?" I almost missed the look of relief that washed over Jordan's face as I turned to head back to his office entrance. Or compound entrance. *Whatever it was.* I couldn't miss my own relief, however, that sense of rightness that washed over me at being back with my boys. My skin didn't feel too tight. Jordan's weird vampire scent mixed with wood smoke was becoming almost comforting. It made me nervous. Both of them were temporary additions to my life. Ephemeral.

They wouldn't *stay.*

But then Jordan asked, "What did you just call him?" and I wanted to throw him through a wall again.

"*Nothing.*" I gritted out.

His laugh was unabashedly relieved, and I fought down the bubbles of happiness the sound created inside me. "Those clothes look good on you," he said as I turned and walked away, heading back toward the entrance with a clingier than usual dragon wrapped around my thigh like a little barnacle. He seemed even bigger than yesterday.

"You have this really bad habit of disappearing constantly," I groused at Jordan, not bothering to raise my voice. "You know that, right?"

"And how can I make that up to you?" he asked in a mischievous tone, much closer behind me than I had expected. I hadn't heard him follow me.

I paused as his words registered, and he passed me to open the front door for us, staring at me with his twinkling eyes as he leaned over to grab the handle. He pulled it open and continued to watch me as my mind whirled with possibilities. He was hinting at sex, *obviously*, but I could get that anyway. What could he give me that he probably wouldn't want to? "Are you going to Elara's wedding this weekend?" He'd better be going. I knew for a fact that she'd requested a night wedding specifically so he could be invited.

His mouth pulled down into a frown and the twinkle left his eyes. "Yes."

I tried to imagine how he would look in a tux and it did funny things to my insides. Even without trying, he dressed neatly and always had his hair so irritatingly perfect. Picturing Jordan when he *tried* to look nice? Yum. "Then you owe me a dance," I said, hauling my flapping leg warmer past him to knock on the inner door. A spectral flickered in the air in front of us, and then the lock clicked over to let us in.

"I don't dance."

I pushed the inner door open and dragged Huck inside with me, turning to scowl at Jordan as he entered. He slowed to a stop just inside as the door closed behind him and I prowled back toward him, willfully ignoring the fact that I was walking like I had a peg leg—since it was hard to move with Huck clinging to my thigh and his tail dragging along behind us. With mere inches between us, I stopped and glowered at him, raising my chin defiantly.

This weekend I was going to be wearing the prettiest dress I'd ever worn to anything, ever. I was going to spend *hours* with Elara getting our hair and makeup done. I was going to be primped and prepped within an inch of my life. I was going to feel *pretty* all dressed up, and I wanted to dance with Jordan while I did. "We're going to dance." I raised my lips for a brief kiss, and he narrowed his eyes at me—clearly not in agreement about my declaration—but he gently pressed his lips to mine.

Chapter 26

WE SPENT THE NEXT two days in roughly the same way, with me heading into Seattle to work in the shop in the early evenings and then joining Jordan later to scout and help with Huck. He let me accompany him both nights to search for the missing dragons as long as I stayed in my bird form to avoid recognition. Just thinking about how long Huck's siblings had been in Phantom hands made me incredibly anxious.

I didn't leave during daylight hours because it was so difficult for Jordan to stay awake—being a young vampire—so I didn't want to risk Huck being without any supervision in the compound. Augustus, his creepy old boss, was old enough to be able to wake up whenever he wanted and cheerfully offered to not only watch Huck if needed during the day, but to keep him for us during Elara's wedding. I hadn't taken him up on the daylight hours thing—he wasn't fireproof like Jordan—but leaving Huck with him for Elara's wedding couldn't be avoided. It was either this or beg Allie to watch him again since my brothers were all attending the wedding, and after he blew her eyebrows off when he escaped the first night, I didn't think she'd be down for that.

I held up the baby carrier in Jordan's room on Friday night. "Do you think we could convince Augustus to wear Huck in the carrier? Tell me that wouldn't be hilarious."

Jordan paused while unpacking a bag of takeout he'd brought back for me. "Sidney, I know you live for messing with people, but Augustus is off limits."

I narrowed my eyes at Jordan. "Off-limits" wasn't generally part of my vocabulary. "Why?"

He lowered his voice to a barely audible level as he handed me the dumplings he'd picked out for me at a local food cart. "Not only is he my boss and my mentor, but he's a twelve-hundred-year-old elvish vampire with mixed-sylvan ancestry who can *'un-alive'* anyone he has a visual lock on by making fungus explode from their body cavities. Please don't irritate him."

"*Gross.*" But point to Augustus. "Noted." I took a quick bite of a dumpling, trying not to scald myself on the soup inside. "I'm glad we're on the same team."

Jordan gave a subtle nod.

I WAS ENTIRELY AWARE that Elara's wedding wasn't about me, but this was quite possibly the best day of my life. I'd been dancing around everywhere I went, unable to stop swirling the skirt of my dress and flouncing about no matter how hard I tried. Between the plunging neckline and the corset-back lacing, this thing did *amazing* things for my figure.

Elara looked positively resplendent. The royal decorum with which she carried herself had been baked into her at the expensive girl's school that moneyed elvish families always sent their children to. Her dress draped behind her, the filmy white gauze and gold detailing catching the candlelight with every movement. While she normally wore jewelry in excess simply due to its pragmatic magical functions, tonight she'd selected pieces for their beauty and elegance. The effect was striking as her train trailed behind her down the aisle and her jewelry glittered in much the same way it had in the dusty wreckage of our college campus the first day I'd met her. *My girl was growing up,* I thought with a pretend tear wipe.

Regardless of her regal bearing, Elara was still jittery about the event, being the consummate introvert that she was, but spending the day getting ready with her had caused me to give her nerves a side-eye more than once. She'd seemed more emotional than usual, and it struck me as an odd reaction from her. When I caught her getting glassy eyed as the hairstylist pinned her hair back, I'd zeroed in on the tiny teardrop that escaped. "What is this? This isn't ceremony jitters. What's wrong?" I'd reached out and taken her hand, and when she grasped me back like a lifeline, I was on high alert. Elara wasn't the clingy type like I was, so my anxiety was pinging. "Who do I need to kill? Or did you already do it and there's a body to hide? Just tell me where to find it, and I'll take care of it, El."

She'd huffed a watery laugh. "Everything's fine. I don't know what's wrong with me."

I'd frowned in confusion. This wasn't stage fright. Elara wasn't the type to crumple under pressure even if she didn't care for crowds and attention. "You're not concerned about marrying Levi, are you? You already did that once, and anyone can see you two are madly in love with each other." I could take him out if I had to, but I'd rather not since I liked the guy, and it was obvious he adored her.

"No, of course not." She'd given her head a little shake, careful not to disturb the hairstylist. "Of course not," she'd repeated. "I think I'm just afraid of things changing, and you know I don't do well with change," she'd admitted. I'd searched her face, looking for anything hidden or hurt, but she just seemed... well... emotional. "I miss you," she'd huffed and squeezed my hand. "I had to leave for weeks to help the sprites, and now you're gone with the baby dragon." She wiped her eyes. "The elvish government contacted me this morning with requests for more magical emitters like my prototype, and I don't know how I could build those and continue to run the shop."

"Elara!" I'd squealed, startling her and the hairstylist both. "That's fantastic! That's great news!" I'd told her, genuinely happy. I didn't know where I fit into this future she painted, but I couldn't have cared less at the moment. "This is huge, Hon. Those emitters can save so many lives." The shop was great, but this would change the way Boundlands citizens were rescued in the Void.

I'd wrapped her hand in mine and squeezed. I'd realized as I stared at her, though, that I understood her fear of change. It hadn't bothered me before, because change was a constant thing and I'd always known the things that mattered most to me wouldn't change. I had my family, and that was all that I'd ever feared losing. But I had more than that now, and I didn't want to lose what I had.

Jordan had a tendency to disappear on me, and that was one thing I could see myself fighting him on, because it scared me. Losing him to the shadows again was a thought I found I couldn't tolerate. And I didn't want to lose Huck, even though I knew it was best for him to grow up and fly free. But one thing, at least, that wouldn't ever change was my friendship with Elara.

"No matter what happens, Elara, I'm always going to be here. No matter what." I let my eyes shift between hers before jumping for the tissues. "Stop! No crying! You're going to make your face all puffy!" We'd spent the rest of the day being primped and polished by lovely hair and makeup artists, and even though it wasn't my usual thing, it was girl time that my soul had truly needed. I was already tired, but I intended to enjoy every moment of this event.

Her parents had invited everyone they'd ever known and their entire extended families to their sprawling castle estate on the edge of Golden Laurel. It was an outdoor wedding with big, beautiful flower arrangements and gauzy fabric dripping down the stone walls of their home and outbuildings. There were fountains and musicians and fifteen-foot pikes topped with streamers and garlands. Torches and double full moons provided dreamy, cozy lighting for the ceremony. I was in the company of more important people in one place than I could count on a dozen hands. Government officials, high-society socialites, famous musicians, deeply respected scientists and healers… Everywhere I looked, there was someone new to schmooze. I was having a blast. At least until the ceremony started.

Grim, as Best Man, escorted me down the aisle like a complete gentleman, and stood opposite me as Elara and Levi said their vows for the second time. Only, this time, I couldn't understand a word of what was being said because it was all spoken in Old Elvish. Grim obviously understood it from the way he was paying attention to every back and forth, and Elara had mentioned that he'd helped tutor Levi on what words to say and when. There had been a lot more rituals this time too, a handfasting and several other old elvish customs I hadn't paid much attention to. It was all way more buttoned up and stuffy than any shifter wedding I'd ever attended, which was mostly a bunch of drunken shenanigans. I'd wager you were more likely to wake up with your pants on your head or a bad tattoo from one of those than any of these staid elvish affairs.

As much as I'd tried to pay attention to what was going on, I was in the perfect position to watch the crowd, and I had a bead on a sneaky-ass vampire who had slipped in the back just as the ceremony began. Elara felt guilty about Jordan not being able to attend their elopement with us the first time, hence the night-wedding request this time. Jordan was wearing a perfectly tailored black tux, with his hair—as usual—styled just so, and *damn* but if he didn't look good like that. I couldn't wait for the ceremony to be over because I'd already decided I was going to hunt Jordan for sport tonight.

Levi's voice carried such a strong enchantment that he managed to pull me back to the present as he returned his vows to Elara. His voice was strong and clear, and even if he stumbled over a few words, and I couldn't parse their meaning, I could hear the triumph in his voice and see it written on his face. This was a man hopelessly in love, and I couldn't help the burning feeling that creeped up behind my eyes as I watched my best friend smile at him with tears pouring down her face just like she did the first time they were married. Even Grim wore a soft expression as he gazed at our two friends.

Their kiss was gentle and short. Too short, if Levi's blazing eyes telegraphed his desires correctly, but they had the rest of their lives to muss each other up properly. Elara was too shy to make out with her husband in front of a crowd of beaming well-wishers. By the time the officiant announced the bride and groom, and Grim and I followed them down the aisle, I was ready to be out of the spotlight myself. I slid my gaze to the arrogant vampire in the back row on my way out. He owed me a dance.

Chapter 27

GRIM AND I WERE seated since we weren't part of the receiving line. It was kind of a bummer because I was incredibly nosy and wanted to know more about some of these guests who were making their way through the line. For instance, there was an elvish girl a little younger than us who looked like the spitting image of Elara's father, Lord Varsalos, but she was married to a guy who looked nearly full mer. So maybe he was related to Levi? But when they reached the front of the line, Varsalos embraced the girl in an awkward but genuine hug, and she looked like she wanted to cry. *Elara's family then,* I decided. I wondered what that was about, but she seemed happy to be here, even if her husband looked a little gun shy and overwhelmed. I made a mental note to ask Elara about her, then scanned the line, looking for my handsome, fanged quarry.

"Sidney." Grim's voice was quiet as always, but I nearly fell out of my chair. I shot him a look that probably showed every ounce of shock I felt since I'm terrible at keeping my inside-thoughts on the inside. It wasn't that I'd forgotten Grim was *there,* because his aura was so overwhelming that it was physically impossible. It was that I'd only heard the man speak two or three times—*ever*—and this was the first time he'd ever spoken *to me.* He appeared entirely unruffled by my behavior, continuing on as if he wasn't some kind of primeval eldritch bogeyman who was choosing the current moment to speak to me for the *first time.* "Do you mind if I ask how you've come to bear a dragon's mark?" he asked softly. He deftly opened the roll of silverware in front of him with one hand, unfurling the napkin and draping it gracefully across his lap. *I should probably do that.* Table manners weren't my strong suit.

"Uh—dragon's…?" *What?* I looked down at my exposed skin, hurriedly checking my arms and inspecting my cleavage for claw marks. Huck had left plenty of scratches on me, but shifter-healing should have meant that they were all gone by now. "Well, he's a feisty little brat," I responded as I removed my own napkin, "but I would have figured they'd have healed up by now. You must have exceptional eyesight," I concluded.

In an effort to pretend like I *also* had manners, I dropped the napkin over my lap just in time for a dwarvish waiter to place an artfully plated appetizer carefully in front of each of us, and then glanced at Grim to find he looked as confused by my answer as I did by his question. He returned my frown. I noticed he had none of the slices of fish on his plate that I had on mine. His only contained vegetables.

My youngest brother gave a little wave to catch my attention as he filed past the raised dais where we were seated in front of the rest of the tables. He'd brought a smaller crow-shifter with a beautiful, dark complexion and a voice I recognized from Josh's late-night calling-chip conversations. He'd found me to introduce his date, Ahmed, before the ceremony, and they both blushed every time they made eye contact with each other. You couldn't wipe this smug grin off my face if you tried. I wanted to smash them together like little dolls and say, "Now kiss!" but I would restrain myself. I wondered if Ahmed danced. *I bet I could get him to dance with me.* That would be a perfect time to interrogate him about his intentions regarding my brother.

The crowd continued to filter into the sunken garden area in the back, where all the dinner tables were set up. Servers drifted between the tables delivering appetizers and wine, and I spotted my oldest brother, Sam, in line for the open bar. I searched the crowd as it grew and found Aaron nearby, mingling with Levi's dad, who seemed like he'd probably fit in better with one of my people's pants-on-head shindigs anyway. Joshua stayed toward the fringes with his date, and my parents were awkwardly trying to make conversation with Ahmed. *Good.* Jordan was nowhere to be seen, though. I drummed my fingers on the table.

Levi and Elara finally had their grand entrance and joined us, and the feast began, but I still hadn't spotted my prey. "Grim," I hissed under my breath. We were friends now, since he had spoken to me. Right? "Where's your roommate?" What if Jordan had left already? I wanted to dance! I flicked a glance at my newly friended collector of souls to find him quickly scanning the seated crowd.

"There." He pointed to an area off to the side that I couldn't see from my seat. I had to lean a little closer to him to catch a glimpse of Jordan, but found him seated with my old friends Hyrak, Solandis, and Alistair, drinking a glass of what looked like very dark wine. *Jordan can't drink wine.* Had the caterers sourced blood for him? I glanced at Grim's vegan meal again and turned to eye the large clan of dryads in the crowd who had supposedly lived on Elara's family's estate for centuries, maybe millennia. Even the giant tree people had some sort of greenish brew to sip on. Elara had certainly worked to make sure everyone had individual attention... but *blood*? Seating Jordan with Hyrak had been an interesting choice, considering they'd never met, but knowing how he felt about old acquaintances, it was a good one. Probably better than some stuffy Head-of-State.

I practically inhaled my food, which was a shame, because I barely tasted it, and the roasted elk and sea grapes paired with the expensive elvish confections were delicious. The servers kept our wine glasses topped off, so I wasn't entirely sure how many glasses I'd had, but I was already starting to feel it. *Finally*, the cake was cut, and the tea was served, and Levi led Elara out to the center of the beautifully landscaped stone walkways to dance in the moonlight. It was all I could do to not melt into a puddle of goo at how romantic it looked and how beautiful they were together. I realized I had my hands clutched together under my cheek like a loon, but they were so lovely!

I noticed as they danced that little sparks, the fire fairies, were darting around their feet, always coming between them and the crowd any time they got close to an onlooker. I squinted, trying to get a better look, but I couldn't make heads or tails of it. "What are they doing?" I whispered to Grim. He didn't respond, staring at me in the darkness with a puzzled expression. "The fairies," I clarified.

He turned back to the spectacle, a minute frown marring his expression as he watched. "I believe they're guarding her," came his quiet response.

"She already has guards," I puzzled out loud. Her father had hired a private security company of elves from Chicago to staff the wedding tonight. Elara had mentioned that some fae had taken up residence in her potted plants and some cabinets after she delivered the leviathan to the sprites and that she'd found a few flitting around whenever she traveled in the Boundlands, but it was hard to tell how she felt about it. Fairies could be rather vicious, but they were also incredibly loyal. Not a people you'd want to anger, for sure.

Fairies have some serious PR in the Void. I've never understood how they managed to convince humans that they look like darling towheaded children with sparkly wings. And *who decided* that teaching children to bargain with fairies using body parts was a good idea? Teeth and bones are old magic. Humans are the epitome of naïve ignorance and their only saving grace is that they'll never get a chance to meet a real fairy, since neither of them can cross a portal and live. So having them pottering around after my friend everywhere made me a little uneasy. I'd have to ask Jordan what he thought.

My eyes flashed to him again for the thousandth time tonight. He looked way too uptight and uncomfortable. The dude needed to find a way to take the edge off. Maybe we could figure out a way to make alcoholic blood. Or maybe I could drag him behind some bushes and find a different way to take the edge off. I wouldn't be opposed to that.

"Shall we?" I almost fell out of my chair again, thinking that Grim was somehow responding to my thoughts this time. His puzzled expression and upturned palm didn't calm my internal freak out. "I believe it's our turn to welcome the guests to join the ball." Oh, right. That. Yes. Dancing!

I set my hand in Grim's, and we rose as one to make our way to the dance floor. *Time to slay.*

Chapter 28

THE ELDRITCH HORROR WHIRLING me about the floor was an excellent dance partner. I don't know why I was surprised by this, but every movement was precisely calculated, every spin perfectly led, every dip gracefully balanced. I still felt that creeping sense of foreboding in his presence, but I let myself relax into the joy of the dance and the excitement of the moment. Dancing with Grim was like dancing on air. He waltzed as if it were second nature to him and was clearly talented in his leading as he drew me through the steps of the dance with ease. It didn't escape my notice, however, that every loop brought us closer and closer to Jordan, who wasn't looking at me at all. He was looking at *Grim*, and he was *mad*. Was jealousy rearing its ugly head again? I nearly laughed.

I followed Jordan's gaze to Grim's face, finding an unmistakable spark of mischief in his eyes as he spun me directly into Jordan's line of sight. I did laugh then, unable to smother my disbelieving cackle as I realized *Grim was acting as my wingman*. Would wonders never cease? Delightful. *Don't worry Jordan, I'm going to drag you out here and subject you to dancing next*, I thought, with evil glee clearly written on my face. But the next time Grim whirled me toward the seated crowd, Jordan had disappeared. *That scamp!*

The song ended, and we faced the crowd, raising our arms in invitation to the floor, and then returned to our table. "That was lovely, Grim. I had no idea you were such a clever dancer." No response, other than to incline his head.

Elara and Levi were mingling with their guests, and I could tell from here that Elara was already starting to feel overwhelmed. Time for a rescue. I scooped up her glass of water and pressed my way through the crowd, dodging around spark fairies and taking her hand to pull her aside. "Hello, sorry to interrupt! I just need to borrow Elara," I said with a fake grin pasted on my face as I handed her the glass and dragged her from the fray. Levi was on his own. Everyone around him looked enraptured by his enchanted words.

"What's wrong?" Elara whispered.

"Nothing. I'm rescuing you. Drink some water." I scanned the crowd again, looking for Jordan.

Elara huffed a laugh before dutifully sipping her water. "Thanks. What are you looking for?"

"Jordan. I'm going to make him dance with me."

She broke into a small grin. "He doesn't seem like the dancing type. You should dance with Rafe."

I shot a frown at her. "Does he still have those birds in his shoulder?" Rafe was one of the clan of dryads—a race of nomadic tree-people—that Elara had grown up playing with because they sojourned on her family's property. I liked Rafe well enough, but the cute little adorable male chickadee that lived in his shoulder was a total *dick*.

Elara's mouth dropped open. "You wouldn't withhold a dance from Rafe just because you're holding a grudge against Dust!"

"I'm not holding a grudge," I grumbled. "I just think the guy could stand to be a little more respectful to his wife."

She chuckled at me. "Puff and Dust have been *mated* for almost seven years now! You need to let it go, Sidney. They're *birds*."

I was aware of that. I could choose to dislike a bird simply on principle if I wanted. Scanning the crowd again proved fruitless. Jordan had seriously disappeared; I couldn't see him anywhere. I would have asked Grim to find him, but he'd conveniently disappeared, too. "Fine." I'd make my own fun while I looked for that sneak. He had to be hiding around here somewhere.

Rafe's twelve-foot frame was easy to spot among the crowd of people. I tried to keep an eye on what was happening around me as I pushed my way through—sparks darting to and fro, a jovial ogre gabbing happily with a goblin in high-court garb, Elara's reserved parents talking to my brash ones, my brothers doing shots in the back with Ahmed, half a dozen attendees mobbing Levi with questions because they were hoping to hear him speak. I rolled my eyes, knowing I'd been just as enamored with his voice the first time I'd heard it and grateful for the ear cuff Elara had provided me to ward against it.

"Rafe!" I called over the din of conversation and music as I approached. He turned gingerly, slowly raising his arms above the height of the crowd as he pivoted, as if he were afraid of injuring someone if he moved too quickly. It was hard to describe a dryad's body language. They didn't really use facial expressions in the way that most people did, but his movements still had an air of expectation to them as he turned to greet me. There were various sized dryads among his clan, and Rafe wasn't the tallest, but he was enormous. Built like a kickboxer, he had a heavy frame that looked like an impressionistic statue made of driftwood and vines welded together by moss and fungus.

"Oh! Sidney! You look splendid," he greeted as his vibrant eyes settled on me. Their eyes glowed faintly green in the dark with foxfire.

I grinned at him, taking in the extra swathes of moss covering his huge form and the tiny white flowers dripping from the small, gnarled looking antlers that sprouted from the back of his head. "You look rather fetching yourself, all done up for the ceremony. Come dance with me!"

"I'm not sure I know much of this dancing, but I would be honored to try. I'll need to be careful not to jostle the little ones out of their slumber." I spotted Dust nestled into a crag in Rafe's bark with his head tucked behind a wing. Puff, his mate, must have been squirreled away in the cavity he'd allowed them to hollow out in his shoulder. If they could handle him running through the forest and training for battles in the mountains, they could sleep through a dance or two. The crowd quickly parted for Rafe, staring up at him in awe as we entered. Even the flowers turned their pretty faces toward him as we passed them by. He paused at the edge of the crowd to watch a few loops of the dance, and then declared, "This dancing is much like a gentle martial art," in his deep, rustling voice. He took my hand, and we were off, whirling our way into the ordered chaos that was a formal dance. His movements were the graceful bow of a tree in the wind and the power of an avalanche rolled into one. He was all confidence and good cheer, and I burst with joy as we spun about the floor. *Why couldn't Jordan do this with me?* I caught a glimpse of him slipping behind a column to chat with Grim and stared him down until the crowd moved between us and he was gone again. Probably sulking in the shadows somewhere.

I spent hours taking turns with Rafe and my friends Solandis and Alistair. Solandis and I turned out to both be terrible dance leads, so we stepped on each other's feet and spun each other about wildly until we collapsed in a fit of giggles. Alistair had left me covered in his iridescent wing scales, and I probably looked like a glittery disco ball, but it had been worth it to smoosh my face into the mothman's soft fur when he hugged me. I couldn't corner Jordan, but I did meet Sadira, the elvish girl from the receiving line. She and her pretty husband seemed incredibly shy, so I brought them shots from the bar and then foisted them upon Solandis. She could show anyone how to have a good time, and they clearly needed it—shell shocked as they appeared.

I also managed to snag Ahmed—my brother's date—and convince him to dance with me, but before I could pepper him with questions, Josh interrupted us. "May I cut in?" he asked, and I beamed at him. *Aww, my little brother wanted to dance with me!* I could have squealed with excitement, except that he wheeled away dancing with Ahmed instead of me. He cast me a mischievous grin over his shoulder as I cackled at his audacity.

But then... *then*, as I danced with Rafe again, I found *him*. Jordan was seated up on the dais with Levi, Elara, and Grim... *in my seat*. I paused in my steps as Jordan stood and buttoned his jacket, narrowing my eyes at him. He spotted me immediately and said something to Levi before stepping off the dais and into the shadows. *Oh, no, he doesn't.*

"Excuse me, Rafe," I growled. "I've got a vampire to catch."

Chapter 29

I was waiting for him in the moonlit courtyard to the south of the party when he tried to slip through, quiet as a church mouse. My voice was more irritable sounding than I meant for it to be when I said, "I've never known someone so big and scary to be afraid of something so trite as *dancing*." Frustration at him and the pervasive itch beneath my skin at being away from Huck for so long had made me agitated.

Jordan froze in his tracks, nearly hiking his shoulders up to his ears as if I had startled him, but I couldn't imagine why. The man could hear and smell things from blocks away. He cast his gaze around the walled garden as if searching for onlookers before turning to face me where I leaned against the stone wall in the corner of the courtyard. His question came without inflection. "You still think I'm scary?"

"I know you are," I answered, straightening from the stone wall and stalking toward him through the darkness. "It's one of my favorite things about you." I stopped in front of him.

His expression flickered through confusion, irritation, disbelief, and amusement before he shuttered it, raising his gaze to the stars above us and heaving a breath before locking eyes with me again. "I'm not afraid of dancing."

"Prove it."

He cast a harried glance back the way he'd come. "What? Like, here?"

"Right here."

"There's no music," he hedged.

He couldn't fool me. "You can still hear the music."

Jordan huffed a disbelieving laugh and cocked his head at me, pursing his lips like he was trying to school his features. But he lifted his hands to take one of mine and brace the other on my waist. "This is what you want?"

I beamed at him as he led me through the beginning steps of a popular modern waltz. *These well-bred rich boys and their formal educations.* I could see the appeal of including dance lessons at those fancy schools. "Yes," I answered, taking a deep breath of his smoky vampire scent and holding it in my lungs. After a few moments of rote steps and enjoying each other's presence away from the crowd, Jordan finally began to relax. He seemed to find solace in the solitude of the moonlit garden, his shoulders loosening and his expression softening. His hands gripped me a little tighter.

"What is it you like about dancing?" he asked quietly, studying my face as he spoke.

I gave him a cocky grin. "The showmanship of it," I answered. "It's a very dramatic form of courtship, don't you think?" A gentle shrug punctuated my question as he walked me in a large circle on the manicured lawn.

"Courtship?" he repeated.

I shrugged again. "I *am* part bird." Was a simple dance too much to ask? At least I wasn't some animal that fought for dominance as courtship. "You see now? This isn't so bad, is it?"

His fingers tensed on my back as he quickly glanced toward where the reception was winding down. "It's not so bad, no, away from all those eyes."

My words came out before I even processed the thought. "What if I wanted you to claim me in front of all those eyes?" Joshua thought the family would blow up over him bringing Ahmed, but so far, at least, that hadn't happened. I was a little jealous of their seemingly easy acceptance of my brother's choice of date. Maybe it could be just as easy for me and Jordan. What if I was overthinking everything and it could just be simple between us? I'd always pictured myself with children, but was that because I wanted them? Or because my society expected me to have them? What if my family just accepted him because I—my brain stuttered on the L-word, and I chose something safer—*wanted* him?

His gaze warmed and grew intense as our paces slowed, but then he shook it off, his eyes growing guarded. "You didn't seem to be having any trouble with a lack of dancing partners. I suppose the dryad could give you any number of nice sticks." He pressed his mouth into an unhappy line and stared over my shoulder into the garden, as if he were unaffected.

My laughter bubbled out of me. "Are you... jealous of *Rafe?*" The idea struck me as absurdly funny. He didn't respond, and my jaw dropped. "Jordan, he's a *plant.*" A really lovely sentient plant, of course, but... a plant, nonetheless.

"And I'm a *vampire!* Doesn't that take me out of the running just as much?" We both stopped dancing, holding each other in the moonlight while he tried to calm his agitated breathing. I watched the frustration and pain and denial flicker across his features, wanting to answer carefully, so that I could be sure I spoke the truth to this beautiful man with ink-colored eyes who had been so thoroughly broken.

"No," I said slowly. "I don't think it does."

"Why?" One word, spoken like a retort, not a question.

"Because you make me... happy," I settled on. Maybe Elara was right, and happiness was all that mattered. Even if it couldn't work in the end—if he couldn't grow old with me and I couldn't live forever with him—did that mean we should throw away the potential of what we could have? I felt that I would be ruined either way, so why not take my happiness while I had it? Jordan wasn't my type—at least superficially—but he fit me. He didn't let me push him around. He wasn't put off by my crazy. He rattled my screws in the best way. I felt whole when I was with him.

Jordan didn't move—I couldn't even tell if he was breathing—and it seemed like the gears in his head were stuck as he stared at me, stunned. He opened and closed his mouth quickly. "Sidney, I—" His expression was torn, and he never did finish his thought because shouts echoed from beyond the garden wall. He stiffened, turning toward the sound, his entire demeanor shifting in an instant.

A group was running, thundering across the grounds like a herd of elephants, then a singular shout and a thud like someone had been tackled. More shouting and cheering, then raucous laughter. I narrowed my eyes because those voices sounded familiar.

"Sidneyyyyyy! Sidney, where aaarrre youuu?"

I was going to kill my brothers.

"Put me down!" shouted Sam angrily, the oldest and *supposedly* most mature.

"I love you, man." That was Aaron.

"Dude, you're just drunk." That sounded like... Ahmed?

"We should get matching tattoos," replied Aaron.

"What if she's hiding?" asked Joshua.

"In the bushes?"

"She's been eyeing that vampire all night," said Sam. "Does he look familiar to you?"

"Sidney had better not be hiding in the bushes with some vampire!" Aaron yelled, slurring his words.

I flinched, knowing if I could hear them that Jordan had heard every word. His hand was jerked from mine, even as I tried to grip him harder. "Jordan, don't—"

"I can't, Sidney. It's bad enough getting judgment from my own family. I won't stand for it from yours too. I can't do this." And then he was gone. His scent hung there, taunting me, but he was *gone.* He moved so fast that it was like he had stepped into the shadows and disappeared.

I gritted my teeth, my eyes narrowing into angry slits, and balled my hands into tight fists as I whipped around to stomp toward the incoherent shouting coming from my brother Sam. I stormed down the path and through the garden gate, finding the whole gaggle of them in the next courtyard. Aaron was staggering around with Sam hanging over his shoulder, with Sam's head covered in some kind of dark sack. Ahmed was trying to argue with Sam—through the sack—that the airspeed velocity of a crow was higher than that of a magpie. And Joshua was lying stretched out in the grass behind them. *This, right here, is my villain origin story.*

"We found Sidney!" Aaron shouted triumphantly, too drunk to register the simmering rage on my face.

"I am going to pluck you like a Sunday chicken," I growled, kicking off my high heels, and then charged him at a dead sprint. *Some dudes just need their heads knocked,* I thought as I launched myself into the air.

It grieved me that Ahmed had to witness me taking my dipwad brothers to the ground like an angry lumberjack. Although, there's something to be said for knowing what you're signing up for when you date a person, so maybe I was just doing him a favor by revealing early on what our family life was really like. That was my justification later, at least, as I whacked the dirt from my dress and wiped my hair out of my face with the back of my hand, giving him a once over to make sure he hadn't been harmed in the scuffle. At the time, I'd just been *angry.*

"You've got a little—" Ahmed motioned to my cheek. "—dirt... right there."

I wiped my cheek on my shoulder since my hands were filthy. "Better?" I asked.

He nodded. "Better."

"Thanks." My smile for him was genuine. I kicked Sam in the ribs on my way out.

"Hey!" Sam hollered. "What was that?" The sack remained on his head, so it hadn't been a fair fight, but I never claimed to fight fair.

"That didn't *hurt,* you giant manbaby. Next time keep your gossipy suppositions to yourself, ok? You interrupted an important conversation."

"Is that what the kids are calling it these days?" Aaron asked from beneath the pile of Sam.

"Can you guys keep it down? I'm trying to take a nap," Josh said from where he was sprawled spread-eagle on the grass.

Only Ahmed was still standing, but his drunken lean told me he wouldn't be for long. *Whatever, they can sleep on the lawn tonight.* I had a vampire to catch.

Chapter 30

IT TOOK OVER AN hour of traveling to get back to Jordan's compound, and I felt like I was running on fumes by the time I arrived. I should have just gone home, but I wanted to talk with him about his reaction, and I missed my dragon. Imagine how irritated I was when I stomped my way into the building, and neither one was there.

"Where is my dragon?" I asked the dark elf, Cyrus, who manned the station of swirling spectrals and piles of calling chips in the main room.

"Hello to you too," he replied with faux cheerfulness, casting a glance at me from the hazy crowd of images whirling in front of him. "Last I saw, the little beastie was with Augustus, but he hasn't been back yet."

I hesitantly leaned on his desk. The guy still gave me the creeps—they all did, except Jordan, of course—but I was pretty sure he wouldn't eat me. "Where's Jordan?" There was no new scent of him in the entrance or stairwell, so unless he came in a window, he wasn't here. Tracking him all over town seemed inefficient when I had direct access to his office's security guy with a desk full of calling chips.

"He's at a wedding," he replied, not taking his eyes from the spectrals this time.

I squinted at him and then gestured wildly at my ballgown with my dirty hands. "I was *with him* at the wedding." Did he think I wore a getup like this on a regular Saturday night? How old were these vampires, and how quickly did ancient vampires fall out of touch with current fashion standards? "He is no longer there. You don't keep tabs on your people?"

Cyrus watched my irritated flailing with a bemused expression. "Why would we keep tabs on our employees? I can send him a message if you like, but I'm sure he'll turn up before the daysleep takes over. He is very young. He's probably out doing young people things."

I narrowed my eyes farther at the elf and his assertion that Jordan would be out doing "young people things". I wasn't even sure what that would be. Partying? Chasing girls? Running amok in the streets? What had young people done whenever this guy had been young? "How old are you, Cyrus?"

"I have two hundred fifty-six years as of my last naming day," he said proudly.

"Wowsers," I replied, trying to keep a lid on my sarcasm. It wasn't Cyrus's fault I was cranky. He wasn't terribly old for an elf, but he'd confirmed my suspicion of him being out of touch. "Congratulations? Uh, yeah, could you please send Jordan a message saying I want to talk to him? I'm going to crash in his room in case he or Augustus comes back," I said, motioning over my shoulder with my thumb.

Taking a shower was necessary even though I fell asleep standing up twice. I'd been awake since early in the morning to help with the wedding, running on not much sleep to start with, so staying awake to wait for Jordan was impossible. I was out the moment my head hit the pillow, and though I didn't remember the specifics of any of them, my sleep was plagued with nightmares. I startled awake just after noon to find myself alone and the bed empty. There was no fresh scent of Jordan in his room.

My stomach immediately sank. I'd trusted him not to ghost me and disappear again, but maybe that trust was naïve on my part. He'd made it clear that he had problems, and he'd had a habit of disappearing on me from the moment I'd walked back into his life. But was my brother recognizing him really a line in the sand?

I flopped over the side of the bed and stuck my head under to verify what I already knew—there was no dragon in the room. I hauled myself up and pulled my new leathers out of the backpack I'd left on the floor, dressing quickly with an uneasy feeling in the pit of my stomach. I didn't like this. Poking around in Jordan's office during the day felt like poking around in a crypt, which I liked even less. The common rooms were empty, so I decided to head into Seattle. At least I could keep my mind busy at the shop, since it wasn't like Jordan or his boss would come rolling in during daylight hours.

Was this who I was now? Was I obsessing over some boy and a tiny-tot dragon? *Arg!* I squeezed my eyes shut in frustration, took several deep, calming breaths, shook myself out like a dog, and jerked open the front door to the shop. "Why are you here?" I asked Elara. It was Sunday, and not only that—it was *the day* after her wedding.

"One could ask you the same question," Elara responded distractedly, her focus directed at whatever she was working on. *I should probably know what that is.*

I stalked over to her desk—giving her annoyingly sexy husband a secret handshake on the way—and grabbed the planner to catch myself up to speed. "I'm distracting myself, so I don't turn into a pathetic wretch or do something violent."

Elara set her tools down and turned to face me fully, her eyes narrowed and full of concern. "What's wrong?"

I rolled my eyes at myself and dropped heavily into my chair. "Nothing. Jordan just didn't come back to his office last night, and I'm feeling some kind of way about it, I guess. He's probably just at his apartment or tucked away in some bolt hole somewhere, but it makes me angry that he wouldn't just *talk to me* about it if something is wrong. I want to yell at him, but he's not around to yell at."

Levi's chair squeaked, and I slid my gaze over to find him leaning forward intently. "You never caught him last night?" he asked, a spark of humor in his eye and his magic buffeting me with every word. *Was I really that obvious?* I frowned at him, annoyed that I'd forgotten my enchantment ward and unwilling to explain that I had caught him, and then have to rehash that Jordan had overheard my brothers recognizing him. "He won't answer a text this time of day even if he's here in the Void, but I can go see if he's at the apartment," Levi offered quickly. I wasn't sure whether to be grateful or suspicious, but he was out the door before I could shake off the enchantment of his words.

"I need to start leaving my enchantment ward here," I grumbled. "Now, why are you working? Shouldn't you be on your honeymoon or something? Your wedding was *yesterday,* for Pete's sake. Is this my fault? Have I been slacking so much that you need to work overtime? I thought we had your schedule worked out."

"We do. It's fine." Elara seemed flustered as she returned to tinkering with—I checked the notes again—a necklace embedded with a power well. "We had a few days at the Bed and Breakfast we rented in Whitewave after our courthouse wedding. That counts as a honeymoon. I don't need a second one just because we had another ceremony for my family. I'm *not* working too much. This is fine. I'm fine. I just want some sense of normalcy right now."

All of my alarm bells went off at her little speech. I swung my chair around so I could glare at the side of her head without having to move more than my foot. She did her best to ignore me, but I continued staring lasers at her head until she finally acknowledged me, setting her tools down gently and swallowing thickly.

She heaved a huge breath before announcing, "I'm pregnant."

I rocketed up out of my chair so fast it slammed into the desk behind me with a crash. "You *what?*"

"Grim gave me a baby gift last night and told me I was pregnant, and when I got home, I took a test and confirmed it." She covered her face with her hands.

I was so conflicted my brain couldn't even process a thought. On the one hand, I wanted to scoop her up and jump up and down while squealing. On the other... "*How?*"

Now it was her turn to glare at me. "You know very well *how*," she said stubbornly.

I held my finger out at her. "I'm not asking for *details*. But I know dang well I put a bulk pack of condoms in your camping equipment. If you already ran out, I could have just made another Costco run!"

Elara covered her face with both hands again. "I didn't feel like it was worth using them. We were already married. We figured we wanted children *eventually*. Elvish and mer people both have notoriously low birth rates, so it didn't seem like it would make that much of a difference if we let whatever was going to happen... *happen*."

I erupted in laughter as I collapsed back into my chair. "But you're not *just elvish,* Elara! He's not just mer! You're both half human!" Elara was one of the smartest people I knew, and yet... *and yet*. My laughter was uncontrollable. I laughed so hard that Elara eventually lowered her hands and began to smile with me despite herself. I launched forward—quick as a cat—and snatched her against me, smushing her face to my bosom. "We're going to have a baby!" I squealed. I could already picture it. A little squishy baby with a mop of her pretty dark hair, or a tuft of Levi's blonde.

"We?" Her voice was muffled against my chest, so I released her so that she could breathe.

"Yes, *we*," I emphasized. "I'm going to be the best wine-aunt that ever lived. This child will want for *nothing*. I'm going to spoil them rotten."

She laughed at me, and I squinted at her.

"Are you a little bit excited?" I asked, trying to gauge her emotions.

"I am," she confirmed. "I'm also nervous. I really hadn't expected it to happen so fast. It's just one more thing that's changing, you know?"

Biting down on my lip as I nodded kept me from telling her under no uncertain terms that we were closing the shop and moving her permanently back into the Boundlands with a dozen guards. "So... what are your thoughts moving forward?" I asked as diplomatically as I was capable of.

"I think we're going to have to figure out another way to do this," she said with a sigh, glancing around the shop.

Oh, thank goodness. "That does seem wise," I answered as evenly as possible. "Especially if you're going to be moving towards focusing on building emitters for the government instead of this stuff, anyway, right?" I asked, gesturing toward the necklace on her desk.

She gave it a rueful glance that told me everything I needed to know about how she felt—she didn't want to give up making jewelry completely, but removing customers from most of the equation would be nice and the emitters were more important overall—but before we could discuss it, she perked up and turned toward the door.

It didn't take long for Levi to walk in with a concerned look on his face, and I braced myself for his enchantment. "Jordan isn't at the apartment."

Chapter 31

I ASSURED LEVI THAT I didn't need his help and that I'd prefer he stay with Elara. I had a weird feeling in the pit of my stomach, and the last thing I wanted was her getting involved in something shady if it came to that. Maybe Jordan had a bolt hole somewhere—some quiet, safe space he went to when he was stressed, where he was tucked away, out of the daylight. Maybe he just needed some time to himself. I hoped that was all it was, even if I didn't like it. But a creeping sense of dread crawled up my spine as I made my goodbyes and headed to the Gate in the late afternoon sunshine.

I fought with anger and anxiety the whole way to his office. He'd better not be ghosting me. Now that he'd firmly entrenched himself in my brain and my heart—had made me *feel things*—I'd have a devil of a time getting him out. He'd given me a *stick*, and now my silly crow-brain had decided that he'd made me a *promise* and he was *mine*. There was going to be hell to pay if he'd suddenly decided he didn't want me just because my brothers were jackasses. I was amped up and ready to kick something by the time I made it into his office entryway. Staring hard at the security door, I was trying to decide if I wanted to try to kick it in or knock on it, except it opened before I'd made up my mind.

"He's been taken," Cyrus said as he stepped through and pulled the door shut behind him, backing me up against the main front door to make room for him. I blinked at the dark elf, trying to make sense of his words as he crammed the black helmet over his flowing white hair. "Jordan," he clarified, his voice muffled by the helmet. "We think the Phantoms have him." He reached over my shoulder to push the entryway open, and I stepped out to clear the way for him.

"How is that possible?" I asked, fear sending my heart sprinting in my chest. I was already making a mental catalog of the weapons on my body and regretting the lack of bombs. Jordan was the strongest, fastest person I knew, other than maybe Grim. For someone to capture him... I couldn't even picture what we'd be up against.

Cyrus turned toward the side of the building to open a small hangar style door, answering me as he went. "Lucas found the location of the dragon hatchlings last night and asked Jordan to meet him there in the Old Town District." I knew where that was. Jordan and I had been scouting there together this week. Cyrus ducked inside a large garage and approached a row of pricy looking Voyagers—smaller, single person conveyances similar to Voider motorcycles. Of course, Enforcement groups needed to get around town, but I'd always thought these were a ridiculously frivolous expense. Something this size couldn't hold a conjuring stone large enough to power it over any worthwhile distance, like a train could, but at least he could transport my gear for me.

"Pop your storage compartment and keep talking," I said, stripping out of my jacket. He lifted the seat to reveal a mostly empty storage space, and I piled my jacket inside, followed by my boots, my knives, my extra knives, my back up knives, and the rest of my clothing and hair ties. *Can't forget the hair ties.* I deeply regretted that my handgun was at the shop—the Boundlands were sketchy about gun ownership in general, so I tried not to be in the habit of carrying it in—but I let it go.

"Lucas and Jordan decided to go in after the dragons themselves, but it was a trap, and the Phantoms were waiting for them. Lucas just now escaped and called for backup. That's all I know right now. Why are you naked?"

What is it with these people and nudity? "Where in Old Town?" I asked, ignoring his question.

"The Obsidian Trust building," he said, indicating an abandoned bank building. "But you should stay away from there. There's going to be—"

"I'll see you there," I answered, seizing the magic that allowed me to shift forms and snapping my wings into the air with bone crunching speed. I was out of the garage and rocketing toward Old Town before he'd even managed to back his vehicle out. Like I was going to sit around waiting for them to *hopefully* rescue Jordan? *I don't think so.*

The bank building was one of the places we'd noted increased activity around, and my stomach clenched as I thought about how hard it would be to breach the exterior. If the Phantoms were using it, they'd chosen well. The sun was just beginning to set as I sped over the dusty city, fear driving me ever faster, all my senses on high alert. The building was three stories tall and probably had several layers of basements, built of stone and wood, with windows covered in metal security bars. It was clearly in disrepair after years of disuse, but still stood stalwart on the low skyline.

I turned sharply as I coasted over it, cataloging the surrounding blocks. In front of the bank was an abandoned construction site. Other nearby shops and buildings were either closed or empty. Several streets away, a team of orcs and ogres were suiting up in what looked like Enforcement riot gear, but none of them were Jordan's crew members. Catching an updraft allowed me a wider view, and I spotted Cyrus speeding quietly along a parallel road toward the bank. He slowed and pulled into the loading bay of an old grocery warehouse down the block, and I took one last slow spin around the bank, taking careful note of the windows and what I could see inside. The front doors were heavily barricaded and most of the people I saw were trying to barricade the back entrance. What was their game plan here?

I was just turning to head for the grocery building when I heard a familiar coo from a nearby rooftop. *Oh no, Pidgy!* He fluttered his wings happily and launched into the air after me, following me all the way to the warehouse and landing on the street outside as I flew in the door that Cyrus had pulled his vehicle through. *I don't have time for your bullshit right now, little dude.* He could go find someone else to flirt with.

Crates and boxes had been pushed to the sides of the storeroom to make room for a makeshift planning area and medical triage. Augustus stood in the middle of the room talking to Cyrus and a very large ogre in an Enforcement uniform. Lucas, the lorelei, was propped on a bench, sucking on a blood bag while a medic looked at some cuts on the side of his face. *Shouldn't all vampires have rapid healing?* They were famous for it, after all. Tobias, the goofy giant guy, slept sprawled on the floor in the corner of the room with Alejandra next to him, both in full gear with helmets on. *At least, I assumed they were sleeping.* The sun was still setting, and Jordan had mentioned they were the next youngest compared to him, so they probably hadn't been able to shake off the sleepiness yet.

Huck was hanging from the baby harness on Augustus's chest, and when I flew into the room, he started flailing frantically, flapping his wings, and causing everyone to step back. The surge of affection I felt for that little monster made me breathe a little easier, but only slightly. I didn't even have it in me to appreciate the humor of staid, old Augustus wearing a dragon in a baby harness. I shifted forms and landed next to Cyrus.

"Oh, thank heavens," Augustus said by way of greeting, trying to corral Huck's wings with his arms to keep from being clobbered in the face. "He was quite fractious outside of your presence."

"Thanks for keeping him," I answered, already starting the process of plaiting my hair out of my face again. Two tight Dutch braids were probably best if I were going to end up in a fight today. "Let me get dressed, and I'll take him back from you. Cyrus?" I glanced at him, but he was already heading for his Voyager. The ogre just stared at me, confused. I gave him a grim smile. "Don't let me interrupt."

Cyrus brought me my stack of clothes and held them for me while I finished with my braids and dressed, his eyebrows drawing together as I replaced the knives in my boots, sleeves, multiple pockets and down my back. I zipped up my leather jacket and turned to Augustus, holding my hands out for Huck, and trying not to be too distracting while the ogre filled him in on where his Enforcement teams were planning to station themselves around the bank.

Augustus unstrapped Huck while I held his wings and the little dragon fought and flailed to get to me, finally launching himself onto me once he was free and clinging to my waist. I stroked his head between his horns, glad to have him back with me again.

"Are you sure you don't want us to go in first?" the ogre asked. "If they've got vampire specific traps that slow you down and keep you from healing, wouldn't we be a better fit to go in? They're barricaded in and waiting for you."

Augustus shook his head. "We'll go in. He's my crew and my responsibility. The ones with more experience will be able to fight through the blood-magic. I won't have squishy mortals sacrificing themselves for us," he explained as he continued to unhook Huck's carrier and hand it to me. The thing was pretty much done for at this point, with split seams and soaked in flammable dragon drool.

"Why are you going in at all?" I asked Augustus. "Is there anyone else in there we want, other than Jordan and the two dragons? Just set the place on fire and wait them out. The three we want are all fireproof."

The ogre stared at me like I had two heads, but it was a good plan. Augustus had his mouth open like he was going to protest and got stuck. "Hopefully it won't come to that. Our superiors generally frown upon wholesale destruction and loss of life when we have the means to send a strike team in," he finally explained. *Lame.* I wandered over to Lucas while they discussed boring stuff like logistics. The front was too heavily fortified, so they were going to go in the back, even though it meant an obvious fight. The ogre's teams would be waiting to arrest anyone who came out of the building. Since Augustus wouldn't let the Enforcement officers help, I knew he wouldn't allow me to come in with him, which meant I was free to do whatever I wanted.

Chapter 32

"You put Jordan up to this?" I asked Lucas while the medic finished taping up his face. Huck was still clinging to the front of my jacket, so I pushed him down onto my leg where he'd be less in the way. I tossed his baby carrier in a nearby trash bin—he was way too big for it now anyway—and returned my glare to Lucas.

The big lorelei sighed. "We weren't expecting the blood-magic runes, and he was too young to fight off both the enchantment and the daysleep, since it was so close to dawn. I thought we could slip in and out with the dragons without being noticed, but the Phantoms were ready for us. I promise I'll get him out. And the dragons." He looked a mess. His dark skin was crisscrossed with hastily taped, jagged cuts that made my stomach churn.

"You're going back in?" I asked doubtfully. "Why aren't you healing? I thought vampires healed nearly instantly. The blood magic runes stop your healing?"

He nodded and held up the empty blood bag. "The runes were strong, and I hadn't fed in a while. This just needs time to absorb."

"The sun is down," Augustus called. I turned to find the ogre gone and Alejandra sitting up. "Cyrus, can you see yet?"

Cyrus crouched at the table, pivoting handfuls of calling chips from one pile to another as dozens of spectrals swirled in the air around him. "I've got them," he confirmed, staring ahead at ghostly images of the bank building, the entrances, the orcs and ogres waiting on the surrounding streets to catch any runners.

"Splendid. Alejandra, I want you and Tobias in the back. Lucas, with me. They are going to know we're coming and are funneling us into the only viable entrance, so it's going to be an all-out brawl. I don't want any slip-ups tonight. Let's go get the new recruit." I frowned at him as he muttered about new immortals always thinking they were invincible. They suited up and headed out as a single unit, clearly well practiced, with decades of training together. I didn't want to get in their way or cause them problems, but I figured I could help in my own way. Counting down from thirty, I waited until they were gone before I started after them.

"Hey, where are you going?" asked Cyrus, throwing me a concerned glance over his shoulder while trying to pay attention to the tornado of spectrals.

"To get my vampire back."

"You should stay with the dragon," he argued.

"Sure thing, boss." Huck had a good grip on me, and he was a pretty sturdy little guy. *I'll bet he can give some Phantoms what-for.* His tail dragged behind me as I hobbled toward the exit.

"That's not what I meant!" Cyrus called. "You should—"

"Tell that orc team the crazy blonde girl is with you!" I hollered, cutting him off.

Pidgy was waiting for me when I stepped out onto the sidewalk, and Huck eyed him with interest. I tapped him on the snout. "Don't eat Pidgy. Birds are friends, not food." *Voider movies have the best quotes*, I thought to myself as I scanned the empty street in front of the bank. I wasn't concerned with being stealthy, I was on a different mission. Right now, I wanted to be as obnoxious as possible. If Jordan's team was going to have a hard time getting in the back because all the Phantom's attention was focused there, I could try to bring some of their attention to the front.

The abandoned construction site looked promising. I removed Huck from my leg and set him on the sidewalk next to me so I could kick open a rusted gate, hoping he wouldn't eat the empty-headed pigeon that continued to hop along behind us. Three strong kicks and it was broken, so I pushed it open and headed straight for a nearby pile of bricks. They were too large to fit between the metal bars covering the windows, but smashing them on the street reduced them to smaller chunks that I lobbed repeatedly at the second-story windows, causing Pidgy to flutter away finally. *Good riddance.* I'd never had the best aim, and most of them bounced off the metal bars anyway, but I did manage to crack two of the windows. "Hey, assholes!" I yelled at the front of the building. No response.

Looked like I needed to find a way to be louder if I wanted to provoke something. I stomped back into the construction site and spotted a three-foot length of rebar laying in the dirt. *Now we're talking.* Rebar was great because it had a good heft to it, and it was long enough that if I needed to fight with it, I could keep someone bigger and stronger than me out of arm's reach. But it would tear up my hands quickly, so I dug into my jacket pockets and pulled out my new leather gloves—*thanks Jordan*—sliding them on and snatching up the rebar along with a metal trash can lid.

Pidgy was already back on the sidewalk in front of the bank when I emerged, Huck eyeing him hungrily. "Shoo, Pidgy," I said distractedly, waving my rebar at him while I watched the windows. I'd feel guilty if Pidgy died because my pig-headed dragon toddler ate him, and I'd be even more irritated about Huck making the connection that birds could be eaten, but right now getting Jordan out took up all my brain space. I slammed the rebar into the trash can lid repeatedly like I was playing terrible cymbals. "Hey! I want my vampire back!" I yelled, hollering at the top of my lungs at the building.

I saw movement in several second-story windows and one of the first-floor ones, people peering at me from behind old curtains and stacks of whatever. "Yeah, you!" I yelled at the one on the first floor, pointing my rebar at him. "I'm talking to you, asshole! Give me my vampire back!" I dropped the trash can lid, wound up like a batter, and slammed the rebar into the metal grate in front of the window. The thing had no give, but it made a satisfying clang and the guy in the window jumped back, disappearing from view. I made the rounds of all the first-floor windows, smacking the grates with rebar and trying to make as much noise as possible, whatever I could do to be a distraction.

When I walked past Pidgy again, he fluttered out of my way, flying up into the alcove for the big entryway to the bank. His movement triggered Huck's prey drive, and Huck scrambled after him, shooting flames that arced up into the air and sprayed across the front doors. "Huck, no! We don't eat Pidgy!" I yelled as he chased after him, beating his wings and actually managing to make it several feet off the ground before crashing back to the sidewalk again, shooting flames all the while. *My baby was flying!* I tackled him anyway. "Don't eat birds, you dingus!"

The sound of crackling flames made me lift my head. Fire coated the solid wood front doors. Well, that would surely get their attention. The doors were sturdy and thick, and probably wouldn't have burned easily if not for the sticky accelerant in dragon drool, but even the boards that had been nailed over the entrance began to catch as I watched.

"Hey, Pidgy, come back here," I mumbled half-heartedly. He made good bait.

I climbed off Huck and picked him up, dropping my metal bar and trying to balance him, feeling along his throat. "What do you think, buddy? Can we get some more of that lighter fluid?" I asked him. There was a pair of lumps under his jawbone that I tried squeezing gently, and liquid shot out of his mouth, so I aimed him at the front door and sprayed until the fire had built into an inferno. Someday I'd have to figure out a way to train him to do this on command. I didn't want to drain his glands completely, so when I was satisfied with the roaring flames, I set him down and stepped back to survey my handy work. Within seconds, the entire alcove was blackened, streaks of soot reaching up the front of the building. "Good work, Huck. Even if you were just trying to murder Pidgy..."

I gave him a quick pat on the horns, but he just blinked at me a few times, obviously confused. I grabbed the rebar again, holding it like a spear and using the end of it to ram the glass from between the metal bars on the windows. It was reinforced with some kind of film, but a few good whacks and a little elbow grease yielded some cracks that I could chip away at. I continued hammering away with the end of the bar until holes had opened up in several of the windows and I could hear shouting inside. More airflow was always good for fire, right? Mostly I just wanted to be as big of an annoyance as possible, and I wanted to get *inside*.

I punctured through a third window and a man appeared in front of the glass, grabbed the end of the rebar, and tried to wrench it away from me, cursing a blue streak and calling my mother all kinds of dirty names. She would have laughed. I jerked the metal out of his hands, hopefully shredding his palms in the process. "Why don't you come out here and say that to my face, you pathetic piece of shit?" Why weren't they coming outside?

I jumped up to grab ahold of the metal grates and hauled myself up, bracing my feet against the wall and pulling with all my might, but they wouldn't budge. I dropped to the ground again and paced back to the front door, studying the framework and pattern of the fire as it ate through the wood. The door was solid and it would probably take a long time for the fire to ruin it completely, but the wood that had been used to board it up when the bank shut down was already coming apart. The gap between the two double doors had smoke pouring out from between them, so I focused on the spot next to the locks in the center of the doors and kicked with all my strength. It didn't open, but I felt the wood crunch, which was satisfying, so I kicked again and again until the door finally cracked and fell open about a foot. There was something behind it blocking it from opening all the way, but the fire from the door would spread to whatever it was leaning against.

I counted to ten, trying to give it time to spread, but all I could think was that Jordan was in there somewhere, probably injured, and I wanted him out, *now*. Kicking the other door forced it open too, widening the opening between them to about two feet. While I was trying to figure out how I was going to get inside, Huck pushed past me and scrabbled his way through the doors.

"Ack! Oh no, you don't!" I grabbed his tail before he could disappear. "The entire point of this is that we're trying to get the dragons out!" He thrashed and one of the flaming boards nailed to the doors came loose, falling close enough to my face that I was forced to let go of him. He disappeared into the interior of the building. Screaming sounded from behind the door. I stood up and kicked harder and harder—grateful for the leather boots and pants Jordan had given me—putting all of my weight into it until the open door was slamming into whatever was behind it, pushing it back a little at a time. I finally made an opening big enough to fit through and could see a large desk that had been wedged against the back of the doors. One more hard shove and I was in. I picked up my rebar and headed into the darkened front room, coughing as it filled with smoke. Several large shapes jumped over a long counter, running from Huck as he spit fire at them, and disappeared through a swinging door in the back of the room.

More shouting filtered in from the exit they'd left through. We were in a small, dirty lobby area, and Huck quickly scrambled over the wooden counter, scoring large claw marks in the carved façade as he went. I followed him over, heading for the exit in the back of the room. Huck was already sniffing at the door, which had swung shut behind the men, and just as I got to it, a heavy-set guy at least a head taller than me jerked it open again. I didn't recognize him, and he didn't have an Enforcement uniform on, which meant he was the enemy. Huck spit fire on his feet, and I hauled back—channeling every drop of fear and anger and adrenaline into my swing—and cracked him across the head with my rebar. He dropped like a sack of rocks. "That's going to leave a mark," I panted.

Chapter 33

Jordan

I OPENED MY EYES, but nothing changed since there was no light in the vault. Every breath felt like sandpaper in my lungs and a belt around my rib cage, but I knew the sun must have set because it wasn't such a fight to stay awake. I couldn't even sleep to escape the incessant pain because they might come in to try to drag me out of the vault again. The smell of charred flesh assaulted my nose from the last time they'd tried, but I took another slow breath anyway to try to focus myself, disgusting smells be damned.

The mental fog that held me in its grip while the sun was up had finally begun to clear, so I tried to take stock of the situation. Normally, I'd already be up on my feet and ready to fight, but if I had energy enough for that, I'd have had energy enough to blow this whole place sky high once Lucas had gotten out. So, I was as much on high alert as I could be while lying in a heap against the wall, fighting off the last of the daysleep, but I didn't have it in me to do much more than remain slumped in the back corner of the old basement level bank vault I was trapped in.

I closed my eyes as I thought about how much heat I was going to catch for breaking protocol with Lucas and coming in after the hatchlings without backup. His magic was all based in stealth and illusion, which is what made him such a good scout. We figured we could be in and out with the dragons and back to the compound with time to spare before daybreak. *Mission accomplished!*

My sardonic laugh turned into a rattling cough as I tried to clear some of the blood from my lungs. We hadn't counted on the Phantoms recruiting a blood mage. This was just a temporary safe house for them—a place to hide which had been thrown together after the loss of their main bunker—so it shouldn't have had any well-planned defenses. It was just bad luck that someone had tipped them off to my crew hunting them and that they'd had access to blood-magic hexes powerful enough to cripple vampires.

I'd fought through the daysleep multiple times already, just trying to stay alive. Listening to the Phantom's muffled arguments about what to do with me and Lucas after they'd trapped us, and how they'd wished they'd sold the dragons to the first prospective buyer and gotten rid of them already, and then finally their increasing panic as nightfall grew closer and they knew we'd "awaken" from our slumber soon. They hadn't realized that by that point Lucas was already awake and ready to go, and when they tried their luck right before sundown, it hadn't gone well for them.

The hatchlings shifted against each other, still curled up together in the other corner of the vault, where we'd found them. I hadn't gotten a good look at them—since there wasn't any light down here—but their breathing was labored and occasionally they sounded like they were shivering. I'd tried to create some warmth for them after we'd first been locked in, but once it became clear that Lucas and I couldn't get out, and I'd need my fire magic to defend us until we could, I'd tried to reserve it for those times the Phantoms came in while we were "sleeping".

They hadn't learned their lesson the first time, or the second or third, and the fourth time resulted in the two piles of bones still smoldering next to the vault door. Luckily, Lucas was older and able to shake off the daysleep quicker, coherent enough by the last time to camouflage himself and bolt through the open door. We'd argued about it more than once. He wanted to take me with him, but I didn't want to risk leaving the hatchlings and them being moved again. I could protect them as long as I stayed here and kept the Phantoms out of the vault, so he promised to return quickly with backup. But now I was questioning my choice to remain behind, as I choked on my own blood and tried to ignore the stinging gouges lingering on my back and shoulders.

The one *single* thing I appreciated about being a vampire—being able to heal from injuries in seconds—laid to waste by some frustratingly well-placed hexes.

Banging noises coming from outside the vault made me sit up and seize my magic, ready to torch the next person who opened the door. This time I'd hit them so hard there wouldn't even be bones left. The screams of the last intruders still rang in my ears. One more sound to add to the cacophony of my nightmares. I realized I was hissing and swallowed painfully to silence myself, straining my vampire-enhanced hearing to its limit, listening for any clues as to what was coming for me. It hadn't been that long since Lucas left, which made me suspect it wasn't my team. The taste of fear was bitter on my tongue.

"Yeah, you! I'm talking to you, asshole! Give me my vampire back!" The words were hard to make out from inside the vault—even to my hearing—but I could swear that sounded like Sidney. My heart seized as I worked to fight down the upwelling panic. What was she doing here? I'd kill anyone who touched a hair on her head.

I listened for every step, every word, every sound that could give me a hint. Two-hundred and thirty-six breaths later, a gentle tapping sounded on the outside of the vault door. I pushed myself to my feet, fighting through the pain that tried to force my throat closed and my body to the floor, ready to immolate whoever was on the other side.

"Young Jordan," came my boss's voice. "I am going to open this door, and I will make you a joyous deal. I'll promise not to make mushrooms explode from your body, if you'll promise not to make fire explode from mine."

"Deal," I answered, sagging against the wall in relief. Lucas had done it. He'd gotten out and gone for help. I lifted my gaze toward the ceiling, searching for sounds of Sidney as the lock mechanism clicked over. Blue light flooded the interior of the bank vault as the door creaked open, painful brightness adding to the pounding in my head as I squinted, trying to shut it out.

"Are you well?" he asked, shielding the crystalline torch with his fingers to spare my eyes.

"How do you stand it?" I asked hoarsely. With the blood-magic hexes choking me, making breathing, moving, and simply existing an agonizing experience, it wasn't any wonder that I'd completely succumbed once the sun rose. How was Augustus standing here like it wasn't bothering him at all?

"With age, you will learn to tolerate many uncomfortable things," he replied. His expression was visibly relieved, and his mouth twisted into a wry smile. *Great.*

I coughed and spat blood on the floor, making him wince. "Come, we have medics waiting. Allie? Tobias?" he called over his shoulder. "Be careful as you remove the hatchlings. These do not appear as robust as the one the shifter cared for."

I glanced at the dragons, finally able to get a look at them now that the space was illuminated. They were curled into a tight clump, their heads buried beneath each other's limbs, but they were smaller and more gangly looking than Huck. Maybe they were females. Or maybe the Phantoms hadn't been feeding them. The crew would take care of it. "Why is Sidney here?" I asked at the mention of her. Why was the smell of smoke growing stronger? The realization that I could hear the distant roar of flames had me staggering for the door.

"Ah, yes," Augustus answered distractedly as Tobias pushed past him into the vault. "She should probably be removed from the premises. I don't expect it will be sound for much longer."

Tobias shouted as one of Huck's siblings shot fire at his legs, but I had other things to worry about right now. I left them to deal with the dragons and stepped out of the vault, pausing to take in the vaguely person-shaped piles of pale colored fungus strewn across the basement. Two outside the vault and one slumped halfway up the stairs, completely engulfed in mushrooms. I made myself look away, not wanting more fuel for the nightmares that already plagued me. *Daymares?*

I mounted the steps, careful to avoid the fallen body littering the stairs, and then launched through the door above as I followed the sounds of Sidney's shouting about wanting "her" vampire back. The smoke was thicker up here. The fear-fueled flare of energy pushed me past the pain and fatigue, past the dread sitting like lead in my gut as I ran by offices, hallways, an old boiler room. I burst into an old work room and froze, my eyes wide at the sight of her—the object of my obsession. Soot on her face, her expression fierce with beautiful fury, Huck spitting fire while wrapped around her right thigh, Sidney was on a *rampage* with a piece of rebar longer than my arm.

Longing for her sucked the air from my lungs, and I wondered if my infatuation was as obvious to everyone else as it was to me. She swung at a wide-shouldered mountain troll like a rabid five-year-old who wanted to make sure she got every single piece of candy out of her birthday pinata. She was so focused on keeping him and a smaller goblin out of arm's reach that she hadn't even noticed that they were covered in burns and massive blisters, and she should have been too. Fire coated the far wall, the flames a deafening roar, and the smoke was thick and choking, but she was absolutely intent on her attackers. The room was *hot*, far too hot for her to be in here without injury, and fear for her safety nearly overwhelmed me, but she didn't even seem to notice.

I'd tried to stay away, not wanting to admit my desire for her. Not wanting to become attached and then be forced to endure the endless stretch of immortality without her—this one chaotic spot of hope and pleasure in my life. I was still bewildered by how quickly she'd become the center of my every waking thought. Like a moth to the blaze of a desert bonfire, I'd danced around the periphery of her. Not wanting to get too close and touch the flame, but ever lured by the brightness of her personality and beauty. She reminded me of a spark, which seemed fitting, because most people were afraid of the little fire fairies but I'd always found them charming. Sidney had that same explosive energy, the same untamed edges, the same ferocious zest for life. She was such a blinding light that it would be a form of blasphemy to snuff that out, to change her. To woo her into a life of vampirism and darkness just for the sake of my own happiness, making her an immortal so that I would never have to say goodbye. I'd only paused for a fraction of a second, but it was enough for me to see the flames licking her face and spewing from Huck's mouth, and it spurred me into action.

She coughed once, and my heart lurched, wondering what this smoke was doing to her. I lunged for the goblin closest to me and snapped his neck.

Chapter 34

Sidney

THE MOUNTAIN TROLL GAVE as good as he got. Huck was clinging to my leg again, severely impeding my ability to kick the snot out of this giant meathead with no neck and his little goblin friend. They were blocking my way into the back of the bank. Since Huck was acting as my personal flamethrower again, I decided to leave him where he was. Out of the corner of my eye I saw a flicker of movement, so I whacked the troll on his raised forearm to give myself time to glance over my shoulder. He roared at me as Jordan dove out of the farthest doorway and snatched up the goblin, quickly dropping him once more in a broken heap before I could blink.

"Sidney, what are you *doing here*?" Jordan asked as the goblin left his hands, his voice a strange rasp as he tried to make himself heard over the roaring flames.

I hit the troll again as hard as I could to make him stagger back. I needed more room. "I'm saving the princess!" I answered Jordan. "Toad had better not tell me she's in another castle!" Tiny mushrooms blossomed across every inch of the troll's exposed skin, unfurling into giant fist-sized caps as he crashed to the floor, and Augustus stepped into the room behind Jordan.

"That is *disgusting*!" I shrieked over the roar of the spreading flames, just as Jordan dove for me and Huck. He scooped me up like a child, pulling my arms around his shoulders and gathering Huck in his other arm so he could get my legs around his waist. There were cuts through his jacket all across his shoulders. "What are you doing?" I asked. This was the closest I'd been to

Jordan's neck unimpeded, so I turned my face away and tucked my head to give him more space.

"Don't shift!" was all Jordan responded with as he took off running with us in his arms.

Augustus followed Jordan as he practically flew through the building, running at the now-flaming cashier's counter in the main lobby. "How is that more disgusting than beating someone to death with rebar?" Augustus asked me, sounding miffed.

Jordan ignored him, gritting out, "Don't shift, don't shift," into my ear like a mantra as he leapt over the counter with me in his arms. His strength was otherworldly, but his voice shook, and his steps felt uneven.

The entire lobby was engulfed in flames, and I cringed away from the inferno, trying not to jostle Huck. Part of the ceiling fell in as he landed, and I felt my magic flare hot, right on the edge of shifting, but his hand came up and clamped the back of my neck—firm and possessive—stopping my shift in its tracks. But the warmth moved elsewhere, pooling in my lower belly as he rushed from the building, clutching me to his body. He didn't stop until he reached the grocery warehouse, collapsing against the wall and finally dropping onto the sidewalk in front of the building with me on his lap. I tried to climb off him, but he wouldn't let me up, tightening his arms around me and pressing his mouth to the top of my head. My brain short circuited.

Huck decided he'd had enough and squirmed out from Jordan's arm to flop onto the sidewalk. Augustus blew past us toward the side of the building. "I'll get the medic," he called.

I tried to sit up, wanting to remove my weight from Jordan. I needed to assess his injuries since he was covered in bloody cuts, but he clutched me tighter, holding me against him. "Don't leave," he said, but his words were hoarse.

I wrenched myself up anyway, his worries triggering all of my righteous indignation. "*You* left *me*," I bit out, suddenly horrified to find hot, angry tears were escaping down my cheeks. Horrid *feelings*! I took in how tired he looked and how deep some of his cuts were, and it made me even angrier. "You left me in the garden! And then you came down here and nearly got yourself killed!" I scrubbed furiously at my cheek with my shoulder, infuriated with both my brothers *and* Jordan for being dummies. It was all I could do not to bare my teeth at him in rage.

"I'm sorry," he rasped, trying to pull me closer. It was probably the only time I was going to get to cuddle him this close to his neck, so I let him, but I wasn't happy about it. My adrenaline was still pumping, and I wanted to *fight*.

"Why couldn't I shift? If you were going to insist on carrying me—wrecked as you are—it would have been a lot easier to carry a little bird." He'd still managed to jump over that counter while holding me, but why make things harder for himself?

"Smoke is bad for bird lungs," he said quietly, repeating the answer I'd given him when he'd offered me a cigarette. *You poor, sweet, foolish boy.* My heart clenched, and I melted against him, all the fight draining out of me.

"You and I are going to have a long talk once we're alone. And if you bolt on me again, I'll hunt your ass down."

He didn't respond except to press his mouth to the top of my head again, which made my heart flutter in a way I didn't care for.

Augustus came back around the corner with a uniformed medic in tow, and I turned to see Tobias and Alejandra coming up the block from the other direction with squirming dragon babies in their arms. Lucas was bringing up the rear. Tobias was cursing and trying to keep his dragon's head pointed away from him, and Alejandra was desperately trying to get her arms around the wings of the one she carried so it couldn't club her in the face.

I tried to get up again when the medic crouched to talk to Jordan, but when he tightened his hold again, I just accepted it and drooped against his chest. He needed his safety-blanket right now, and I supposed that was me. The medic would have to work around me. I eyed Augustus as he fussed over the two new dragons and brought the one from Alejandra's arms over to me.

"These do not appear as hearty as yours, I think," he stated, holding it up to Huck as he lounged on the sidewalk. He was right. Their ribs were showing, and they were noticeably smaller. They had the same black scales as Huck, but where his were shiny with an iridescent gleam, theirs were dull and rough looking. I held my hand out toward it, and Augustus brought it closer so I could feel its bone structure under its scales. Nothing seemed out of place or broken, but it seemed weaker than Huck, so I pushed some of my magic into it to give it some strength.

"The Phantoms might not have fed them," I sighed. "Try some burned rats. Hey, what's wrong with your skin?" I asked, noticing that Augustus's face and neck were covered in blisters where his leather jacket didn't cover. They weren't wearing their helmets now that the sun was down, but maybe they should have been?

"The room you were in was very hot," he said, stepping out of the way so the medic could get past him. I had to sit up after all so that Jordan could get his jacket off. Augustus glanced at my face and neck and then did a double take. "How is it that your skin is unmarred? Do you have fire resistance like our Jordan?"

My mouth dropped open, and I pressed a gloved hand to my face. I hadn't felt any pain?

"I wondered that myself," Jordan replied as the medic taped one of his deeper wounds shut.

"What does that mean? Of course I'm not fire resistant. I've gotten burns all my life," I said. Huck had flambéed both me and Joshua the night he started flaming. I pulled my glove off to wipe my face and found it black with soot, but I got distracted by the medic as he taped up some of Jordan's deeper wounds. "What are you doing? And why is he still not healing?"

The dark-haired man shot me a glance as he worked, saying, "I'm just pulling the edges together to make sure they'll heal properly once his magic kicks back in. Give him a few hours away from those hexes and he'll be just fine. Sir, we need to move you so I can check you over and address the cuts on your back."

Jordan winced as he stood, and I gritted my teeth as I caught a glimpse of how bad his back was torn up.

"Are all of the Phantoms in that building dead?" I asked. I'd go back there and finish the job if they weren't.

"All of them," Augustus agreed, trying to keep his squirming dragon contained.

"How much trouble am I in?" Jordan asked as he hobbled toward the warehouse entrance.

Augustus shook his head with the smallest sigh. "Every new immortal gets one free pass for idiocy. If that's not written in the immortal's contract, it should be. There will, however, be a department-wide mandatory meeting about following protocol to limit damage and loss of life where possible." Tobias groaned and Alejandra muttered something about newbies under her breath. "Unfortunately, Lucas has already used up his free pass." He shot a droll look at Lucas, who returned an unamused one.

I blinked a few times before patting my leg for Huck to follow us inside. "There's an immortal's contract?"

Jordan laughed. "No."

Chapter 35

THE NEW DRAGONS DISLIKED water as much as Huck had, but their dull looking scales concerned me, so I had them soaking in some warm tubs with a little antiseptic in Jordan's shower back at the compound. At least I'd gotten some food into them, although the vampires had *lost their minds* at the burned rat smell in the kitchen. *Oops.* We were stuck with them until Augustus could arrange proper rehab because I wasn't letting them go back to the refuge that allowed them to be stolen in the first place. Huck was completely uninterested in his siblings, slinking under the bed to sleep in a pilfered pile of my clothing while I got cleaned up.

I exited the bathroom and stared at Jordan, silently eyeing the taped-up cuts still crisscrossing his shoulders as he sat hunched on the edge of his bed with his forearms braced on his knees. The cuts were healing about as fast as a shifter heals, so they'd be gone before too much longer, but the fact that they were still there threw me off balance. Jordan had seemed so un-conquerable and invincible—a quiet menace who was quick as lightning even in his youth. He was faster than that now, but his speed and competence was what had drawn me to him even then. The extra dose of power and strength, paired with his new imperviousness to harm, looked good on him. But seeing him with injuries in spite of all that did something inside me. It made me mad. It made me want to protect him. It made me *crazy*.

The spark of anger flickered back to life, deep in my gut. I still hadn't forgiven him for bolting on me last night or for going after the dragons the way he did. I knew most of my anger should be directed at the men who hurt him, but it was hard to be angry with people who were already dead.

"Maybe you should bite me," I suggested.

Jordan's head shot up, his inky black eyes instantly locked on mine with a ferocity I hadn't expected. "What?" The word hit me like a whip.

It wasn't something I'd ever expected myself to offer, but staring at Jordan's lingering cuts made my chest hurt. I crossed my arms. "The medic said taking blood would help you heal faster. I'd assume fresh would work better than that old, bagged stuff."

I was flat on my back on the bed before I could blink, with Jordan looming over me and a scowl on his face. The way my stomach swooped and tightened and my heart started racing irritated me to no end. I took a deep breath, trying not to be obvious about pulling his scent into my lungs, basking in the warm, rich smell of *him* layered under the sharp, spicy scent of his blood magic. "Don't offer that to me, or anyone, ever," he said, his voice pitched low. "I will never do that to you."

I blinked at him and narrowed my eyes. His purring, velvety tone was at direct odds with his blunt words and his scowling expression. "If it's consensual—" I started, but he cut me off.

"One drop of my venom in your blood would damn you to the same darkness, the same diet, the same shadow of a future that I have. I have some control over its release, but that is not a risk that I will ever take with anyone, let alone *you*. It won't ever happen. Don't offer it again."

The desire to be obstinate just because I didn't like being told what to do warred with my racing heart, which told me just how much I liked his bossy tone. Only the knowledge that this subject was a trigger for him and I shouldn't push him on it made me bite my tongue. *What is happening to me? Who is this person who cares what someone else thinks?* My whole thought process derailed when Jordan leaned down and pressed the lightest kiss to my forehead, then brushed another across my cheek. "I'm healing just fine," he said, with a hint of humor in his voice. "Have some patience. It's taking about three hours instead of my normal thirty seconds." His quiet humor made my blood race. Until he skimmed his lips down my cheek and pressed them to my mouth—then it felt like my heart stopped altogether. I know I stopped breathing, not wanting to make any sudden moves and startle him.

He pulled back far enough to look me in the eye, and I ran my hands up his arms, wanting to maintain some level of contact. "You came for me," he stated quietly.

"And don't forget it," I said. "Nobody takes what's mine. I will chase you down every time." I gritted my teeth as that flare of anger took hold again, and Jordan seemed puzzled by it. There was something behind his eyes that I didn't understand. Some emotion that he seemed to be struggling with.

"Why?" he asked.

My fingers clenched lightly around his biceps, and this time I did bare my teeth, glaring daggers at him as I cringed into the bed. "You know why." *He had better not—*

Jordan shook his head, narrowing his eyes at me as the hint of a smile played at his mouth. "Tell me why." It was the quietest murmur I'd ever heard from this stubborn man.

I took another deep breath and made myself force the words out through my teeth. "Because I'm in love with you, jackass." I hated the wave of defensiveness that swept through me. "You gave me a *stick*," I said by way of explanation—or maybe excuse—feeling every bit as petulant as I sounded.

Jordan's laughter rang in my chest as he cupped my jaw and kissed me, softly at first and then deeply and hungrily. His lips were covetous and jubilant as he smiled against my mouth. He tightened his grip on me, and my body finally relaxed, melting into the mattress beneath him. Enjoying the feel of his heart beating against mine. This was what I needed. "I could kiss you like this for the rest of my life," I murmured against his lips, my eyes suddenly stinging. "I just wish I could kiss you for the rest of yours as well." The piercing ache at the thought of the disparity of our lifespans sucked the breath from my lungs and

I kissed him harder, a kiss that surely tasted of desperation and heartache.

Jordan broke our kiss to hold me still, comforting me and waiting for me to calm before pulling back to whisper, "You have utterly wrecked me." He stared into my soul as he said it, but the intensity in his eyes gentled and faded as he watched me, and his expression made it hard to breathe at the forlorn sadness suddenly painted across his own features. "But I can't give you what you need, Sidney. Or what you deserve. I can't give you a life, or children, or happiness."

I shoved him off me. I needed room to sit up because I wasn't having this discussion on my back. "You," I started, as I pushed myself up to face him squarely, "are worth more to me than the children we can't have." I spit the words out as I thought them, but once they were out, I realized how much I meant them. Biological children with Jordan would have been lovely, and I knew I would need to grieve the loss of that possibility at some point. But he mattered to me as a person, and my disobedient heart was too attached to walk away from him over that grief. As for my family, well, I didn't owe my genetics to the future generations of my people. I didn't have to please anyone but myself with my choice of mate. My life was *mine*, and my happiness was one more thing I wasn't going to let anyone take from me. "If you want children, we can figure that out together," I argued huffily, "but you already make me happy. And why *can't* that be enough?" I said it to myself as much as to him. I had recognized the wisdom in Elara's words adequately enough to pass them on to my brother, but it had felt selfish and fruitless to apply them to myself. *Why?* Why did *Josh* deserve happiness, but I didn't? Why couldn't I take my own advice? Jordan was enough for me.

He looked like he wanted to argue, but I cut him off. "I don't have all the answers, Jordan. I don't know how it's all going to work. All I need to know is that you'll be there for me, and you'll stop disappearing on me. Just *be with me.*" *For as long as we have.*

His mouth opened and closed several times, his gaze locked with mine as I brushed my fingers back up his arms, coaxing, pleading. His expression was torn, but I could tell he was thinking hard and fighting his own defensiveness.

I huffed an agitated breath as he wrestled with his thoughts. "Please, let me talk to my brothers. You'll feel more comfortable if they're on your side and you aren't feeling like they're out to get you."

Jordan's eyebrows pulled together in a frown, and he started to pull away from me. I slid my hands down to his wrists, keeping contact but loosening my hold so he didn't feel trapped. "They aren't going to like me," he finally responded with the slightest shake of his head.

"Sam has always liked you. He was your teammate!"

Jordan grunted, the unhappy sound so like my own brothers that I had to bite my lip to keep from smiling. "That was before... all this. I heard them say that you'd better not be with a vampire while we were dancing." I started to argue, but he kept talking. "No. I cut out my own family so that I wouldn't have to listen to their abuse. I won't put up with it from yours either." His posture was all rigid tension as he sat back on his heels.

I rubbed my thumbs lightly across the back of his wrists and worked to keep my voice gentle and beseeching. "Jordan, listen to me. I understand your choices. That's completely fair, and I agree. But I'd like the chance to *try*. I haven't even discussed you with them because you wanted your privacy, so they had no idea how I felt about you when Aaron said that. Let me talk to them and smooth things over. If they can't be kind, then you don't ever have to see them," I assured him, and I meant it. I wouldn't subject him to unkindness, even from my own family. *Especially* from my own family. "We can buy a cabin in the mountains somewhere and go be hermits together."

He stopped pulling away, but he still looked doubtful.

"But let me try. My brothers—my family—are important to me, and I want to give them a chance to get to know you without you disappearing when they inadvertently say something they shouldn't. It might take me talking to them a few times before they come around to the idea, but I believe in them." I would burn the world down for my brothers, but I was grown enough to make my own decisions, and I expected them to respect those decisions. The same went for the rest of my family.

"Come here," I said, tugging him back down with me so I could play with his hair while he thought about what I'd requested and the dragons finished soaking. Jordan was enough for me... even if we had some work to do.

We lay quietly, lost in our own thoughts as I ran strands of his hair through my fingers until he broke the silence to ask, "If I played Mario Kart with Sam, would he let me play Peach?"

This felt like some kind of test I didn't understand. "He'll let you play whoever you want, because if he doesn't, I'll pinch his nipple off."

He sat up and looked at me like *I* was somehow the crazy one.

Chapter 36

WE LEFT AT DUSK to take the first night train into the foothills. It had taken a week of searching, but Augustus had finally found a dragon-specific wildlife refuge with space for our babies. My heart was broken, and I was exhausted. I'd tried to prepare Huck for the inevitable transition, but the more I'd tried to distance myself, the more stubbornly he had clung to me. If I was laying down, he wanted to be next to me, and if I was up, he wanted to be in a nest of my clothing or following me around the compound. He hadn't even let us cage him for transport, thrashing and flaming so much that we'd all caved and found a harness for him so he could ride alongside me on the train. But of course, even that hadn't been enough, and now he was trying to prove he was still egg-sized by cramming his scaly bulk into my too-small lap. I pushed his snout over my shoulder so it wasn't in the way and stroked his neck. *It's not like I'm ever going to get to do it again.*

Lucas lifted the wool blanket covering one of the sibling's cages to peek in and immediately got flamed in the face for his troubles. "Ow! Shoot, ow!" He scrubbed the sticky accelerant off his face with his arm, and I watched with fascination as the burns healed nearly instantly. Too bad his eyebrows and the front clumps of his dark hair would take longer. Augustus watched the entire interaction with little more than a sigh before returning his gaze to the darkening windows. I guess when you'd known each other for however many hundreds of years, it wasn't worth your breath to tell someone to knock it off.

The brakes engaged with a screech, and Jordan reached over to give my arm a reassuring squeeze as we slowed to a stop at our station. I didn't respond as I waited for Augustus and Lucas to wheel their two cages out, my jaw set and the backs of my eyes burning. I hated this. My skin prickled as I stood and adjusted Huck's grip on the front of my jacket, hoisting him up higher so he could see over my shoulder as we walked. *I probably shouldn't have gotten him used to being carried like a baby in the first place,* I thought as I pushed his wings out of my line of sight again. This was going to be a good change for my little dragon. He was a wild animal, and he needed to be able to *be* a wild animal. I just had to trust that this place would treat him right and rehabilitate him well, and he'd have a long, happy dragon life—which I didn't *want* to trust anyone else with.

We stepped off the train into a little town nestled in the Ardac Mountains called Thranum's Reach. It was nearly full dark as we made our way through the town to the outskirts where the rehab facility sat on a rocky hillside. Only the double moons lit the road between the scrubby bushes that dotted the otherwise barren ground. A tree line in the distance separated the tall, wrought-iron gate that surrounded the sprawling property from the mountain peaks in the distance. A large guard with tusks and light-green skin met us at the front entrance and called for someone inside. *So far, so good,* I thought as Huck squirmed to get down so he could sniff around in the dirt. Several large mastiff-type dogs, like the ones that Elara's dad bred, came loping up to the fence while we waited for entrance, barking and making a ruckus until a dark figure approached from behind them and called them off.

He was a big, burly, handsome older man who wore his hair in flat twists against his scalp with a gray-streaked beard and a proud nose, his skin bearing a warmer brown hue than Lucas's grayish cast. He grabbed the thick metal bars of the gate and gave us a warm grin, quickly cataloging our group and the cages as he hauled it open with the help of the orcish guard. I patted my thigh to call Huck, not wanting to risk a violent interaction between him and the dogs.

"Neven Vargas?" Augustus asked the newcomer.

"That's me. Welcome," he greeted. "You'll have to forgive me for the lack of staff. We don't normally do intakes after hours, but I'm happy to make an exception for your group."

Huck clambered up my leg to wrap around my thigh, and I reached down to rub the scales between his horns as Augustus introduced the four of us and ushered us through the gate. "I'm not trying to end up with canine barbeque," I told Neven as I eyed his dogs. They were hanging back to keep some distance between us but remained intensely focused on all of us.

"Oh, don't worry about them. They're only concerned about people. They know to leave the dragons alone." He waved a dismissive hand and raised his voice slightly to address the whole group. "Why don't we head for the intake office, and I'll get some records and take a look at what we've got." The dogs dropped back as he led the way up a hard-packed dirt path to a squat stone building, talking as he walked, and explained that all the buildings on the property were fireproof and built to withstand the wear and tear that comes with caring for large animals. "I've already sent the rest of the staff home for the night, so it's just me tonight, other than the guards. Normally we have lots of hands around to help," he explained as he let us into the darkened office and turned on the lights.

Neven lifted the covers on the cages with an expectant expression as we entered, taking quick peeks in each of them and expertly keeping out of flame range when one of them got feisty. He guided us into what looked like an oversized exam room and made sure Huck's tail was in the door as it dragged behind me before letting it close.

"This is our triage and exam area. Once we're done in here, they'll move into the quarantine pens, but let's see what we're working with first," he said cheerfully, pulling out a folder and opening it to a stack of papers to make some notes. "Alright, let's do this," he said, eagerly rubbing his hands together, clearly excited about hauling a feral dragon baby out of her cage. He opened the first cage, ignored the flame the little dragon shot at him, and gripped her gently by the back of the neck to pull her out. "Looks like we've got some little Lesser Black Highlands dragons! This one is a little girl," he said as he checked her over, confidently handling her as he turned her this way and that.

He kept her wings restrained without hassle, pinching a bit of her skin on her back to check hydration. I was pleased with how shiny her scales were after they'd shed over the last few days. He calmly checked her eyes and didn't even flinch when he opened her mouth to check her teeth and she flamed him again, wiping his face with his arm without comment.

"She looks pretty good," he said tentatively, feeling along her bone structure as I had, palpating her belly, and working each limb and wing to check mobility. "A bit small for her age, but she should catch up with regular feeding. Okay now, let's put you back in your cage while I look at your sister," he told the little dragon as he put her away and then pulled the next one out to give her the same exam. "Yeah, they're both a little small, but I think they'll be okay." He cast a sideways glance at me. "So, who are your people?" he asked as he felt her bones.

It was the shifter way of asking which clan I belonged to, and it wasn't my imagination that Jordan shifted his weight so that he was closer to me. If my heart hadn't been hammering out of my chest, waiting for it to be Huck's turn, I might have laughed. *Jealous prat.* "I'm from the magpie clan."

Neven simply nodded as he loaded the second dragon back into her cage. "I'm from the bear clan. It looks like you've got a healthy little boy there," he said, gesturing to Huck. He scribbled for a few minutes in his notes and then started to put the folder away, confusing me.

"Aren't you going to inspect Huck?" I asked, pointing down at my scaly leg barnacle.

He put the folder away anyway and turned to look at me. "Oh, sure, I can if you want me to. Set him right up here," he said, patting the metal exam table.

I frowned at the man as I set Huck in front of him, but he only had eyes for my dragon, cooing at him and checking over his body. For his part, Huck sat somewhat patiently, looking like a disgruntled cat while Neven gave him his exam. I turned to glance at Augustus, who merely shrugged and looked as confused as I was.

"He looks great!" Neven concluded, handing Huck back to me with a smile that looked like he was trying to be reassuring. "Good size, beautiful scales, a very calm personality. You've done a great job with him. He's going to be a very large male someday—for his species," he clarified.

Jordan coughed. "So, large house sized instead of small house sized?" he mumbled.

Neven nodded. "Exactly so. Perhaps you all could help me take them over to the quarantine pens, and I can show you the grounds as we go? I don't normally give tours, since we're trying to limit the dragons' exposure to people in an effort to rewild them, but since they're sleeping now, we should be fine." He led us out of the exam room to the back door of the main building and held the door for us as we filed through. I hoisted Huck against my chest, wrapping my arms around him with my heart in my throat, grateful for a few more minutes to say goodbye.

The pack of dogs found us and trotted at a respectful distance as we followed Neven through wide, meandering paths between enormous, sturdy-looking pens with high roofs made of iron bars to keep their occupants inside.

"Can you tell me about your facility's security measures?" Augustus asked Neven as we walked, pushing the wheeled cart with one of the dragon cages in front of him. "Have you ever had any dragons stolen from the property?"

"We've never had anything stolen, and I'd have a hard time imagining anyone trying. We have the fences, and the after-hours security team, and the dogs live here full time, but all of that is rather redundant in my opinion. Anyone who stepped foot on the property unannounced would be dragon food," he explained dryly. "Here we are," he said, approaching an outbuilding with a small, fenced yard. "This is one of our quarantine areas for new residents." *I guess this is goodbye.* I couldn't hear what else he said over the blood rushing in my ears as I squished Huck against my chest and Jordan rubbed light circles on my back with his hand.

Chapter 37

"Yes, so this is where the girls will stay for a few weeks," Neven said in response to something Augustus had asked him, "and then after their quarantine period is over, we'll move them nearby some other dragons they can learn from. They'll stay in a caged run while they practice hunting and put on a little size, and then we'll eventually release them farther up in the Ardacs."

"Just the girls?" I asked, suddenly panicked as I latched onto his remark. "Where is Huck going to go?" I was already picturing him in some cold, dark pen all by himself... making his squeaky baby dragon cry to call for me in the middle of the night. No one would keep him company or pet him between his horns when he was lonely. My fight-or-flight response was nearly overwhelming, and since I couldn't shift and carry Huck in my bird form, I was ready to start donkey kicking every person within kicking range. *Except maybe Jordan.*

Neven turned to me with his eyebrows pulled together in confusion. "Who? Your little guy?" he asked, eyeing the way my hand wrapped around one of Huck's tiny horns as he rested his head on my shoulder. The older man shook his head at me. "Oh, no, that dragon isn't releasable. You're stuck with him."

I stumbled backward into Jordan's chest in my shock, and he braced me with a hand on my waist. "Why isn't he releasable? He can hunt! I've seen him do it! I know he's habituated to me, but that's why they spend time here without contact with people—to *rewild them*."

But Neven was already shaking his head again. "That dragon is yours, ma'am. If he hasn't already marked you, I'll eat my hat."

I frowned at him because he wasn't wearing any hat. "What mark?" I asked him obstinately. But that reminded me of something Grim had said. *"Do you mind if I ask how you've come to bear a dragon's mark?"* I didn't have any marks!

"A dragon's mark." He nodded down at Huck. "You didn't realize?" he asked, searching my face with a hint of incredulity. "Dragons mark their favorites—especially shifters—by sharing their magic with them. Their resistance to fire and disease, their near immortality. If you think about it, it wouldn't do for a dragon to have a beloved hoard that wouldn't last as long as he did! He's clearly imprinted on you. You gave him some of your magic at some point, didn't you?"

I tried to think back, sure that I had, but I was still trying to make sense of what he was saying. I gave my magic to any Boundlands creatures that needed it. Why be stingy with something that I could regenerate? "I did, yes, when he was still in his egg. I gave my magic to all three of them, but more to Huck. He was so fragile, and we didn't think he would make it." I hugged him closer, remembering how Elara had panicked at how weak his presence was inside the shell when we'd found him. Huck snarled at me indignantly to let me know my grip was too tight, and I loosened my hold.

Neven nodded. "And you've noticed that it's hard to be away from him, right? It feels like something's wrong?"

"But that's just because I'm worried about him!" I argued. "He's so little, and he cries for me when I'm gone," I explained, but my voice was already faltering because I wasn't sure I was right anymore. "But I can't be resistant to fire because I got burned by him when he first started flaming a few weeks ago!"

Jordan cleared his throat behind me. "You stood in those flames at the bank that blistered Augustus's skin from ten feet away."

I shot a look at Augustus to find him staring back at me with a calculating expression. But Neven just shrugged. "It can take a few weeks for the mark to develop fully."

It felt like bile was rising in my throat. "Did I ruin his life?" I asked, clutching Huck a little tighter again. Sure, I loved having the little guy with me, but was this the best thing for him? Wouldn't he be happier living wild like he was meant to?

Neven gave me a crooked grin. "It sounds like you *gave* him life. If he was already dying and wouldn't have made it, then you did the best you could for him, and this is a better life than no life. It's just going to be a much longer caretaking task than you anticipated. Much, much longer."

"How long?" I asked, feeling lightheaded.

"Well, we suspect they live for hundreds of thousands of years, but because their life span is so long, we haven't been able to track it accurately," he said with a slight chuckle.

"And you think I'm going to live that long?" I squawked.

Neven's whole face transformed into a wide grin, his eyes crinkling at the sides like he thought I was adorable. "I do believe so, yes. Especially if what your vampire says about the fire is correct. I'll be happy to sign off on the paperwork you need to finalize for permanently keeping the little guy, since he surely won't tolerate anyone taking him from you." My heart fluttered at the way he said "your vampire", racing at the implications of what he was saying. Was it truly possible that I would be able to love Jordan not just for the rest of my life, but for the rest of *his*?

"But how can you be sure? How do you know all this?" I asked, fervently wanting to believe him, but afraid to get my hopes up. I couldn't even look at Jordan, or Lucas, or Augustus. It felt like I had tunnel vision and the whole world had narrowed down to Neven's amused face.

"Oh, well, because I have one myself," he answered with a self-deprecating little shrug. He placed two fingers under his tongue and whistled shrilly, and then the ground began to rumble. I felt the small hairs on the back of my neck stand up as a large shape lifted into the sky just behind the tree line, the sky darkening as it rose and blocked out the distant moons. Enormous leathery wings created a breeze over us as it cruised low above our group, pulling them up sharply to slow its landing, and then a flurry of beating that allowed it to touch down softly. The ground still shook when the huge dragon landed on the wide path just beyond the quarantine pen, his muted red scales softly reflecting the moonlight. The whip of his tail flicked out and smacked the metal bars and his slitted pupils, so much like Lucas's, narrowed on our little group as he loomed over us in the darkness.

My body decided I was too close to being a dragon snack as I watched flames flicker in the back of his open mouth and smoke curled out of his nostrils, but just before I felt my bones crunch with the snap of my shift Jordan's hand flew out and clamped on the back of my neck. It felt like my brain reset at the contact, but considering I was holding Huck, it was probably for the best that he kept me from shifting.

"How do you do that?" I hissed at Jordan, unable to tear my eyes from the dragon's gleaming teeth or the sharp jut of horns that rose into the night sky.

"I can smell your adrenaline spike," he muttered.

The dragon's shoulders were probably fifteen feet from the ground, with his head towering above that on a thick, meaty looking neck that was covered in overlapping spikes. I couldn't imagine trying to feed something that big. Huck beat his wings and thrashed in my arms, and the girls joined the chaos by sending panicked spouts of flame in the direction of the towering dragon.

"Sorry, I forgot how insecure the little ones can be around Ashtaroth," Neven said, quickly leaning over to adjust the covers on their cages so that they couldn't see out anymore. "Sorry Ashtaroth! Go on home. We don't want to scare the babies," he called, waving a lazy hand at the massive creature.

I expected the dragon would launch himself back into the air, but it released a puff of smoke and bent its mass nearly in half to turn around on the pathway and lumber back the way it came. Huck was still flailing dramatically, so I pinned his wings and clucked at him to try to calm him down. His little heart was racing even faster than mine.

"How long before they get that big?" I asked, turning to Neven with my eyes wide.

"Oh, I got Ash a little over six thousand years ago,"—I choked on my own tongue— "but I'd say he reached maturity at around the century mark. Dragons get big fast because their bulk helps protect them from predation by other dragons, and your little guy will end up bigger than Ashtaroth. By the end of his first year, yours will be about your height at the shoulder, and within ten years, he'll be the size of an average bedroom. Then he'll slow down a bit and end up about the size of a large house in a hundred years."

It seemed impossible that Huck would grow that fast and live that long, and that I was supposed to be part of that journey with him. "I'm going to need a new place to live."

Jordan, Lucas, and Augustus helped Neven load Huck's sisters into their new pen while I stood, holding Huck, who was finally starting to loosen his grip on me. I let him slide down just a little bit so I could stare at his adorable, squeaky, disgruntled face in awe. Did he love me? Could dragons love? He was sharing his magic with me, and he wanted to be with me, so to me that seemed something like love. I leaned down and kissed him right on his little dragon snout, and then promptly coughed and spat on the ground because he tasted like kerosene smells.

"Feel free to come back any time," Neven told me when he waved us off. "I'll help you with your paperwork and answer any questions you have."

Our group was quiet as we made our way back to the train station, and I was grateful for the time to sort through my thoughts, until Lucas said, "He's got a badass dragon named Ashtaroth, and you named yours *Huck*?"

I stuck my leg out and tripped him.

"You deserved that," Augustus said dryly as Lucas stumbled.

Once we neared the train station, Jordan took my arm and pulled me aside, telling the others, "You guys go on ahead. We'll catch the next train." I was startled to hear a tremor in his voice, and when I looked up as he tugged me into the shadows around the side of the building, I was shocked to find his eyes glassy.

"What's wrong?" I asked through the sudden tightness in my throat as he settled against the stone wall and tried to gather me into his arms. Huck gave a resentful squawk at being crowded and quickly ditched out to wrap around my leg instead, freeing up my front for Jordan.

"I just... I'm having a moment," he said, his voice tremulous and breathy. He pulled me closer and tucked my head under his chin, wrapping his arms firmly around my back, so I snuggled in and wrapped my arms around his waist. "Everything that man said is a dream come true for me," he paused to press a kiss to the crown of my head before continuing, "but I'm half-afraid of believing him. It sounds ridiculous when I say it out loud." He held me tighter and rested his head against mine. "And I never thought I'd be so grateful to some rowdy, winged lizard," he said, giving Huck a little boop on his snout with his finger. "I need a few minutes to put my heart back in my chest before dealing with anything else."

A few minutes to snuggle Jordan in a dark alley was definitely something I could do. In fact, it sounded like I might even have a few thousand years to spare for such activities.

Chapter 38

Jordan was becoming more comfortable with me riding on his shoulder when I was in my bird form, but even so, he didn't like sudden movements. I was doing my best to hold utterly still at the moment anyway, as his team filed into a meeting room together and took their seats around the conference table. I didn't know what it was going to be about, but since I wasn't part of his team, I didn't really belong here, and I was hoping they wouldn't realize I was a fly on the wall—err, magpie on the shoulder—and kick me out. Because I was nosy. Augustus took his seat directly across from Jordan and made direct eye contact with me before smirking and going back to his notes. *Ha!* That meant I got to stay. I puffed up my feathers in triumph.

Elara was in the early stages of selling the shop to a human lady who was hoping to keep some of our magical customer base and wanted to keep some of our products stocked on a consignment basis. This was great for Elara because it allowed her to keep making the occasional jewelry or magical trinket, but she wouldn't be taking custom orders anymore and that freed up her time to spend on building magical emitters for government rescue services. She still needed me—I sourced materials for her and ran her books—but since we didn't have customers to deal with, I'd been spending a lot more time tucked away with Jordan during the day and bumming around with his team at night. I was like the magpie mascot they never knew they needed.

Jordan reached up to stroke my feathers, and I flattened against his shoulder, tilting my head to achieve maximum petting benefits. *Aw yiss.*

Augustus cleared his throat. "New assignments," he began. "Tobias and Alejandra,"—he passed them packets of papers as he spoke—"a suspected ring of Phantoms is moving fairy dust in South Sands. Lucas and Jordan,"—more packets doled out—"lengthy Enforcement investigations haven't found any evidence that portal guards allowed the dragon eggs that Sidney found into the Void. There's a possibility that a new portal maker has been recruited by the smugglers, and if that's the case, I need you to find out. That magic is exceedingly rare, but that doesn't remove the possibility. Oh, and"—one more packet landed in front of Jordan—"do take Sidney with you. Bird shifters used to work as scouts in ancient times, right? I figured, since she'll be sticking around anyway, we might as well put her to work. It'll be nice to have a pair of eyes in the sky." His eyes betrayed a small smile that didn't quite touch his lips. Jordan opened my packet and held it up for me to see a hiring contract. He also wore a hint of a smile, which meant he was in on this. *That sneak.* I bristled with excitement, but had one hang up.

I poked my head above the page so I could see Augustus. "Part time. I still have work to do for my current job."

He inclined his head in acknowledgement. "Whatever you need." *Yay!*

Scratching sounded at the conference room door, and Allie stood to open it, letting Huck into the room. He'd been sleeping under Jordan's bed and must have just woken up from his nap. He trotted in, dragging a pair of my pants like a kid dragging a blankie, and quickly settled under the conference table as Augustus went back to doling out instructions for our future assignments.

And Jordan resumed his petting.

"So, what do you think?" I asked my oldest brother. Sam stood at a distance with his hands on his hips, looking out at the gorgeous view afforded by the hill we stood on. Craggy, sand-covered hills, dotted with the occasional low scrub brush, stretched for miles around us. The sun silhouetted his short cropped blond hair so that it looked like he was glowing when he turned to look at the ramshackle stone house again.

"I think it looks like a dump," he said gruffly around the twig of honeywood he was chewing on.

"Right... but is it a fixable dump?" I asked. It looked like an exciting dump that was chock-full of possibilities to me.

Elara had completed the sale of the shop and moved her operations into her townhouse. It was crowded and not ideal, but it was a temporary solution while we worked on a long-term fix. This parcel of land—we were hoping—was the long-term solution. It was a massive piece of property in the Ardac foothills with a reasonable commute to Dry Gulch. Elara and Levi were discussing building some kind of mansion farther down the hill, but she said this little stone house that was left over from some long-ago hermit would just sit empty unless I wanted it. And I *wanted* it.

I needed somewhere to escape to, and soon. Jordan's company living quarters were a nice place to crash, and his team was great, but I'd quickly agreed with him that living there permanently wasn't sustainable. I loved living with my younger brother, but I couldn't keep Huck there, and Huck wanted to be with me. Jordan had his apartment with Grim in the Void, but we couldn't take Huck into the Void, and Jordan *also* wanted to be with me. Hence, the dilemma. This, a stone house that wouldn't burn down around us, close enough to Elara and Levi's new residence that Huck would eventually consider their house part of his territory—and thereby worthy of his protection—with enough land that he could rampage around without destroying civilization sounded like the perfect solution.

Sam stretched his bulky, muscular frame before ambling over toward the old stone construction again. "Plumbing it won't be fun, but I think we can do it." Having family in construction was such a blessing.

I squealed and tried to jump up and down, making Huck squawk and flap his wings as he clung to my leg. He'd been fine on the train ride out here, but once we made it to the wide-open skies in broad daylight, he had scrambled up my leg and refused to let go. No good places for a little dragon to hide out here, I guess. Luckily, there were some rocky overhangs in the cliffs right behind the house that were sizable enough for him once he got too big to fit into the house with us.

"You gonna carry that little guy around everywhere?" Sam asked, gesturing at Huck with his twig.

"I'm hoping he'll return the favor once he's bigger," I muttered, reaching down to stroke Huck between his horns as I hobbled up toward the house to look inside again. It was just a few rooms with stone walls and the clay tile roof had fallen in, but that was repairable and there was space to add on to the house if we ever wanted to later.

Sam dusted off the rocks that made up the framing for a front window and leaned on them to look inside. "It's gonna be a lot of work, but I guess it's better than living somewhere your new pet could torch."

"He's not a pet," I said primly, with a little pat on Huck's snout. "He's my key to immortality." I raised my nose in the air, pretending to be haughty, and then ruined it by stumbling over Huck's tail. My brother laughed at me and helped me hobble over to the entryway so we could use the front step as a seat. It was a tight squeeze since he was such a moose, but he put his arm around me to make room. I laid my head on his shoulder and snuggled against him, enjoying his freshly showered scent and the dab of aftershave he always wore. There was nothing quite like big brother snuggles. Or maybe just Sam-snuggles because you couldn't pay me to snuggle with Aaron. He was always trying to stick his armpit in my face. Huck took the opportunity to climb off my leg and dart into the ruins of the house to look for rats.

"Yeah, I guess immortality's worth putting up with a little house torching," Sam teased.

I wrinkled my nose.

"It's not worth the house fires?" he questioned in response to my facial expression.

I shook my head. "No, that's fine." *What's a little house fire now and then, anyway?* "I adore Huck, and if he can't be released, I'd keep him no matter what. Immortality feels... scary. Like it's too big. I don't know what eternity *means* for me yet. I love that it ensures I don't ever have to say goodbye to Jordan, but I don't like the thought that I'm going to outlive everyone in the family." A lance of pain stole my breath at the thought of my loved ones growing old and eventually passing without me, and I suddenly had a taste of the separation Jordan felt from society. I could keep him, but there was a cost.

Sam had been crushed for Jordan's sake when I told him what had happened to him, but still seemed unsure about me *being* with him. As I suspected, Sam had been too drunk to recognize Jordan at Elara's wedding reception. Or perhaps Jordan had done too good a job of hiding. My brother had promised to try to have an open mind, not only for my sake, but because he cared about Jordan and wanted good things for him too. Aaron and I were still at odds about it, but we were always at odds, so that was nothing new. He'd come around eventually. I still needed to talk to my parents and the rest of my family, assuming Aaron hadn't run and tattled to them immediately—which I wouldn't put past him. Josh was firmly in my pocket and promised to back me up whenever necessary. *I should sic him on Aaron... or maybe our mom.*

Sam squeezed me a little tighter. "Ah, Sid. You were always going to outlive everyone in the family. You're the only one of us with any sense," he said gruffly. He lifted his arm to wrap it around my head and squish my face against his burly chest. I tolerated it for two seconds before jabbing him in the ribs, making him release me. "But look at it this way," he continued, "you'll get to be the family matriarch who swoops in every few hundred years to give the great-great-grandkids dragon rides. That's pretty cool, right?" His boyish smile made my heart squish. Sam was such a cutie. I loved my brothers so much.

I sighed as I settled back against his side. "Well, it won't be *my* great-whatever-grandkids, but I suppose I could be convinced to keep an eye on yours." The picture he painted did sound pretty badass. Jordan and I could travel the world, keep an eye on our families, flit in to drink all the wine and give people something to talk about, and then flit away again. That didn't sound half bad.

"Does that bother you?" Sam asked with that twig clenched between his teeth again. "That you won't have kids?" he clarified.

"I don't think it's really sunk in," I answered honestly. "I'd always assumed I'd have kids, and part of me is sad that I won't get to realize that assumption. But mostly I'm sad for Jordan because it seems like something he wanted, and it was stolen from him like everything else. If we decide we want to grow our family in the future, there are always other options we can look into, but I think for now I'm content to just *be.*"

We sat for a while, watching the setting sun tinge the sky pink, until Sam finally grunted. "Alright, sis, I love you, but I'm getting hungry." He gave me another squeeze before hauling himself off the step.

"You're always hungry," I grumbled. But I wanted to get back to Jordan. He'd been more likely to wake up ready to fight ever since he'd been captured by the Phantoms, and I didn't like the thought of him being alone when he was sleeping. I knew he was safe at the compound, and it had been necessary to bring my brother out to the property so we could look at it in the daylight, but I still felt uneasy. "Let me find my scaly little rascal," I said as I rose from our stone seat.

"Come on, Huck," I called as I stepped into the rubble of the front room. He clambered out from behind the pile of debris and tiles littering the floor and came right to me. "That's a good boy," I told him with a little pat on his head. Before we could leave, there was one thing I wanted to do. I pulled one of the sticks Jordan had given me out of my jacket pocket and laid it on the ledge of the windowsill before weighing it down with one of the broken clay tiles. It wasn't the first stick he'd given me—that one was too special, still tucked away in my vase at home. But this one was me putting our first mark on this little house and calling it mine.

"That's a nice stick," my brother commented, and then we made our way back down the hill.

Epilogue

Jordan

THE EVENING SUN IS finally beginning to loosen its grip on me, and I stare at the ceiling, trying to sort through the scents and sounds assaulting my senses. There are too many people in my new house, and they all smell like they're related to Sidney. Well, most of them. I also smell Levi and Elara, which means I can expect to find a picture of the wolf-boy from Twilight taped to the underside of my toilet lid. Or maybe he'll switch it up and use Bigfoot again.

Sidney's footsteps approach our door, and she quietly cracks it to peek in at me. I close my eyes again, pretending to sleep. The door creaks open farther, and a flurry of footsteps give me just enough warning to brace myself for her impact as she lands on top of me.

"I know you're awake," she says quietly, though her arrival was anything but. "Your guests are waiting."

I frown at her in the darkness of our room and wrap my fingers around the back of her neck in the way I know she likes, enjoying the feel of her shiver. "They aren't *my* guests," I mutter, pulling her toward me so I can taste her mouth. Her lips are hope and pleasure as she relaxes into me and matches the pace of my kiss, and I could swear this is what love tastes like. The sound of her heart rate increasing as her tongue flicks against mine and her chest heaves against me turns my hands into grasping things that want to clutch her tightly and haul her deeper into the darkness where no one will bother us. "Let's just stay here until they all go away," I growl against her mouth.

She laughs, and my heart flutters pitifully at the sound. "We can't. It's our housewarming party. My grandmother cooked for you. I don't know if you can actually eat any of it, but just make some appreciative noises and pretend to be grateful," she whispers against my bottom lip. She laughs again as I groan out my dismay.

This is one of the hazards of becoming a magpie's mate, I suppose. Social creatures that they are, they come with an extensive accompaniment of *family*. Especially this one. Sidney tells me not to pout as she climbs off the bed and tries to pull me up, careful not to bump the precious vase of sticks on her nightstand. As if I can't just give her more. "It's just a few hours," she says, "and then you can drag me back to your lair and have your evil way with me."

With that promise, I haul myself from our comfortable bed and trip to the bathroom to make myself presentable. As I suspected, a teenage werewolf stares at me from under the lid of the newly installed toilet.

A few moments later, I creep into the living area to find Levi and his heavily pregnant wife seated on the couch. Sidney's youngest brother, Josh, is in a chair nearby, peppering Elara with questions about the dragon magic she can feel on my mate. In the small kitchen, Sidney's diminutive, white-haired grandma is bent over the table instructing Josh's boyfriend about something she's pouring into a baking tin. Sidney's mom—a stocky, muscular woman with tanned skin and short, blond hair is getting a workout pulverizing something in a mixing bowl. There are a lot of people in our small house, and I can hear more in the yard.

The kitchen door slams open, and Sidney's dad stomps in, bringing in the scent of meat cooking on the grill, and pulls his hat off—whacking it against his thigh to knock the dust off. James is balding, and about the same height as Sidney and her mom. I have no idea where her brothers get their towering height from. "Sharon, I give up!" he grouses. "These boys are squirreling around every which way, and I'm not going to stand out there waiting for them anymore."

Sidney's mom glances at her husband and shrugs. "I don't know what you're expecting me to do about it. They're your kids through and through," she says with her usual level of exasperation before returning her attention to her mixing bowl.

"Dad, sit down," Sidney tells him as she breezes into the kitchen. "This is supposed to be a party. You guys have been out here nearly every day for months, working on the roof and the plumbing and everything else. Let them have their fun." She presses a kiss to the top of his head as he takes a seat at the table and pours him a drink of lemonade. Such a different relationship than I had with my own parents growing up.

Boisterous laughter echoes outside five seconds before the door is thrown open again and Sidney's dark-haired brother Aaron steps inside clutching a cloth bag with something moving in it. "I've got a bird in a sack!"

Sidney jerks upright, instantly angry. "You leave Pidgy alone!"

"Who's Pidgy?" Aaron asks. "I've got Sam." He's clutching the top of the sack closed while the bottom flops around, muffled squawking sounds coming from inside.

"What's up with the flirty pigeon anyway?" Sidney's dad asks over his shoulder. "He's fixing to get eaten by that dragon."

I move to the window to look outside, knowing Sidney will be unhappy if he eats a bird. Huck is laying on some exposed rock next to the house, enjoying the residual warmth from the sun. The pigeon in question is sitting on Huck's back, currently being thoroughly ignored.

"He followed me here from Dry Gulch one day and never left," Sidney grumbles. "They seem to have made some kind of peace." As I watch, Pidgy jumps down and begins to do a weird little dance in front of Huck, bowing and vocalizing. Huck doesn't even bother to open his eyes.

The energy in the kitchen is a little too overwhelming for me, so I slink back over toward my old roommate and take a seat in a chair across from Josh as he excuses himself to grab a drink. Elara looks mildly uncomfortable, though whether due to her stage of pregnancy or due to also being overwhelmed by watching Sidney's family hustle and bustle about, I have no idea. Levi is ignoring all of it, engrossed in the Chuck Tingle novel that Sidney instructed me to hide in his room.

"What are you reading?" I ask, feigning ignorance about the book he's holding.

Levi reaches up without looking and pushes the embroidery hanging behind him askew. It's the terribly stitched, "Home is where the vampire is," gift he made for me. Sidney insisted on bringing it to our new house when we moved in.

"I'm just killing time waiting for you to get your ass up so we can play some Settlers," he mumbles. He reaches into a duffle bag at his feet and pulls out my favorite board game, setting it on the coffee table in front of him, and then turns the page of the book.

This party just became a million times better. "I guess it's good that Grim couldn't come," I joke. He's the *worst* sheep thief.

Levi smirks because he *knows*. "He sent a housewarming gift." This time he does set the book down, balancing the open pages on his knee so he doesn't lose his place, and reaches down to pull out the gift. A package of rock salt, a little pot of sage, some strongly scented incense.

"What the hell?" Sidney asks from the kitchen, stalking into the living room to peer at the objects on the coffee table. "Is he trying to tell me our new house is haunted?"

Levi picks the book back up and finds his place as he answers her. "Is that what salt means? I'm pretty sure he just wanted to gift you some cooking and house stuff."

Sidney jerks back, blinking at Levi repeatedly before shaking her head to clear it. "I forgot to put my ear cuff on," she says, referring to the enchantment ward she wears to block his siren's magic. I've never had a problem with it myself, so I guess blood magic must block it on its own. She stumbles toward our bedroom, where she keeps her jewelry, pointing at the table as she goes. "That's ghost stuff, Levi! People use that to keep ghosts out! A reaper would know that, right?" Levi shakes his head and continues reading, and I exchange a look with Elara, because now we're going to be fighting all night about whether there are ghosts in my house and Grim is subtly trying to tell us something.

Josh drops back into the seat across from me again, cup in hand this time. "Oh, I love this game!" he says excitedly. "I can't wait to steal all your sheep!"

"Jordan!" Sidney's grandma walks to my side, handing me a wine glass full of blood that she probably shouldn't be handling. I don't know her real name; she instructed me to call her "Grandma" the first time I met her. "I made you a blood pudding, and a blood sausage, and some blood cakes," she says, patting my arm.

Her family has been more welcoming to both me and Josh's partner than any of us expected them to be, Sidney included. But her mom still declared that she didn't care how it happened but she expected some grandchildren from someone, at some point, and no, Huck didn't count. Sidney's response had been to nominate Sam for that job and run from the room.

"Thank you so much," I tell the older lady, oddly touched that she would try to make food that I might be able to eat, and she smiles.

"You're a good boy," she declares, nodding to herself, and walks back into the kitchen.

Sidney threads herself through the living area and drops into my lap, the ear cuff now firmly in place. "Aaron!" she hollers, even though the house is the size of a shoebox. "Let Sam out of the sack and come play Settlers with us! Hm, I think we're going to have to play teams." She leans back against my chest as Elara whispers to Levi that she wants to learn how to play and picks up the instructions for the game... and my heart is strangely full.

*

Want more of the Boundlands crew? Keep reading for a preview of Grim's book, Seduction of a Psychopomp!

Preview for Seduction of a Psychopomp:

Erogenous Hand Holding and Other Ways to Tame your Reaper

Grim

It was snowing when we exited the portal into the southern courtyard of my family's estate in the Boundlands, and I let my staff dissipate along with the portal behind us. Snow wasn't unexpected this time of year, as the castle had been built into the craggy slope of a northerly mountain, but the chill felt unnaturally sharp tonight. Loud clanging from an outer bailey rang through the night air as we made our way to the main keep, indicating there was a sparring match in progress even though the sun wasn't up yet. Someone was restless. My sister 'tsked' at the noise but held the door open for me with only a glare toward the bailey.

The smell of my childhood home greeted me—cold stone and warm bread—and I felt some of the tension I always carried in my shoulders loosen as I stepped inside. The familiar halls of the keep were open and vaulted. They had been updated to the Renaissance-Gothic style that had been in favor during my mother's youth, but even the original castle had been built large enough to be comfortable for someone my size. My sister was considerably smaller than me—though she was tall for a woman at just over six feet—but even she looked perfectly suited to the space as she walked beside me. At just over seven feet tall myself, I was always relieved to return to the places in the Boundlands that were sized appropriately... whether they were meant for other reapers, orcs, ogres, or giants. Humans in the Void built structures that seemed so small, comparatively.

Yelena led me past the sculpted bust of an ancient elvish ruler whom my great-grandfather had been friendly with to a servant's staircase tucked away in the back of the keep, likely trying to dodge small talk with anyone who might be up. She swept up the stairs ahead of me, shoulders back and head held high as she turned into an upper hallway and knocked on the door to our grandmother's study. I turned a questioning look on my sister as we waited to be granted permission to enter, but she ignored me, looking for all the world as though she were preparing to march into battle. Maybe she was.

"Come."

Yelena pushed the heavy door open and paced into the study without a backward glance. Grandmother Zdenka was seated at her oversized wooden desk, writing with an old-fashioned quill in one of her ledgers, the space lit only by candlelight. I'd provided her with numerous modern pens, but she always said she preferred the feeling of a well-made quill tip as it scrawled across the page. Now, as I watched her cap the pot of ink and replace her quill in its holder, the image was charming enough to make me regret my prodding. Let her enjoy her old things.

My grandmother wasn't the soft, round, wrinkled woman that most people called to mind when they thought of "grandma". She was sharp angles with an ageless grace, a tall woman with the same raven-dark hair that she'd passed down to all her grandchildren, currently worn in a low twist at the nape of her neck. Her skin was smooth and unblemished, and to glance at her you might be forgiven for assuming she was perhaps close to my own age—somewhere in her early thirties, maybe a few years older or younger. But once you looked into her eyes there was no mistaking the millennia of wisdom she carried. Those same eyes fixed us with a familiar intensity as we entered her study.

Low burning coals in the fireplace told me she'd been in here for hours and, despite the chill in the air that her thick curtains hadn't managed to keep out, hadn't bothered to stoke the fire by adding more wood. She had servants to do such things for her, of course, but only the cooks would be awake at this hour. She was perfectly capable, but she was often preoccupied with her work.

"Well, this is a surprise," she said, lacing her fingers together as we took our places in front of her desk.

A spike of frustration flared inside me at her words. She hadn't asked for my presence as Yelena had said, and we were here wasting her time. "Forgive us. I was under the impression that you wanted to see me," I murmured, carefully trying to avoid directly implicating my sister in this breach of etiquette but knowing my grandmother would probably read between the lines anyway. I gave a small bow and leaned over to take my stubborn sister by the elbow, ready to haul her bodily from the room with me.

"Stay," my grandmother said, stilling my movements.

The look Yelena sent me was triumphant as I snatched my hand back, and the scowl I sent her only served to please her more. I was going to throttle her.

"I do want to talk to you. Though, I was waiting for a more appropriate hour to send for you." She turned a wry look on my sister, who stood silent and unbothered. As reapers, we didn't sleep much—a few minutes here and there—but manners kept us from straying too far from a normal daylight schedule, want- ing to respect mainstream society's quiet hours and nocturnal habits.

I lifted my gaze back to my grandmother to find her giving me a considering look.

"I have a... proposal of sorts for you, Victor." The wryness in her expression returned and a niggling thread of anxiety wormed its way into my chest. I waited silently for her to continue as she studied me for another moment, before purposefully shifting her posture and directing her full attention to me—making it clear that my sister was not a part of the conversation. "Or perhaps a new assignment, if you're not amenable. But I would like for you to marry."

My heart rate sped up at her blunt words. I'd always expected that my family would arrange a marriage for me. It was the custom of our people. We lived so long that the choice to bind yourself permanently to another wasn't something to take lightly, and I'd heard the older generations scoff that it wasn't something they would want to leave to something so foolish as *feelings*. I knew this, but I hadn't considered that it would happen this soon.

"No," my sister interjected, her voice calm and resolute. "Absolutely not." The racing of my heart only increased with her refusal. I didn't care to be caught between the two most headstrong people in my family.

My grandmother continued as if she hadn't been interrupted, and I had to strain to hear her over the pounding of my heart. "If you're not willing to do so, then I would like for you to, at the very least, retire your position in the Void and take on guardianship of the girl while she seeks treatment for her illness here in the Boundlands."

"He's a child!" my sister interjected again, the calmness slipping from her voice.

I slid my gaze to my sister without turning my head, unimpressed with her appraisal of me. She might have been more than 400 years older than me, but that didn't mean she needed to call me a child.

Grandmother pressed her lips into an unhappy line, finally giving my sister her attention. I couldn't imagine the quarrels they'd gotten into over the past 436 years, but no doubt they were many. "Does he look like a child to you, Yelena? I seem to recall that he's been besting you in the arena since he was fifteen years old. He's thirty-two now, has spent the past decade fighting monsters in the Void, and is perfectly capable of speaking for himself."

Yelena ignored the barb about her fighting prowess, though I knew she would try to take it out on me next time we sparred. "He only gets one chance to find a mate, and you would give it away! He has the rest of his life to find someone on his own! Someone he likes."

"Like has little to do with love, Yelena. The older we get, the more set in our ways we are, and the harder it is for us to intertwine ourselves with another. You didn't want a marriage when one was offered to you, and I respected that. But I would like to give your brother a chance to make his own decision without you hovering about insisting he's somehow tied to your apron strings." My grandmother's patience with my sister's interruptions was wearing thin, and by the end of her reply her words were clipped and her tone short.

I swallowed thickly and tried to breathe past my fraying nerves. "What did you have in mind?" I asked my grandmother, hoping to keep the disagreement from escalating.

She studied my face again before answering, and I could practically feel my sister bristling beside me. "Queen Danica Morningstar of the Kingdom of the Rising Sun approached us about a possible arrangement for her granddaughter, Princess Celeste of the Dawn Court. Loathe though they are to see their precious children leave Faery, the princess is a special case. Her health is failing, and it seems no amount of treatment there is helping, so she's been placed in a magically induced stasis to buy her more time, though she doesn't have much. Since your magic would heal her, and she would provide you a nice wife, I think it could function as a lovely arrangement."

"That is preposterous!" Yelena practically shouted. "Why him? Ask Nikolai!"

To my sister's credit, my cousin Nikolai did seem like a better fit. He was 125 years old and had always seemed to draw the eye of the women around him.

My grandmother addressed my sister but never let her eyes stray from mine. "I believe Victor and Celeste would be better suited for one another. They're of a similar age, and I think it has potential to be a perfectly agreeable arrangement between our houses."

"Grandmother, mortals die all the time! Must we cry over every spent blossom that falls from the cherry tree?"

Grandmother's gaze snapped to my sister. "We do if it's our cherry tree that we've planted in our yard and tended carefully for many years."

"Then maybe we should take more care not to get attached to things that die," Yelena replied hotly.

I wondered at my grandmother's words. It wasn't uncommon for immortals to get emotionally attached to certain mortals, or even an entire family lineage. I thought of my friend Levi and his wife, Elara. From the first moment I saw her, I saw their life together. I saw their children, and their children's children, and I found I already loved these people who didn't even exist yet. Because they belonged to my dearest friend. I knew from the first moment I laid eyes on her that I would go to great lengths to care for these descendants of theirs, could easily imagine my future-self pulling strings and arranging marriages with my own descendants—if that's what it would take to ensure their well-being—simply because they were his. Therefore, I could not begrudge my grandmother her affection for this fae family, if that was what it was.

But my sister wasn't finished and sighed as she pinched the bridge of her nose. Her voice turned beseeching. "He gets one chance, Mama Zdenka. Even in an arrangement he brings a superior family line and immortality to the table. What does she bring?"

Our grandmother was unimpressed with Yelena's gentler tone. "As a princess of the Dawn Court she has a direct royal connection to the Kingdom of the Rising Sun and good genetics, Yelena," she explained as if my sister was particularly slow of mind.

"Obviously not, if she's dying," my sister snapped.

Grandmother merely shrugged, unconcerned, and waved her hand dismissively. "Victor's magic will resolve her of any pesky mortal afflictions. But she has a pretty face, and she'll make pretty babies for my favorite grandson." I nearly choked on my tongue. "She's a sweet girl and the pride of her grandmother."

"And this has nothing to do with the fact that Mom attended said grandmother when she began her reign," Yelena retorted sarcastically. *Ah, there it is.*

"Your disregard for the partiality of others smacks of hypocrisy, considering how jealously you guard your younger sibling," Grandmother replied.

I closed my eyes to block out the bickering, wishing I could close my ears as well, and then took a deep breath. This probably had less to do with my mother's attachment to the Queen of the Dawn Court and more to do with her and my grandmother scheming for a way to get me out of the Void, since the high fae were terribly vulnerable there, but either way, I'd always known that this day would come. I would never deign to shirk my duty to my family, to refuse what our matriarch thought best for us. I realized that the room had grown silent and opened my eyes to find my sister and grandmother staring daggers at each other, until they both slowly turned to pin *me* with those stares. I gave my grandmother my gaze and nodded.

"I am willing," I responded, resolving to be just that.

But what was I supposed to do with a wife?

GRAB YOUR COPY OVER on Amazon. To stay up-to-date on release dates and more info please sign up for my newsletter at www. elsiewinters.com, follow me on Facebook or Instagram, or join my reader group, Elsie Winters Boundlands Babes!

Green-Eyed Monster

HE'S AN ORC STUDYING for his accounting exam. She's a forest faerie trying to salvage her botany project. There's a magically animated stone sentry crashing through campus like a two-story tall wrecking ball.

The first time Hyrak lays eyes on Solandis, he's too immersed in the chaos around them to notice her soft beauty, but once she's in his arms, he's enchanted by the opinionated little fae's passion. Can gentle Hyrak control the fiery possession scorching through his veins? Does Solandis really want him to?

GREEN-EYED MONSTER is a short (10K word), fun Fantasy Romance with a guaranteed HEA. Content warnings include adult language and consenting adult romantic scenes.

Get a free copy when you sign up for my newsletter at elsi ewinters.com!

Leviathan's Song

I knew he was trouble before I even laid eyes on him.

Levi Navarre has magic in his voice, a literal siren's lure... not to mention he's leanly muscled and tattooed with a smile that makes my brain melt.

Fortunately, I have a ward against that sort of thing - both his magic *and* his infuriating charm.

*Un*fortunately, I need him.

Levi has some major hesitations about assisting me, but there's a civilization on the line, an entire underwater city that desperately needs my elven magic - and I desperately need his help.

Needing his help and needing *him* aren't the same thing at all... *right?*

Available Now

Seduction of a Psychopomp

Erogenous Hand Holding and Other Ways to Tame Your Reaper

I won't live to see my 29th birthday unless I make a deal to marry Death.

An arranged marriage to a grim reaper? Whatever keeps me on this side of the dirt.

My new husband Victor is formidable, built like a god, and ... is scary supposed to be this sexy? Because it's kind of sexy. The problem is he doesn't seem to *get* this whole marriage thing. Every time I approach him for company, he scampers off like a disgruntled cat. I'd be fine with letting him have his space, but I can't help being reminded every time I look at him that a girl has *needs*. How can I lure my new husband into bed? And is it even possible to win the heart of a reaper?

Available Now

Live, Laugh, Lurk

NOTHING COULD BE WORSE than having to take a temporary job in a spooky old college town. Until I realize I'm living downstairs from a terrifying Mothman.

The only thing I want is to get back to my old life as soon as possible, until I realize that the most terrifying thing about the mothman is his obsession with well-made lamps—and I notice how good his butt looks during our shared yoga class. Slowly, he wraps himself around my heart like one of his chunky, hand-knitted blankets. Will I be able to shake off the sparkly moth dust when it's time to go home?

Available Now

Also By Elsie Winters

Green-Eyed Monster

Leviathan's Song

Magpies & Mayhem

Seduction of a Psychopomp

Live, Laugh, Lurk

Acknowledgments

I am so thankful for the wonderful people who hold me up and keep me going in my writing community. I want to thank Susan R., Melissa M., SL Prater, Erin Vere, Colleen Cowley, and Vela Roth for all of their time, logistical help, and emotional support.

Amira Naval brought Sidney and Jordan to life on my cover. Leigha Wolffe-Stoirm provided *much* needed edits and has unending patience with my ineptitude regarding commas.

About the Author

Elsie Winters writes sweet, cozy comfort reads with a dash of spice and a dollop of fantasy. Her favorite pastimes are feeding the birds who knock on her window for snackies and spending way too much money on plants. She also reads paranormal romance books like they're going out of style and collects monster art that she has to hide from her kids.

Never miss a story! Check out my website to sign up for my newsletter or follow me on social media!

Contact info:
www.elsiewinters.com
elsie@elsiewinters.com